About the Book

In **Cunning Killer**, a professional female assassin plays cat and mouse with the male CEO of a giant corporation.

A figure popped up from behind his vehicle. Both Webster and Murphy let out gasps and stopped short. Murphy reached for his weapon and Webster heard a muffled "putug!" Murphy crumpled to the pavement. Webster, puzzled, took a quick look down at the immobile Murphy and then back to the figure.

His heart immediately went into overtime. What the hell is this? he asked himself. What's going on?

"That should have been you, Mr. Webster!" said the figure. It was a woman's voice!

He stared at her but it wasn't bright enough to see any details. She looked ghostly.

The woman laughed and began a slow walk toward him. She was tall -- taller than him. She was slim. She had something over her face that blurred her features.

She walked closer. Webster's instinct was to run. But where could he go? There was no place to hide. If he ran, she could shoot him in the back.

In this thriller, we introduce the colorful private detective Odie Gallop who is charged with tracking down this elusive villain. Readers will also find many of the other characters that appeared in "Naked Greed."

***

In **Naked Greed**, a satellite is launched that has the promise of eliminating destructive world weather patterns. But man's insatiable greed may lead instead to a cataclysmic result.

The entire project now raced through his mind -- the months of total dedication he and his team had devoted to bringing the Energizer and its Searoc Beam to these final seconds. The project had cost him his marriage.

Webster's faded red shirt was wet. Perspiration stains spread under his arms and along his spine. Tie loosened, sleeves rolled, he stood with arms spread-eagle on his desk, eyes following the motions of each technician at the terminals. Five years of his life were wrapped up in this project. It had started when he discovered it was mathematically possible to reflect the sun's energy into a beam of light onto the earth that in turn could act on the atmosphere and modify global weather patterns.

Thus begins this fast-paced thriller just before a project backfires and thrusts catastrophe onto a small New England town.

Cunning Killer

A Novel of Suspense

by
Gerald Seaman

To my grandchildren who
provided me with so much love and
entertainment over the years

Danielle
Darci
Kelly
Charlotte
Nate
Stowe

Also by Gerald Seaman

Naked Greed (2012)

December 24

At midnight Christmas Eve, a mysterious and powerful light broke through dark, heavy clouds. At first, it was like a gigantic searchlight from some sort of silent, unseen aircraft.

Worshipers, emerging from their traditional late-night church services, looked up and were blinded as if looking into the noontime sun. Some fell on their knees, shaken to the core, certain this was the second coming of Jesus Christ.

Late-night revelers, roaming noisily through the city streets singing seasonal carols, were immediately frozen into silence. They stared upward, stung by a totally new stimulus on their already addled minds.

For all who witnessed the scene that night, it was a unique, terrifying experience.

The light, as bright as day, expanded rapidly and within only one hour dispersed the clouds over the entire New England region. It warmed the surface air to midsummer temperatures and ended the horrific snowstorm that had immobilized the area for more than a week.

This Christmas Eve phenomenon came to be known as the "Hole in the Night."

Not surprising, the Hole in the Night inspired a variety of emotional reactions.

"It was a divine miracle," Reverend Richard Breeze proclaimed on Christmas Day from the pulpit to his one thousand parishioners at a church in Manchester, New Hampshire.

"Most of you saw the heavenly light soon after our Midnight Candlelight Service. This, my believers, is the proof we have been waiting for. Jesus is coming.

"Yes!" he said raising his voice. "Jesus is coming!"

And the congregation repeated it, "Yes, Jesus is coming!" They all raised their arms and shouted, "Hallelujah!"

News of the strange light spread quickly around the world. Astronauts in the International Space Station had a unique view of it. They immediately contacted Houston and sent a video from their perspective.

Airline pilots circling to land on a snowy Logan runway aborted their approach and made another turn while frantically demanding answers from the control tower.

Cable TV stations corralled panels of experts who agreed on nothing -- except that the light *had* to be man-made. On the other hand, they pondered, what man-made machine could possibly do what this did?

George Spitzer was among the only witnesses who *knew* what was going on. "The aliens have found us," he preached, standing between snow banks outside the Park Street Station on Boston Common. "There is no question now that the aliens are coming. You saw their light! It came right from their spaceship. They have found us. They'll be upon us soon. Get down on your knees and pray they don't take us away."

A leading Washington, D.C. newspaper declared on the front page, "Another Administration Boondoggle." The administration, they editorialized, is flaunting its dirty secrets once again.

The press in New York City asked, "Who's in charge of monitoring space activity now that NASA is playing second fiddle to corporate space jockeys? We're getting no answers from Houston."

The Hollandson Weekly *Bulletin* headlined, The Winniposkeg is near flood stage, and added, "The eerie light and heat of Christmas Eve speeded up the snowmelt."

Late January to Late June

Nat Webster felt a violent stab in his right arm. He fell forward in his chair to his desktop from the impact. He recovered, raised his left hand to his triceps, looked and then felt the warm dampness through his flannel sleeve.

He was startled at the blood that came away on his hand, still not fully realizing what had happened. He turned in his chair to look behind at what might have hit him and saw the shattered windowpane, and glass shards spread across the floor.

It took only a moment for him to realize he had been shot. His heart broke into a sudden flutter and fear overtook him.

He quickly rolled out of his chair onto the floor to get out of sight. From there, he looked up at the window again. It was dark outside. He could see nothing. There was no sound, just an eerie, nighttime silence.

A thousand thoughts raced through his brain. What the hell is going on? Someone's shooting at me? Maybe a hunter? Not at night!

Oh, God, he thought. Of course. It's the death threats.

If he stood, he would be a target again. He crawled to the next room, inching along on his knees, bending his right arm to his chest and supporting himself with his left. He noticed the pain for the first time. He moved down the hall and into the bathroom. No windows there. He sat on the toilet seat and felt his arm again. A bloody sleeve. He removed his flannel shirt and looked at the wound. It could have been a lot worse.

He ran cold water, wet the shirt and carefully wrapped his arm in it.

Help. He realized he should call for help. Time was wasting. He didn't know what was going on outside -- someone might still be out there, waiting for him to appear again.

His cell phone was on his hip. He called 911.

"Yes. This is Nat Webster. I was in the other day and showed you people my death-threat notes. Let me speak with the chief."

"The chief is gone for the day. How can I assist you?"

"Oh, damn! Well. Now it's happened. I've just been shot in the arm -- but I'm OK. I need you to send someone out here to look at things. They shot me through my office window in the house. I'm really on edge.

"Oh ... and have them bring a big bandage, he added."

"We'll get someone out there right away, Mr. Webster."

"Thank you." He hung up.

In spite of Ellen's nagging, Webster hadn't paid a great deal of attention to the threat notes he'd received. It wasn't until the newspaper headlines began printing his name and implying he was a monster of some kind that he began to take notice. It was then he went to the police and showed them the threats he hadn't yet thrown away. The cops were the ones who reminded him that every threat should be taken seriously and he should "be careful."

What the hell does "be careful" mean? How do I be careful when a stranger is tracking me? he asked himself.

Blood was running down his arm again. He looked at his wound in the mirror. It tore cleanly through his triceps muscle. No broken bone. That's good. No vein hit. That's even better. He flexed his arm. The fingers flexed. Good. It worked. He guessed he was OK. He smiled.

He washed the wound again, this time with warm water. He dried it with a towel and rummaged in cabinet for a large bandage. None. It was still bleeding. He pulled out his handkerchief and wrapped the wound. Can't tie it with one hand, he grumbled. He pulled the points of the handkerchief as tight as he could with one hand and his teeth, and then wrapped the cloth around itself. The bleeding slowed to an ooze. He was glad to be alive.

* * *

The town of Hollandson, Massachusetts was recovering from a devastating storm that, within a single week in December, dropped up to six feet of snow throughout New England. The region was paralyzed. Buildings collapsed. Vehicles were buried along highways. Many people died.

New England was shocked to learn recently that this storm was not only unnatural, it was created artificially by a reputable corporation located in Hollandson itself. That company was Scan-Man. It was responsible for what was now called the "Hole in the Night," a startling weather-modification event that was noted worldwide.

The late January sun and relative warmth had now allowed for the clearing of roads and highways. Residents had removed the snow from their driveways and sidewalks. Schools were back in session and most the Hollandson population was in high spirits.

But, contrary to the above, favorable weather was being blamed for allowing an invasion of Hollandson. Scan-Man and its new director Nat Webster were under siege. The press and television crews from organizations worldwide had descended on the little town looking for answers. Why was

Scan-Man fooling with Mother Nature? Scan-Man, they now knew, was responsible for several untimely deaths and who knew how many millions of dollars in property damage throughout the region.

* * *

Maggie Billings and Ellen Bloodworth arrived at Thompson's Truck Stop, aka the diner, soon after it opened. This was a regular stop to take a break following their morning run. To their surprise, a line had formed outside and they didn't recognize anyone. Jack Thompson noticed the women and signaled them to bypass the crowd and come in.

"Mornin' Black an' White," Jack greeted the duo. "Your table is waitin' as usual."

"What's with your sudden popularity, Jack?" Maggie asked as they took their seats.

"They're all newspaper and TV folk. They want to know what Scan-Man's doin' with the weather. It was on the news last night. Did ya see it?"

"Sorry, Jack," Ellen said. "I was watching PBS."

"They're a real pain. They tried to push in here with one of those TV cameras, but I bounced 'em out. They took up too much room in this little place.

"They're all upset that we don't have any hotels for them. You know -- with the Motor Hotel now out of commission."

"Did they interview you, Jack?" Maggie asked.

"They tried to, but I told 'em I was too busy feedin' their faces. I've called in all my girls. This place is a madhouse. It's too much. I don't like it. My regulars feel like they can't doddle over their coffee and do their yackin'.

"I told 'em to doddle all they want. Phooey on the others!

12

"The regular for both of you?"

"The regular, Jack. Thanks."

The women settled in and took note of the locals who had somehow been able to get in before the media. Outside, the line was growing.

"What do you make of this crowd, Ellen?"

"Nat mentioned the reporters when he got home last night. They all want information on the Hole in the Night. He says the media was clamoring at Scan-Man's gate all yesterday. He's granted a few interviews, but says that to cope with the volume of people would be a fulltime job."

"What can he do?"

"That's what he's deciding. He's put out a short news release, but that doesn't seem to satisfy."

"I drove by yesterday. It looked like there were more than just the media at Scan-Man. It looks like you have protesters as well," Maggie said.

Ellen looked concerned. "Actually, I'm very worried for Nat. He's really on the hot seat. He's got a lot going on."

Phil and Maggie were co-owners of the Hollandson Weekly *Bulletin*. The office was part of their home, in an attached, renovated garage. Maggie was the editor and her husband Phil was the financial guy, and responsible for advertising sales. He was also the part-time photographer. That allowed him to slip out of the office periodically.

Ellen and Webster, a mixed-race couple, worked together at Scan-Man. She was a meteorologist and oversaw the information that eighty-four satellites pumped into her department. Webster had been with Scan-Man since its early beginnings nearly twenty years ago. He was the inventor of most of the technology that these satellites carried. Recently, Webster had the stockholders vote for a new board of directors. That board then voted him chairman.

Current media attention had to do with a new satellite Scan-Man had launched in mid-December. The satellite was named Scanner XII and it was loaded with new technology. One of its capabilities was weather modification.

Ellen had good reason to be worried. Something sinister was going on in town as well.

* * *

Hollandson Police Chief Paul Wilson and Officer Commerwitz arrived at Webster's home within ten minutes of his call.

"I'm surprised to see you, Chief. They said you weren't in the office."

"I wasn't. They called me. Your call was too important for me to miss."

"I appreciate your attention."

Webster's office was methodically examined. Photos were taken. They saw the dried blood on the chair. Lining up the window and the desk, they found the bullet. It had penetrated a dozen of Webster's favorite books on a shelf above his desk and had stopped dead, lodged in the American Heritage Dictionary on page 1689. The head of the bullet pointed at a photo of Joseph Stalin.

The chief recovered the bullet as well as the threat to Mr. Stalin.

Officer Commerwitz went outside with a large flashlight. There were tracks in the snow. The cartridge casing was recovered from a small hole melted in the snow. It was about ten feet to the side of where the attacker had spent some time and had trampled the area.

Because of the location of the ejected cartridge, it appeared the weapon had been fired from the trampled area, about 150 feet from the window.

"Why do you think he fired from so far away?" Webster asked.

"He's a marksman," the chief said. "If he was, let's say, at your window, the rifle would have been less accurate. He probably didn't bring a handgun with him. It's likely he hadn't scouted the area previously and didn't know how close he would be to you for the shot. You may have been at a second-story window. Or, because of undergrowth and trees, he just figured he'd have to fire from a distance. Most likely, how far away he was didn't matter.

"The tracks go right up to your window. I can't tell if they were made before or after the shot. We noticed also the tread of the footprint was surprisingly small for an average male."

"A woman?" Webster guessed, surprised.

"It would be strange, but it could be a woman, of course. But we can't rule out a small guy."

"It seems this guy had no intention of killing you," the chief continued. "The weapon was probably a rifle. Most likely it had a scope. The shell casing is a Remington 223. The bullet itself is solid pointed and that's probably why it cut through your arm so cleanly. A Remington bullet can also be hollow pointed. That would have ripped your arm apart."

"Why would he only want to wound me?" Webster asked.

"Maybe just to scare you. A good scare," the chief said, "can often be more satisfying to a madman than a killing. What fun, the madman thinks, when he knows his target is terrified and on the run."

Webster looked glumly at the officers. "If that's the case, he certainly succeeded. But why? Do you think he'd try this again?"

"I'm sure you can answer that yourself. He might very well," the chief said. "Do you have someone you can stay with for a while?"

"I have a friend."

"By the way," the chief said. "You'd better have that arm looked at."

* * *

"Oh my God. I can't believe it. Of course you can stay here," Ellen said to Nat. "I'll come get you."

"I should be OK driving. I'm going to swing by the hospital."

"No way!" Ellen said. "I'll be right over. I'll take you there."

"Let me see the arm," was the first thing Ellen said when she arrived at Webster's house.

"I've got it wrapped. It's nothing. See? I can move my arm and my fingers. It's just a flesh wound."

"Yes, but you can get an infection from a bullet."

"I could get an infection from the hospital!" Webster half joked.

They checked into the emergency room, filled out a few papers and were led to a bed in a curtained area. Fortunately the ER was not busy.

The doctor asked questions. "How did this happen Mr. Webster?"

"I was shot," he answered with a smile.

"Shot?" The doctor looked surprised at Webster's answer.

"Yes. But it's just a flesh wound."

"I can see that," the doctor said. "How'd it happen?"

"Do we need to go into that? I have just spent an hour with the police chief."

"I need the information for my records. It's not often that we have bullet wounds here in Hollandson."

"I hope not."

"Well?"

"If you need information, your best bet is to call for the police record. That will be more accurate than listening to me."

"You are a difficult man, Mr. Webster."

"Thank you. I don't try to be."

"Your name is familiar," the doctor said while bandaging the arm. "Ah, I know. I saw it in the papers. You're the Scan-Man man."

"You guessed it. I'm the man."

"I'm sorry I pressed you for that information," the doctor continued. "I don't envy your situation."

"How so?" asked Ellen.

The doctor turned and looked at Ellen.

"I'm Nat's girlfriend."

"I see." The doctor paused. "The press is being pretty aggressive toward you."

"That goes with the territory, doctor. You try something new that people don't understand, and they're all over you. You see that in medical research, don't you?"

"True. But I haven't seen this much response in my field since the advent of birth control pills."

Webster laughed. "I like you doctor. Thanks for patching me up."

"It was nice meeting you, Mr. Webster, and you ma'am."

They stopped at Webster's house on the way back and he picked up important papers, financial documents, some clothes, and a few books.

It was after midnight when they finally arrived at El-len's condo. The moment they entered her apartment Ellen threw her arms around him.

"Watch out for the arm," Webster warned.

"You said it was nothing."

"It is nothing, but I don't want to hurt it."

"I'm so glad you're safe, Nat. What a horrible thing to happen."

"Do they have any clues as to who did this?" Ellen asked, emotionally.

"I didn't ask and they didn't say. They just suggested I find somewhere else to stay for a while."

"Well, you can stay with me as long as you like." Ellen put her arms around him again. "I'm just so happy you're OK. Let's go to bed and I'll nurse your aches and pains."

"I'm for that," Webster laughed.

* * *

Scan-Man is a giant international conglomerate. Its business is monitoring the environmental health of planet Earth. The company employs some two hundred thousand people worldwide, fifty-six thousand of which are scientists in all specialty fields.

Scan-Man headquarters is located in Hollandson, Massachusetts, at Peters Field, on the edge of the famous Rte. 128 and Interstate 95.

The company has a network of eighty-four satellites performing a variety of functions. Some carry the familiar tel-ephone, television, tracking, telemetry and data transmis-sions. Others measure the weather activity locally over seven-ty-eight percent of the Earth's surface.

At any location within the U.S., Scan-Man can meas-ure the ground surface temperature, water temperature, and radiation hot spots. It can measure also the surface barometric pressures and wind speeds.

Weather prediction and modification has always been a primitive science of trial and error. Scan-Man has now elevated this to an exact science. The practical function is to provide this information to governments and commercial enterprises. NASA is highly dependent on Scan-Man information. The weather forecasts we see and hear on commercial broadcasts are based on information Scan-Man provides.

Nat Webster is the "reluctant" chairman of the board and president of Scan-Man. How could a man of Webster's modesty and sterling character rise to the top of such a large and influential worldwide corporation?

That's the very same question Webster asks himself.

He joined the company some twenty years ago. During those years he exerted influence on every piece of hardware the company introduced. His love is the laboratory where, unfettered by politics and espionage, he is able to devise new technologies uninterrupted.

About ten years ago he was invited to join the board of directors. He was flattered and accepted, perhaps with some idealism of what work this might entail. He found out, resigned after a year, and returned to the lab full-time, although he insisted he be kept in the loop of the board's major activities.

Because of Webster's extraordinary output of ideas and actual products, he continues to exert a strong influence on company activities.

He is a revered member of the National Scientific Association (NSA). Scan-Man is a major financial supporter of the NSA and Webster is usually a featured speaker at one of their two annual conferences.

* * *

The dozen directors, eleven men and one woman, mostly from outside the company, gathered in the meeting room next to Webster's office. There was nothing elaborate about the room or its appointments, yet it was not unattractive. It was Webster-functional and quite different from the director's room Chandler Harrington used as the former chairman. That room was elsewhere in the building and was now used by the employees. Webster sold the huge gold-plated chandelier, the bar and its contents, and the tasteless white meeting table and chairs, all trimmed in neon blue leather. Needless to say, the items were difficult to sell and, in the end, may even have been given away. The former chairman was excessive in every way, long before being fired with the other directors.

Webster entered the room, smiled and shook everyone's hand and small-talked briefly before the board members took their chairs.

"I want to welcome all of you to our first regular meeting," Webster began. "A bit of housekeeping first. You have before you a package that includes the monthly budget and year-to-date figures. You've had this morning to look at the numbers. I think they are pretty impressive considering all that has happened in the last couple of months. We have an excellent cash reserve in spite of the cost of the launching last month.

"Scanner XII has already brought considerable income and recognition to Scan-Man. Its technology brings us into the 21st Century in all respects. I am very proud of that achievement.

"It was quite obvious to all of us when we arrived this morning that the media wants our attention. Last week I did talk with the *Times* and I gave a brief interview with the *CNN* cable channel. I also gave out news releases. Now, it appears, everyone else wants the same attention. I don't blame them, but I just don't have the time or the inclination to undergo that.

"I'm considering a couple alternatives. One, have our Information Office handle the group or, two, ask them all into the big conference room and have me do a one-time recap of the whole thing. Are there any other suggestions here?"

Susan Morales spoke up. She was a character, Webster thought. Her choice of colorful, tight clothing made her stand out like a neon sign in the middle of the desert. She was certainly a contrast to her male peers.

"I think it's the volume of the media that's the real problem," Susan said. "I'd suggest having them work together by electing one representative from the press and one from television. They can then decide in advance the questions they want answered by their representatives.

"Also, I think they should give us their questions in advance of the meeting. Otherwise this could be a free-for-all."

"I like the first part of your suggestion, Susan, but I don't feel right limiting questions. We aren't hiding anything here. There may be some security questions we don't want to answer, but other than that I'm open.

"Lin." Webster pointed to him.

Lin Che-Hsuan said, "You're the one who is on the hot seat, Nat. I don't believe there's much history we new directors can contribute. We will support you as much as we can."

"Thank you, Lin. The proverbial buck stops here.
"Scott."

Scott Padilla added, "I suggest we put out a press release today stating Susan's suggestion. The sooner with the media the sooner they'll disperse."

21

"I agree about going forward with the press release," Webster said. "I want to be sure that the media understands we are not hostile. I personally want to be open and encouraging.

"But there is a danger that the more information we release, the greater the number of questions we will face. At least for the time being, let's be as open as we can be.

"Now, regarding the press release, I'll ask you all to work out the wording, pass it by me, and we'll distribute it.

"Looking ahead, I want to discuss my plans for the use of the Searoc Beam.

"As you know, my prime interest in the Searoc is to use it in a way that aids agricultural production. How can it help? Texas, to mention only one state, has been in a severe drought for more than a year. I believe we can move weather patterns into Texas that will provide enough moisture to encourage crop growth and yield.

"Wherever there is a severe drought, my goal is to help alleviate it. Whatever we do is certainly better than doing nothing. And by doing so, we will learn how to perfect the Searoc and demonstrate its viability.

"Another thing that troubles me are the annual forest fires in the Western states. The solution appears to be the same as the drought problem. Of course the fires rage because of the lack of moisture in the mountains, either because of less than normal snow accumulation or not enough rainfall.

"Those two areas will keep us busy through the summer months.

"Peter."

Peter Posednik spoke. "Regarding the budget. I think the $20 million you've budgeted for R&D is excessive. I'd like to see that cut in half and put into cash reserve for the future."

"I do believe this is a similar suggestion to the one you made at our organizational meeting. I think I answered by asking *you* what you thought was the purpose of R&D. I thought we agreed that both are for meeting future demands. Without R&D, this company is dead. If anything, we should double the R&D budget."

"I still think R&D is excessive," Posednik replied. "I move that we cut R&D by 50 percent and move it to cash reserve."

There was a pause. "Do I hear a second?"

There was no second.

"Does anyone else have a question?"

"I move we adjourn," Susan Morales said.

"I second," said Scott Padilla.

That guy's going to be a pain in the ass, Webster thought.

The meeting was adjourned.

"Thank you, gentlemen and lady."

* * *

Susan Morales delivered the drafted director's press release. She noticed the bandage beneath Webster's short-sleeved shirt. "Oh," she said. "What happened to you?"

"It's nothing," Webster said with a smile. "I met up with an object that was disagreeable."

"It looks awful," she gushed.

"You brought the release?"

"Yes. Lets go over it," Susan suggested, showing her aggressive nature. "I want to make sure it's what you want," showing her eagerness to please.

Webster was surprised when she pulled her chair up beside him, rather than sitting across or adjacent to him at the table. But then again, they could both read the release together. Perhaps she could have made a copy for him, but she didn't. She leaned toward him, not quite touching, as she read the release in her pleasant voice. He couldn't help seeing her ample breasts. They were right in line with the paper she was holding. He had trouble concentrating. Her perfume was a bit strong, but she was an attractive woman and pleasant enough, maybe in her late thirties. He was uncomfortable with her closeness. She appeared all business. He liked her. She had contributed positively to the director's meeting.

Finally Webster said, "Here, let me see it." He put his hand out for it. She handed it to him. He turned to read it on his own. Her breasts were now out of his line of sight. He could concentrate. He read through the release, crossed out a few words, penciled some things in the margin, reread it to himself and returned it to her.

"That seems just fine, Susan. Let's go with it."

Webster stood.

Susan stood. She lingered and small-talked about how well things were going at the company and how well most of the directors worked together, referring perhaps to Mr. Posednik's occasional ripples of self-expression.

Webster listened politely and took advantage of their face-to-face position to study Susan's green eyes and white, even teeth. But he was also impatient to get on to other things. He felt she wanted more from him, and she talked on relentlessly.

Finally. "Please call me anytime, Nat," she smiled. "I'm always ready to be of service."

He smiled back, thanked her and she left, turning as she went through the door to give Webster a little goodbye with wiggly fingers.

Her scent soon followed her, but his image of Susan herself took a little longer to disappear.

* * *

Frank McCullough was a happy man. The snow was melting slowly enough so that the Winniposkeg River had not yet reached flood stage. The edge of the McCullough farm was at a scenic overlook encompassing the river and the fields on either side of it. The river provided the farm with irrigation and a source of water for his hand-dug well.

Frank and Old Rolf, his golden retriever, were on their way down the road to get a good look at what was left of his neighbor's house. The Randolph place had burned down just about a month ago. Ed and Marsha Randolph had planned a large party that night but only two couples had made it. The snowstorm was in full force. Wires were down and the roads were clogged. Other couples failed to show because of these difficult conditions.

Ten people went to bed in the Randolph house that night. They were three partying couples, the maid Alberta, their chauffeur Turk, the houseboy Francisco, and the Randolph's nine-year-old son Robert.

Sometime after midnight, the smoke alarm woke Ed Randolph and Alberta. The two raced through the house shouting wildly to waken the others. It was Randolph's wife, Marsha, who had problems. Ed could not wake her. He couldn't lift her. He had to drag her to the second-story bedroom window and push her out into the deep snow. The flames, already climbing the stairway, blocked the access to the first floor.

Believing everyone else was out, Randolph leaped into the waist-deep snow and, with a heroic effort, dragged Marsha, a few feet and collapsed. It was Turk, a massive man, who came looking for his boss. He picked Marsha up onto his shoulders and carried her, haltingly, around the house and into the garage. He too was exhausted. Randolph finally

25

showed up, breathing heavily. All were wet and icy cold. Marsha, who was still in her nightgown, lay like a limp doll gradually waking to consciousness.

Looking over the bedraggled group in the garage, Randolph didn't see his son. "Who's got Robert!" he shouted, his heart beating wildly once again.

Everyone looked around. No Robert.

He panicked and sprang into action. He tried to get into the house through the metal-clad garage entry door to the kitchen, but when he opened it flames shot out at him. He slammed the door and clawed and crawled his way back around the house through the deep snow to where he had jumped out. He looked up to Robert's bedroom. What he saw caused him to gasp. Alberta's black arm was hanging motionless out the window. Just over her head, flames licked at the outside of the house.

Randolph could only believe his son was still in that room and he had no way of getting up there to rescue him. He crumbled into the snow in despair and released a loud guttural moan.

Then, he thought he heard something -- a small voice. It was behind him. "Father. I'm cold." Still shaken but relieved, he struggled over to his son, picked him up and hugged him. Joyfully, he carried Robert back through the snow to the garage.

The others asked about Alberta. Robert told them Alberta was crying and her clothes were on fire when she had thrown him out the window. The beloved Black kitchen help had saved Robert's life at the expense of her own.

Now, McCullough's head was full of these stories that were told to him in the days following the fire. He and Old Rolf ambled up the drive to the Randolph house, the dog at his side as usual, his tail wiggling and waggling as they slogged along. The Golden Retriever was going to be thirteen this summer. Frank bent slightly and patted his friend on the head.

There was nothing left of the house. With the roads blocked, the fire department wouldn't have been able to respond the call even if they had received it. Now, the huge historic home had fallen completely into its foundation.

Forced out of the garage, the Randolph refugees slogged very slowly the half-mile over the snow-clogged road toward the McCullough's house. The husband of one couple had heart problems and died along the way. He had to be left behind. It was very difficult pushing through the snow. A frozen crust some inches below the surface cut and sawed at their bare legs and feet.

The bedraggled group was welcomed into the McCullough home. Frank's wife, Mabel, a self-trained nurse, brought everyone back to health with one exception -- Ed Randolph. He was acting abnormally, crazy, speaking in an unintelligible babble. It frightened everyone. None of them had ever seen anything like this. He was put to bed without resistance and there he remained for the duration of their stay.

The McCulloughs ran a self-sufficient farm. Whereas most other families lost their power, and therefore everything else modern during the storm, the McCulloughs had oil lamps, woodstoves and every 19th-Century convenience. Life went on without a hitch.

In early January, the fire survivors were rescued and they each went their own way.

Alberta's body was removed days later when disaster crews could get near the remains with proper equipment.

The guest who had died on route was recovered the day after arriving at the McCullough's and placed respectfully in the hay in cold barn until rescuers could manage his retrieval.

Recently, Frank McCullough had heard from Marsha that her husband, Ed Randolph, had been placed in a full-service rest home. As for Marsha, she moved to Naples, Florida and bought a penthouse, leaving the care of Robert to the McCulloughs.

Sadly, Marsha admitted to the McCulloughs that she had never wanted children. Robert for her was an accident. She said she never understood children, had no patience with them, and therefore always had her difficulties with Robert.

In a strange twist, she made a deal with the McCulloughs to let Robert stay with them indefinitely. She offered a regular monthly stipend for Robert's care. The McCulloughs accepted the offer but in fact they put the stipend aside in the boy's education fund.

During his stay with the McCulloughs after the fire, Robert had a wonderful time caring for the animals, playing with the Old Rolf, learning to milk the cow and collecting eggs from the henhouse. He wanted to stay, especially as now his father wasn't able to care for him.

The McCulloughs missed their own children who lived far away and never had time to visit or even write their parents. They had said long ago that they were very busy living 21st Century lives. The McCulloughs didn't understand. Their 19th Century life suited them just fine.

The McCullough's joy of living was increased substantially with Robert's presence. The boy went to school every day. He did his homework faithfully. He was a happy boy in a pleasant family atmosphere.

Frank smiled as he recalled the gold-star day Robert asked if he could call him "Grampy" and Mabel "Grammy." The McCulloughs were ecstatic. It was a major advance in their relationship as a family.

"Hmm," Frank said, with a huge smile. "That would be real fine with us, but only if we can call you 'Robby.'"

It was at that moment the three of them became the family the McCulloughs always longed for. They came together in their first meaningful hug. It was then that Robby said, "I love you, Grampy and Grammy." They were now real family.

Viewing the burned out Randolph estate was depressing for Frank. He and Rolf didn't stay long at the site. He was here now because he wanted to see the place while Robby was in school. There was nothing more to see. Frank felt so sorry for the demise of that family. They had been good neighbors.

Robby would soon be home from school. "Come on, Rolf. We gotta meet Robby at the bus."

* * *

Bob Sivolesky called the selectmen's meeting to order with his characteristic drama.

"Let me start off by welcoming back the other two jokers on this board. Roy and Warren just returned from sunning their butts in the Deep South while the rest of us were wading in waist-deep white stuff."

"Thanks for the kind welcome, Bob," Roy Langer said. "We did our part keeping track of you -- in the papers."

"You had our deepest symphony, Bob," Warren Coulter punned. "You're just jealous."

"We're going to cut the pay for both of you," Bob cracked. "A dollar a day's givin' you too much vacation money."

"You're cruel," Langer added.

"OK. Let's get to business," Sivolesky finally announced. "Maggie," he said, referring to the only reporter who faithfully covered their meetings, "I hear you had some flying time over the holidays."

"That's not exactly business, but yes, I had an interesting flight to Boston that ended with quite a letdown."

Sivolesky turned to the others in the room. "Maggie and her friend Ellen got hold of an Army helicopter. It took them to Boston where they had to parachute out of the chopper in the middle of the snowstorm! But they got a prize for it. They brought home a giant snow cat that saved the day moving people and equipment around in this little town."

"I just want to add for the record," Maggie said, "that the copter and crew were generously provided by Commander Roger Heathside at Peters Field. The snow cat was provided by Governor Kelly Fitzwilliam. It was Ellen Bloodworth who managed our parachute."

"Thank you 'fly-girl,' we're proud of you," Silvolesky said.

"Next on the agenda is Bud," Silvolesky continued. Bud Kelly was road superintendent. "And I have an apology to make to you, Bud. I let you and the townspeople down on providing funds to repair the trucks and plows. I should have gone into the Reserve Funds. But who could have predicted what happened last month?"

"That's OK. None of us could have predicted it," Bud Kelly said. "It was hell while it was happening. Actually, it's all Scan-Man's fault as it turns out. There sure is a lot of damage around town."

"That's a good point you make about Scan-Man," Langer commented. "It is their fault. The top man over there -- what's his name? Webster. He even admitted the whole storm was his fault. I saw it on the TV."

"There are a lot of people around town hurting bad," Coulter added. "Lots of damage. A lot of them don't have insurance. Can't afford it. The town buildings survived pretty good, thank God. It's the little guy who's hurting -- as usual."

"Warren," Silvolesky asked. "Do you think we can get any money out of Scan-Man to help these people out?"

"How would I know? Why don't you go ask them?"

"I don't know," Silvolesky pondered. "I've never been over there. I wouldn't know where to start."

Maggie cut in. She often contributed suggestions when there seemed to be imponderables. "Maybe I can help. Actually, Nat Webster lives in the other side of my house."

"What do you think, Maggie?" Coulter asked. "Any chance?"

"What I think is you had better do an assessment of where and how much money is needed. You're not going to get anything from anybody unless you have some hard numbers."

"You're right," Coulter concluded. "I move that we appoint a committee of five, including two assessors, to tour the town and view the properties and come up with details and numbers for repairs due to the storm."

"Do I hear a second?" Sivolesky asked.

"No," Langer said. "How many structures are there in town? A thousand? Two thousand? The assessors know, but whatever it is, it's too many to tour in the next few months."

There was a pause.

Langer continued. "I move that we run a front-page legal ad in the paper asking those who claim to have property damage from this storm to have the cost of repairs estimated and bring those numbers to the selectmen's office by the end of March. Maybe we should also do a mailing to all households."

Langer's motion was seconded.

"One last thing," Maggie added. "You do the legal ad and I'll wrap an article around it. And I don't think there's any need to mention Scan-Man at this point."

"You can write what you want, Maggie," Langer said. "Our legal ad may or may not mention Scan-Man."

"You might be treading on libelous territory should you call the storm Scan-Man's fault," Maggie pointed out. "Also, if you are expecting some sort of amicable financial settlement from the company, it might be smart to avoid accusations where possible."

"Thank you for your input, Maggie. We'll take that under advisement." Sivolesky said with a smile.

The vote was unanimous.

Maggie left for home. There was nothing more here but routine business. She had mixed feelings about what she should write. Being a friend of Nat Webster and Ellen, could she write an unbiased article about Scan-Man and the storm?

* * *

It is late evening. A Ducati Superbike, devoid of chrome, pulls silently up to the dimly lighted delivery door at the rear of a posh condo tower in Boston. The machine is super muffled, emitting but a whisper. The driver is tall, thin and agile, easily swinging a leg off the bike. Across the back of the rider is a long, slim canvas pouch with a white logo that suggests golf. The machine is carefully eased through a door at the side of the loading dock and guided under the concrete stairway where it is parked.

A cascade of auburn hair falls to just below her shoulders when the rider removes her helmet. She is dressed in a tight black jumpsuit from neck to ankle. She is perhaps in her late 20s and has a women's magazine-cover profile. She removes her pouch, opens a pocket at the bottom, and sets it on the floor. With adept moves she pulls off her gloves and unzips the front of her suit. As she peels out of it, a full, firm, muscular figure is revealed. She is nude except for startling pink panties.

She pulls clothing from the pouch. First is an ankle-length flowered skirt that she quickly steps into. She then twists into a plain white, short-sleeved, button-front blouse. Finally, the black running shoes come off and are replaced with white flats. She unceremoniously stuffs her uniform into the pouch.

Her transformation is dramatic. She quickly fluffs her hair with a shake of the head and swings her backpack over her right shoulder. After a glance at her bike, she crosses the loading area and passes through a door into the Tower lobby. She nods to the desk clerk who says, "Hi Sasha." The bellhop smiles and winks in recognition. She takes the elevator to the top floor. It opens directly into a short hallway that has two suite entrances only. She unlocks and enters one of the doors.

The main room of the woman's suite is large and lavishly furnished with leather, glass, and black metal furniture. The first impression is rich, yet cold. Two long glass window walls meet at one corner. Through them is a spectacular, uninterrupted view of the Financial District and Boston Harbor. Two other walls are adorned with dozens of framed paintings, posters, drawings, photographs and snapshots of women – women of all ages, colors and sizes. Each is in an artful pose of nudity. Above these pictures are 18-inch-high letters printed in gold that read: SASHA + HELENA.

A woman about the same age as Sasha emerges from one of the rooms to greet her with arms outstretched. She is certainly attractive, but her figure is a little heavier than the other woman. She has a length of straight blond hair that reaches nearly to her waist. She too is dressed in a long print skirt and a white blouse. Her countenance is plain, but her facial expressions as she crosses the room exude a warmth and spirit that is magnetic.

33

Suddenly, Sasha screams "Helena!" and sprints three long strides and leaps onto Helena, wrapping her legs around Helena's waist. They fall to the plush carpet in an embrace that is short-lived as they begin a violent wrestling routine, cursing, slapping and punching, punctuated with screams. They rip at each other's clothing, exposing flesh. They squirm and bite, pulling hair and twisting like two animals in a life-and-death struggle. They are breathing hard and the pace cannot continue. The exertion gradually diminishes into a head-to-toe passion of mutual gratification. This lasts for several minutes with groans and sighs as they roll over each other, heads between thighs.

They now struggle to stand and pull their clothing together. Then, arm in arm, in mutual support and smiles, they cross the room to a bar near the windows. Here Helena assembles two martinis, delicately dropping an olive in one and an onion in the other. They sit on stools. Hoisting their glasses, they say their first words to each other.

"To you, Sasha. You must have had a good night tonight?"

"I did. It was very rewarding."

* * *

The school bus stopped at the end of the driveway and Robby Randolph leaped off. He ran to Grampy and hugged him around the waist. He then patted Old Rolf on the head, and the retriever gave him a quick, wet lick on the cheek.

Robby ran toward the pasture, his book bag slapping his back with every step.

Buttercup, the heifer, was out in the field. She saw him coming and lumbered toward the fence, a few stems of hay sticking out each side of her mouth. Robby met her and scratched her head between the eyes and around where her horns had been. "I'll be right back with your grain, Buttercup," he said and continued on to the house.

Into the kitchen he went and dropped his book bag on the couch. Frank and Rolf were not far behind. Mabel was cooking, as usual.

"Hi Grammy."

Robby hugged her and looked around to see what goodies she was creating.

"I've got a snack for you over there, Robby," Mabel said. He ran to the kitchen table.

"Oh. I love strawberry tarts. Thank you." He gave Mabel another hug then sat at the counter munching and watched her roll out cookie dough.

Frank went over to his favorite chair in front of the woodstove. On the floor next to him was one of his whittling projects -- something, if asked, he couldn't yet identify.

Without being asked, Robby ran up the stairs to his room and quickly changed into his work clothes. Then thud, thud, thud down the stairs and out the door to the barn.

Milking time was established between the boy's return from school and dinner. Robby entered the barn and opened the door to the pasture. Henrietta was waiting. She went on her own into the barn and to her stall, placing her head through the stanchion. Robby closed the stanchion and gave her a quart of grain. He then found the three-legged stool and a clean milk bucket by the wash sinks. He washed his hands and bent to wash Henrietta's udders then finally sat down to try his hand once again at milking.

He knew his small hands had a way to grow before the milking technique was perfected. He began squeezing but not much happened. The barn cat stopped by to satisfy its curiosity. Robby tried shooting a squirt in her direction, but it landed on his pant leg.

Then Frank came in. "How you doin' young man? The bucket full yet?"

"I guess I need more practice, Grampy."

He gave up the stool to Frank who then gave Robby another lesson. Henrietta produced about two gallons of milk, including the few squirts that went to the barn cats. Cats were important to the farm. They kept the rats out of the expensive grain.

Robby then led Henrietta from the barn and into the pasture with Buttercup.

It was egg time. Frank had 140 layers and could expect about 100 eggs a day. He and Robby carefully placed them in several wire baskets.

"You girls are feelin' pretty good today," Frank said. "If I counted right, I got 98 of 'em." They both filled the feeder trays and refreshed the water pans.

Outdoors, with Rolf again by their side, they returned to the house with two of the egg baskets.

Much of the McCullough income came from selling eggs, milk and the fancy cakes that Mabel created. Buttercup's ancestors and the hen's relatives contributed liberally to their food bank. Frank had a forty-cubic-foot freezer in the basement. It contained a seemingly endless supply of chicken and beef. Add to that Mabel's canning of the garden vegetables and it all resulted in healthy meals year round.

A generator in the barn was one of the McCullough's few modern conveniences. It had proved its worth when the electricity was off for about a week in December. Propane gas fed the generator and the generator kept the freezer cold. The McCulloughs fed a house full of guests during that unusual snowstorm, the origin of which still baffled Frank.

Propane gas also supplied the lamps when the electricity failed and Frank's woodpile was the source of fuel for stoves and fireplaces when needed.

The McCullough's self-sufficiency often impressed the town's smartphone-toting neighbors who came by to pick up their eggs, milk and cakes.

* * *

Early this year, the Scan-Man stockholders were notified of an emergency meeting where they elected a new slate of directors. At this first meeting Nat Webster was elected chairman. He had no opposition.

All the former directors had been fired. Of those, Chandler Harrington, Ed Randolph and Peter Stevenson were now under scrutiny for attempting to scam the government out of billions of dollars.

As the result of a trial, Harrington, the former chairman of the board, was in jail. Stevenson, a Scan-Man director, was out on bail. Ed Randolph, president of Scan-Man, was judged mentally incompetent and under medical care. All were banned from visiting or interfering in company activities in any way.

Nat Webster was in a different category because of his help to the government in uncovering the scam. Yet he was part of the forthcoming trial because he pled guilty to the charge of implementing a major storm that resulted in death and destruction.

The charges were confusing to outsiders. Webster considered his charge a mere formality.

Webster led the design and implementation of Scanner XII, the most sophisticated weather satellite in use today. Coupled with Scanner XII was a Solar Energizer. The Energizer, powered by the sun's reflected rays, was designed to project a beam onto Earth. Called a Searoc Beam, it had the ability to variably focus the beam from a pinpoint to a broad beam. The Searoc Beam had been a top secret of the former board of directors.

In late summer of the previous year, by way of his friend Senator Conrad Cooper, Webster revealed the board's secret to the President of the United States, his closest advisors, as well as select members of the U.S. House and Senate. Webster was instructed by the President to follow through with the board's secret -- in other words spy on the board -- and over the next several months attempt to trap the directors in their own plot.

Webster had only used the Searoc Beam twice -- on December 19 to activate a major snowstorm and on Christmas Eve to disperse that snowstorm. The action the Searoc Beam created was now referred to as the "Hole in the Night" because the beam from the satellite made a hole in the clouds that expanded rapidly over all New England and evaporated the storm clouds that had caused so much havoc.

* * *

Meeting with the media was new to Webster. He was accustomed to speaking to large groups of Scan-Man employees, and occasionally at National Scientific Association meetings, but this was different. The media were not "his" people. This was not "friendly fire." He was uncomfortable. He was an engineer -- a quiet man. His comfort zone was in the laboratory dealing with inanimate objects.

Although he had recently accepted the nomination to be elected to the top spot in this giant conglomerate, he had not anticipated the sudden thrust into the international spotlight. It was a shock to his self-confidence. He took the leadership position to literally save the company from itself, from its greed and from its broken relationship with the U.S. government. He had the most tenure and general experience of any person available. He knew what the goals of the company should be.

The media had complied with the director's requests. They had elected *CNN* and the *Times* to represent them, and had submitted a list of questions.

Webster and the directors had now read over the questions, discussed them and Webster said he was ready to answer them. The time was now. He steeled his nerves.

* * *

The TV camera was on. The two reporters and Webster were on the monitor.

"Please tell us just what happened Christmas Eve when many of us saw the midnight light."

"Christmas Eve was the *second* use of this technology. The first use was on December 19. The 'midnight light' you refer to is now commonly called the 'Hole in the Night.'

"From Scan-Man headquarters here in Hollandson," Webster continued, "the satellite Scanner XII activated what is called the Solar Energizer that is located in the satellite. The Energizer converts energy reflected from the sun. That energy is transferred to the Searoc that produces a beam. It was this beam, much like a giant searchlight spread out over all New England, that heated and dispersed the cloud cover from the region."

"Does this mean that Scan-Man is now involved in weather modification?"

"Yes."

"Weather modification is a very controversial process. What gave Scan-Man the authority to engage in it?"

"Where is the authority that prevents its use?" Webster answered. "Scan-Man has been intimately involved in weather matters for nearly twenty years. It is a world leader in producing and managing weather satellites. We work closely with the federal government on many projects. Our company recognizes global warming as the new reality. More frequent and more violent weather patterns are, we believe, the result of global warming. Scan-Man thinks it can play a beneficial role in stabilizing these violent weather patterns. We believe, that with the use of our new technology, we can save thousands of lives and billions of dollars in property damage not only in the United States, but worldwide."

"Your Searoc Beam, as you have told us, was used on December 19. The result of that action was disastrous. I don't see how that was beneficial to anyone."

"I agree with you," Webster admitted. "The fault is all mine. I make no excuses. Let me explain.

"The previous Scan-Man board of directors, which by the way is no longer employed by the company, wanted to use the Searoc Beam on December 19 to inundate and cripple all of Europe with a heavy snowfall. The directors' goal was to blame the so-called 'Hole in the Night' on an unidentifiable foreign power. They wanted to convince the President that the United States should fund and create a similar technology, at a cost of billions of dollars, to counteract what the unidentified country was doing. They wanted the government to pay for the development and execution of a technology *that already existed*!

"I was onto their plot. I was the one who led the development of this technology. I directed the activation of the Searoc Beam.

"I totally fought the directors. I took action. I fired the Searoc Beam in a way that I truly believed would send the storm harmlessly into the North Atlantic to fizzle out.

"Unfortunately, in my haste, I did not take into consideration a storm moving up the Atlantic coast from the

Gulf of Mexico. Those two storms collided and, to my consternation, the rest is history."

"Isn't this event over New England a perfect example of why weather modification should never be attempted?" the reporter reasoned.

"No!" Webster was adamant. "It's a perfect example of what can happen if the technology falls into the wrong hands.

"It's a perfect example of why weather modification *should* be attempted. It was the event on Christmas Eve that halted that terrible storm. That action proved its worth. As I said earlier, there are very dangerous storms that can and should be mitigated for the sake of life and property."

Another question. "Why is the beam used at night? It was frightening to those who witnessed it."

"It can be used day or night," Webster explained. "The only governing criteria are the relationship of the sun and the Scanner XII satellite. They have to be within sight of each other.

"In the future, when additional satellites with the Scanner XII technology are in operation, one scanner or another will always be within working relationship of the sun."

"I suspect this Searoc Beam may have some military applications," was the next comment.

"Is that a question?"

"Yes."

"What you suspect is true, but this is an application Scan-Man is not interested in exploring at this time."

"At what time will you be interested in exploring it?"

"Hopefully, never," Webster said firmly. "I will always resist its military use." He paused. "The only function that interests me is weather modification for the benefit of mankind."

"Will you please explain further your resistance to military use?"

"Simple," Webster said. "How many more variations of human self-annihilation do we need?

"Since Alfred Bernhard Nobel's invention of dynamite in 1866," Webster continued, his voice rising in intensity, "mankind has been on an evermore escalating quest to create the ultimate device that, in an instant, will wipe out all life on Earth. *Do we want that?* I will say no more on this."

Webster's last words resulted in a rare media pause. The camera was still running but the audio had nothing to record. The video captured the two media representatives apparently at a momentary loss for words, while Webster adopted an 'I gotcha' smile.

Surprisingly, it was Webster who broke the silence.

"Why does it appear so many of you are interested in the military side of this technology?" he asked. "If indeed we were planning to exploit Scanner XII for military purposes, this would be classified information. Scan-Man is not in the business of developing and producing weapons.

"Applications Scan-Man intends to pursue relate to agriculture," Webster continued, brushing aside the weapons focus. "The Searoc Beam has the capability to move heavy precipitation from an area experiencing floods to one plagued by drought, for example. Unequal distribution of both floods and drought is another factor in global warming. Texas recently experienced a full year of extreme drought, whereas other parts of the country were flooded with precipitation. With weather modification, maybe we can do something about this for the benefit of all."

* * *

Although Ellen and Webster frequently visited each other in their respective homes, having him now actually move in with her as a result of the shooting incident was a new step in their growing relationship.

"I'm thrilled that this is actually happening, but terrified at the reason, Nat," Ellen said. "It takes this horrible shooting incident to budge you. For two years I've hinted at us moving in together at one place or the other. Finally I can watch over you."

"Indeed it is frightening, my sweet," Webster said. "But coming off my divorce only two years ago made me think twice about any new relationship – especially with the conventional warnings about mixed-race relationships."

"Do you still have qualms about that?"

"How could I? I've met your parents and we've had wonderful cookouts together. Your parents are open-minded. Your father's a successful businessman and understands what I'm doing. We've had some interesting discussions. Your mom is fascinating. She's the one, she said, who pushed you to go to school beyond your four-year college education because that would give you the added boost -- and that got you into Scan-Man.

"Yeah, we had good talks about race, about children, about adoption. They are very concerned about your future, as they should be. Your dad was the one who convinced me that, if and when we got married, that adoption of children might be best."

"I know. I know," said Ellen. "They're big on that. I can see their point, but I want my own children."

"But think of the child, Baby," Webster reasoned. "Your dad pointed out a child of ours wouldn't be either race. Where would that place him psychologically among humanity? There is a long way to go in color blindness. In fact we may never get there. Sure race relations are a little better here in the U.S., but most of the world seems far behind."

"But," Ellen reasoned, "that puts us in the position of deciding if we adopt a white or a black or, wait a minute! -- even an oriental child. God, none of us have talked about that! That would be very interesting don't you think Nat? Have you ever thought about that -- about adopting an Asian child? What would *your* parents have thought?"

"Truthfully, I haven't, Baby," Webster admitted. "I don't know what my mother would have thought about our relationship. She probably would have liked you and I know she would like to see me happy with the person I love.

"My father? He was an admitted bigot. I loved him for a lot of reasons. I had a wonderful childhood with him. But if I were looking for faults, which I don't like to do, he was old school regarding Blacks. I grew up with him referring to them as niggers. It was embarrassing. But he held his ground until he died. Somehow I think I survived his bigoted beliefs.

"In the end, our parents were there to lead us in a direction they thought best. Most of their ways were indeed best for me. But that didn't mean I had to respect *all* their beliefs.

"My life has been one of bucking the odds. I like to believe I can make my own rational decisions after weighing all the inputs and options.

"In spite of all the above, I'm in love with a beautiful, intelligent, fun-loving woman."

"Who could that woman be?" Ellen teased.

They were lying in front of the crackling fireplace watching the flames lick at the logs. Webster put his arm around Ellen and pulled her closer to him. "You're the one for me, Baby, for better or worse." He nuzzled her neck and she squirmed.

"Can you think of a better place to be on a cold, winter night?" he whispered, gently running his hand up under her blouse. He slowly caressed her tiny breasts and took her mouth in his.

All Ellen said was, "Mmmmm," and pressed her body closer to his so as to feel his growing excitement.

* * *

"You love that thing, don't you? Helena asked.

"Of course I love it. It's my income, and I love my job."

Sasha was cleaning her rifle, a Ruger Mini-14 with a folding stock and scope. It was considered one of the most accurate 500-yard performance weapons made. Disassembled, the rifle fit neatly into a twenty-four-inch sleeve she carried as a backpack. Sasha was a hunter. She carried a hunting license. Her rifle was registered. She carried an NRA membership card and she belonged the Boston Gun & Rifle Association. She was a distinguished target marksman at the club. She was legal and accredited all the way.

There was one major difference between Sasha and other hunters. Sasha's Ruger was fitted with a noise suppressor.

"What does a girl do with that thing?" Helena asked. "I can't imagine you using it."

"I shoot at targets," Sasha answered. "I am a hunter. I compete at the gun club. I outshoot all the guys. It's fun, Helena."

"I never knew a woman who did that."

"Have you ever known a woman like me?" Sasha smiled.

"I get your point," Helena admitted. "Do you earn money that way -- I mean with the gun?"

"I do."

"You must get big bucks for it."

"You're pushing your luck, Lady," Sasha's voice tightened. "Just enjoy what you've got while you've got it. Forget what I do."

"I'm sorry."

"Come on," Sasha lightened up. "Let's get to the theater before curtain time for once."

* * *

The heavy snow of winter was nearly gone as February approached. Ellen and Maggie were back to their regular early-morning runs. The earlier snow accumulation had slowed them, and actually stopped them in late December. Now, breathing hard, they did their seven-mile circuit along the well-scraped back roads and ended up at Thompson's Truck Stop for their usual.

"Hi Black an' White. Good to see you." Jack slid into the booth next to Ellen.

"We're doing great, Jack," Ellen said. "Just the regular. Coffee, two poached easy on wheat."

"And you, Maggie?"

"Make it the same. We don't want to overwork an old timer."

"Haw, haw, haw. You girls'll be lucky to ever get to my age an' I never ran a day in my life. I been savin' all that energy for now." Jack smiled and winked through his crinkly face and white Hemmingway beard.

"You might be right," Maggie said.

"I ain't never wrong," Jack said, smacking the table. Then leaning toward Maggie he added, "Got any hot news?"

"Jack. The hottest news I get comes from this diner. I should set up my office here."

"That's a deal. I'll set you up in the corner booth."

"Will that include free food?"

"Why not?" Jack laughed and struggled to his feet. "Breakfast comin' up."

The women were silent, arranging their napkins and silverware.

"I don't want to be nosey, Ellen, but I heard a police call to Nat's place."

"Oh boy. What a night. Someone shot Nat in his right arm."

"You're kidding!"

"I wouldn't kid about that. They shot through the window and got him in the right triceps."

"Is he OK?"

"Physically. But psychologically it's bothering him. He doesn't talk much about it. You know all the controversy going on with Scan-Man and the trial and the accusations. Then there's all the shuffling around at the company. He's got a lot on his mind."

"I can see that."

"And last night he moved in with me. You probably saw his car. The police thought it would be smart if he lived somewhere else for a while."

"That sounds nice. Haven't you been trying to get him to move in for some time now?"

"I have. And it feels good to see him more. Maybe I can get him home from work earlier to relax a little. He does get uptight."

"Do they know who did it?"

"I don't think so. But they did find the bullet and the casing from a rifle."

"This is terribly frightening, Ellen. I don't like it. What do you think this relates to?"

"Well, you know he's been getting these death threatening notes ever since he admitted his involvement in the Hole in the Night."

"Yes. But for crimminy creepers, does that admission deserve a shooting?"

"Maggie. You know there are weirdoes out there."

The diner was filling up with the early-morning crowd. Jack returned with two heaping plates.

"That looks fantastic, Jack," Ellen said. "I hope I can eat it all."

"You better. I ain't takin' it back. Enjoy."

The women nibbled thoughtfully at the food.

"When Nat left for work this morning he seemed better. And apparently he didn't have any bad dreams. He was restless, but he said it was his shoulder."

"Let's hope."

* * *

Maggie and Phil were taking a break at the *Bulletin* office. Webster's interview by the media was the topic.

"I was very impressed," Maggie said.

"So was I," Phil said thoughtfully. "But I was surprised by his confession -- his admission of wrongdoing. He had every reason to blame the directors alone. I think he could have done that easily without getting himself involved."

"He's not dumb. I give him a lot of credit for being honest. He stands out in our society like a petunia in the proverbial onion patch."

"You don't think that he'll be punished? He did, after all, cause havoc and lives were lost."

"He may. But we have to believe that good will prevail."

"Maggie, the eternal optimist. I hope you're right."

"You do know that Nat moved in with Ellen."

"Yup," Phil said. "I was surprised to see the VW out there. I didn't know he moved in. Wow. A developing romance?"

"Probably more because of the shooting rather than romance, Phil. Oh, I forgot to tell you," Maggie said. "Nat was shot in the arm the other night. Ellen told me this morning at the diner."

"Shot in the arm?" Phil was puzzled. "What kind of shot?"

Maggie stifled a laugh. "No. No, Phil. Not a vaccination. He got a bullet in the arm. It looks like a sniper got him. You know about the threats he's been getting."

"That's crappy," Phil said. "Is he OK? How much damage was done to his arm?"

"He's OK. Fortunately it was just a flesh wound. Ellen took him to the hospital and he was patched up. Chief Wilson thinks it might be someone who disagrees with Nat's weather modification activities or his stand on weapons development. Who knows? The move in with Ellen was to give Nat a new address until they can find this guy."

"So now they've moved the target to our house?"

"Oh, Phil. Cut it out! Where's he supposed to go?"

"I don't know. Did the chief issue us all bullet-proof vests?"

"Very funny."

"I really don't know how the guy does it, Maggie. He's got so much going and he seems to keep his cool. How's Ellen stand it? How do I stand it? I'm nervous and I don't even have a madman tracking me."

"Ellen's quite emotional about it, which isn't surprising."

"I don't blame her."

* * *

It was no surprise, just a disappointment, to Nat Webster when he received a summons to appear in court for a hearing on Scan-Man's alleged government scam. It was Ellen who took it hard. She broke into tears and lashed out angrily.

"Its not fair, Nat! After everything you've done."

"It's alright, Baby. I think this is just a formality. They have to summon me. I was involved."

"But you were on the government's side," Ellen reasoned. "You were the one who revealed to the government that the company was going to scam them. You were the one who nailed Harrington in the end."

"That's all true and will come out at the hearing," Webster said confidently.

Ellen snuggled closer to him on their couch. "I'm just a worrier. You have so much going on right now as chairman of a new board. And I'm still worried about the guy who shot you."

There was a knock on the door to the other half of the house.

"I think we have company," Webster said hopefully, looking for a change.

It was Phil. "How about some dessert and coffee you guys?"

"Sure, thanks," Webster said. "Sounds good."

Maggie met them and they took chairs at the Billings' dining room table. The house smelled of fresh apple pie.

"I love that aroma." Ellen said. "You just whipped it up?"

"Right out of the oven," Maggie said. "But I did let it cool a bit so we don't burn the roof of our mouths."

"I've done that with hot pizza," Phil added. "It's the cheese that sticks. It can hurt for days."

"Me too, Phil." Webster put in. "I think it's gluttons like us who can't wait long enough for it to cool."

Phil cut and served Maggie's creation. "Hey, Maggie! We have any ice cream?"

"Ooh, good idea. Yes. We have vanilla."

Conversation lulled while forks met mouths and a few satisfying "Mmms" escaped around the table.

It was Ellen who spoke first. "We got a surprise delivered to us today."

Startled, Webster turned toward Ellen. "Nat's been summoned to a court hearing."

"We don't need to get into that, Ellen."

The Billings didn't know what to say. "Ellen's my best friend, Nat. We like to talk things out."

"Well, this is all premature." Webster looked at Phil and Maggie. "Yes. I did get a summons today, but I'm not surprised. And, I'm not worried. I haven't talked with my attorney yet. So, if you don't mind, Ellen," as he took her hand gently, "I'd rather not talk about things we know so little about -- even with our best friends."

"Of course, Nat," Phil offered. "We understand."

"I'm sorry," Ellen said. "I'm just so upset about all that's been going on these last couple months."

An embarrassed silence hung like a bird in a noose.

Finally, Webster loosed the bird. "What's the news in the *Bulletin* this week, you two?"

"It's funny you should ask," Maggie said lightly. "Nat Webster and the media, of course. Nat. You did a masterful job."

"I wish I'd been there," Ellen said.

"Me too," Phil added.

"Maybe one of you can take my place next time," Webster joked.

"The lead story this week is more about the media than it is about your content," Maggie said. "I counted media reps from twenty-two countries in the TV room you provided. According to the people I spoke with, Scan-Man has captured the attention of the world."

"I look forward to the article, Maggie. Do you have the names of those twenty-two countries?"

"Not off the top of my head. But there was China, Russia, most of the Europeans, Brazil and South Korea, not to mention the *Times*, the *Post* and the *Journal*. It was a very impressive turnout. You had more than a hundred in that adjacent room."

"When I saw the number of protesters at the gate," Webster said, "I thought we'd be in for rocky time. I was pleased at how well it went."

"Anyone want another piece of pie?" Phil asked.

"Thank you, Phil," Ellen said. "I have to watch my girlish figure. But it certainly was delicious."

The subject switched to the snowstorm that everyone but Webster had experienced.

"You should have seen these two women, Nat," Phil said. "Did Ellen tell you how they jumped in tandem out of a helicopter into a Boston snow squall and gusts of forty?"

Webster looked at Ellen. "She did. I'm not surprised at anything these two do." He laughed. "I do know Ellen is part of an all-woman team that is going to attack some high peaks in the Himalayas. I'm so proud of her. She's my Baby."

Ellen beamed at Nat's praise. She took his hand. "Isn't he wonderful?"

"You all really did have it rough up here in New England. While in D.C. I read the *Post* write-up and saw the snow aftermath when I returned."

Phil spoke up. "I'm still boggled at the way you ended the storm. Maggie and I slept right through the Hole in the Night."

"I didn't see it either," Ellen said. "I was chained to the computer. There wasn't a window anywhere near me."

"She's my champion," Webster said again. "She and Mr. Polcari carried it all off without a blip -- and that was with the building on generator power!"

"OK, you guys. Enough of this praise," Ellen joked. "My ego is already bouncing off the ceiling."

They all laughed together as good friends. Happily, Webster was now included. This loner finally had a family.

* * *

Only hours after Webster's television appearance with the media, the talking heads of the cable channels and the front pages of the newspapers began their critique.

One international cable channel had five panelists.

"Why should Mr. Webster be treated any differently than the directors? It was Webster who pushed the button that caused the disaster."

"Compare Webster's actions to a murder. There is the guy who pulls the trigger, and there are those who abet him. All are guilty to various degrees. But it's the trigger man who gets the harshest sentence."

"I think he's innocent. He attempted to foil the director's plans by sending the storm out to sea. It was the Gulf storm coming up from the south that actually changed a harmless front into a dangerous one."

"I say he's guilty. He should have been aware of the oncoming Gulf storm. After all, it's his company, none other, that tracks these storms. It was a stupid mistake on his part and everyone suffered."

"Guilty, I say also. Consider that he left town immediately after pulling the trigger and went to Washington to report the bad guys to the President. If Webster had remained at home, he could have broken up the storm just as he finally did, but before it caused its damage."

"I agree with that. He could also have broken it up remotely from Washington soon after he arrived, rather than waiting almost a week to do it."

"Who knows? He might have been in cahoots with the directors all along and it was the Gulf front that redirected the storm that the directors were trying to send to Europe. Consider this. What if, when Webster discovered the original plan wasn't going to work, he said, "I'm out of here. I'm going to tattle on the directors and tell the President.""

"There is one thing the rest of you have failed to consider. The Scan-Man chairman, Chandler Harrington, was caught trying to sell our government a forty-something billion dollar package to create something that already existed. Harrington actually presented the President with a written proposal. This is what Webster reported to the government. To top it off, Webster never claimed innocence. He admitted he did something wrong. He is not in the same category as the directors."

"I agree. The important point is, Webster actually reported the scam about three months *before* the fact. That also sets him well apart from the directors."

"Humbug! Webster still pulled the trigger that killed the victims."

The newspapers were just as indecisive about Webster's involvement in the plot.

* * *

Maggie attended the first day of the trial. Back at the *Bulletin* office, she recapped the day in her own mind while relating the proceedings to Phil.

"Let me summarize the charges:

"The first: Three Scan-Man directors were charged with lying to the government in December when they attempted to sell the government a contract to research and build a new technology that in fact already existed.

"The second: The directors and Nat Webster were charged with terrorism on the people of the United States by causing a winter precipitation event of such proportions that it caused human death and extensive property destruction.

"There were ten other charges that were relatively minor.

"So there you have it, cut and dried.

"As you know Phil, I dislike covering trials. I just don't enjoy it. I guess it's the formality of it and the great length of time it takes to arrive at any conclusion. And, when you know one of the defendants, it makes it all the more difficult. Also Ellen was there with me trying to understand what was going on."

"I've never been a spectator at a trial," Phil said. "Unless, of course, you can count *Judge Judy* shows."

"Very funny. But to lend an aura of seriousness to this, Phil," Maggie continued, "the directors charged were Chandler Harrington who was chairman of the board; Peter Stevenson who was a director but with no company title; and Ed Randolph who was president. They all were active at Scan-Man at the time of the incident.

"Ed Randolph was excused because of his mental instability. The judge was informed by the prosecutors that Randolph was in a nursing home and that he was not mentally able to go to trial. Naturally, he wasn't present.

"To the first charge, all men pled not guilty. To the second charge, both Harrington and Stevenson pled not guilty, but, get this Phil, Nat pled *guilty*!

"At this, the judge and the defendants' attorneys gasped. Webster's attorney simply smiled. The judge asked Nat pointedly if he really wanted to plead guilty, and he said yes, he was guilty as charged.

"I don't know what this means in the long run, Phil. It just seems strange.

"To the eleven other charges, all three men pled not guilty, including Nat.

"What do you make of that Phil?" Maggie asked. "Nat gave no explanation in court, but then he was never *asked* for an explanation."

Phil considered the question for a moment. "You recall that during Nat's interview with the media he confessed that he was wrong, that he pulled the trigger, if you will. I see Nat maintaining a consistent apology."

"It's one thing to apologize to the media," Maggie reasoned. "I think it's a totally different thing to plead guilty in court. It seems like he's asking to go to jail."

"I would hope not," Phil commented again. "I'd say he feels he's on solid ground. Remember, he was working underground for the government -- even at the time he pulled the trigger."

"In any case, they are all out on bail except for Harrington," Maggie concluded. "Now I have to somehow write all this up for the *Bulletin*."

* * *

"I'm really not worried about the trial," Webster explained to Ellen. "I think it's a formality that has to be observed because I was certainly involved."

"Well, I *am* worried," Ellen retorted testily. "You just never know who is going to say what and make your involvement seem far more than it really was. You've read the newspapers. You listened to the cable channels. You never know."

"I have a good attorney with a lot of experience in high-level cases. We talked about my guilty plea and he understood what I was trying to do. I trust him."

"What *were* you trying to do?"

"I was trying to be truthful. How can I say I didn't do something when I did?"

"That's all very well," Ellen argued, "but as you know from the extreme interest of the media, your case is creating sensational headlines. Whatever happened to the good old days of working quietly in the company lab? I know you were in heaven in those days. I was an intern then, worshiping this handsome guy inventing important things. Don't you wish you had that privacy back again?"

"Well, Baby, I think of it this way. I'm proud of the technology I have put together. I am proud of its potential. I know I did nothing dishonest. Sure, we've hit a blip on the screen, but in the end the world will discover how all of this will work to their benefit."

"That's one reason I love you, Nat. You are the true blue idealist with the strength and reasoning of a realist. I believe you will win in the end. But it might be a lumpy road before we get there." Ellen smiled and said. "Give me a nice long kiss and a hug. Who knows, my idealist may be in jail tomorrow."

* * *

When the trial re-convened, Maggie was again reporting. That evening she organized her thoughts by briefing Phil.

"Nat's defense attorney admitted to the court today that his client, as charged, did indeed set in motion a storm that *inadvertently* inundated most of New England. But, he said, he must stress that his client's intent was to send the storm harmlessly out into the North Atlantic, rather than sending the storm into Europe as the other defendants had directed.

"His attorney said Nat deeply regretted his actions, and that he had admitted the same to the media during a highly publicized interview.

"The attorney went on to say there was another important factor. Nat was, at the time, a secret accomplice of the United States government. He said Webster had reported the Scan-Man subterfuge early on and followed instructions to set a trap for the directors. This trap worked when Mr. Harrington attempted to contract directly with the President of the United States.

"'Your Honor,' Nat's attorney said. 'The Scan-Man technology of weather manipulation is an emotional subject. The use of it demanded the attention of the President and members of Congress as well as the military. Webster,' he said, 'dealt directly with the President to apprehend the other defendants.'

"One other significant point he said to the Judge. 'Webster, with the second activation of this technology, personally oversaw and carried out halting the storm over New England.

"'That action,' he said, 'popularly called the "Hole in the Night," has been hailed as a significant step in weather modification.

"'My client, Your Honor,' he said, 'should be exonerated. The charges against him should be dropped.'

"Then," Maggie wrote, "the government prosecuting Attorney General spoke for the plaintiff.

"'Most of what defense says about his client may be true, but the fact still remains the defendant did, with full knowledge of his actions, set the storm in motion that caused the catastrophe in New England. The defendant made that choice. He could have refused to act. There was no compulsion for him to act.'

"Webster's attorney shot back: 'My client did *not act with full knowledge.* In fact he was unaware of the storm coming up from the South.'

"The judge acknowledged the difference in the actions.

"The defense then rested his case," Maggie concluded.

* * *

During the second week of the trial the government prosecutor called Mr. Peter Stevenson to the stand.

"Mr. Stevenson. Were you employed at Scan-Man?"

"I was."

"What was your position at Scan-Man?"

"I was one of the directors at the company."

"What were your duties as a director?"

"I helped run the company."

"What was Mr. Harrington's position at Scan-Man?"

"He was chairman of our board of directors."

"Mr. Harrington led your meetings?"

"Yes."

"Who, among the people on your board, initiated the agenda and made proposals?"

"Mostly Mr. Harrington."

"Anyone else?"

"Actually no one. Well, I guess we all did. We drafted suggestions and Mr. Harrington approved or disapproved them."

59

"Did anyone on your board ever propose a plan that you objected to?"

"Rarely."

"Did Mr. Harrington ever propose a plan that you objected to?"

"Yes."

"What plan was that?"

"The plan this trial is about."

"And what is that Mr. Stevenson?"

"You know. About scamming the government."

"You mean that you objected to the plan to scam the United States government?"

Stevenson hesitated.

"Mr. Stevenson?"

"I objected to his plan. I didn't think it was right no matter how much money we made from it."

"So then. You voted against the plan?"

"Not really."

"Not really. What do you mean? You voted against Mr. Harrington's plan?"

"No. I voted for it."

"Even though you objected to it?"

"Well. There was that veiled threat."

"Explain."

Stevenson squirmed. "We were intimidated by Mr. Harrington. He threatened us."

"Can we conclude then that you, among others on the board of directors, voted in favor of obtaining money from the United States Government because the chairman coerced you?"

Stevenson hesitated.

"Please answer my question."

"Yes, along with the other members."

"You say you were threatened. How were you threatened?"

"Mr. Harrington was known to have a hired gun."

The courtroom suddenly buzzed with whispers. Harrington turned pale.

"What is a hired gun, Mr. Stevenson?"

Stevenson gulped. "Mr. Harrington is a very powerful man. I am ashamed to say we are a rubber stamp for him. He pays us well to do as he says."

"What is a hired gun, Mr. Stevenson?"

"It's a man who is paid to kill someone."

"Do you know the identity of the hired killer?"

"No."

"Do you know for a fact Mr. Harrington has paid to have someone kill another person?"

"I do."

"Can you tell us the name of the person killed?"

Stevenson hesitated. He looked around the courtroom and avoided looking at Harrington.

"Mr. Stevenson?"

"His name was John Ruben. He was an Army general."

"How do you know this?"

"It was announced in Washington papers as well as on TV."

"How do you know Mr. Harrington is responsible?"

"Mr. Harrington likes to drop hints that he is responsible for things he is proud of."

"Drops hints?"

"Mr. Harrington is known for his bragging."

"Please be more specific."

"It was understood by all of us that he could have us killed."

"Thank you, Mr. Stevenson. That is all for now."

* * *

The government prosecutor called Mr. Chandler Harrington to the stand.

"Mr. Harrington. Were you employed at Scan-Man?"

"Yes."

"What was your position at Scan-Man?"

"I am, ah, I was chairman of the board of directors."

"What is the function of the chairman of the board of directors?"

"To oversee how the company is run."

"Then it is you, Mr. Harrington, who is responsible for what happens at Scan-Man?"

"Ultimately. Like a coach and a football team."

"Yes or no."

"Yes."

"Do you know Mr. Stevenson?"

"I do."

"What was his position at Scan-Man?"

"He was a director."

"What does a director at Scan-Man do?"

"He helps me oversee how the company is run."

"Do you and Mr. Stevenson ever disagree?"

"Yes."

"How do you resolve a disagreement with a subordinate?"

"Convince him that I am right."

"How do you do that?"

"By my powers of persuasion."

"Can you be more specific?"

"I simply convince him that my way is the best way and the argument is over. My directors are well paid to follow my direction."

"So you convince the directors through oral debate?"

"You could say that."

"Mr. Stevenson said your persuasion included a threat to his life."

"He is dead wrong. I would never threaten anyone."

"Then you would call Mr. Stevenson a liar?"

"I would."

"Have you ever threatened Mr. Webster's life?"

"Never!"

"Mr. Webster's life was threatened just last week. Do you know anything about that?"

"Of course not."

"Have you ever hired someone to commit a murder?"

"Don't be ridiculous!"

"Is that a yes or a no?"

"It is a no!"

"Have you ever lied, Mr. Harrington?"

"Not that I can recall."

"Last December you made a presentation, representing Scan-Man, to the President of the United States. Is that correct?"

"Yes."

"Correct me if I'm wrong. You led the President to believe a *foreign country* had the technology that caused storm in New England. Yes or no."

"I refuse to answer that question," Harrington said.

"It was you, Mr. Harrington, who directed Scan-Man to create that storm. Is that true?"

Harrington hesitated. "No! It was Nat Webster who caused that storm."

"So, then, the storm was *not* initiated from a foreign country!"

Harrington lowered his head. "Webster disobeyed me."

"You wanted him to send the storm to Europe. Isn't that right Mr. Harrington?"

"I didn't want the storm to go into New England."

"Thank you, Mr. Harrington. You must have been very angry with Mr. Webster."

"I was. He ignored my orders."

"Just how angry were you?"

"I can see where this is going. I did not hire a gun."

"Mr. Stevenson says you hired someone to kill a man by the name of General John Ruben."

"He lied."

"But you have perjured yourself as well.

No response from Harrington.

"You lied to the President of the United States." The prosecutor smiled and turned to the jury. "I conclude that if Mr. Harrington lied to the face of the President of the United States, he could lie about other things -- such as threatening the lives of Scan-Man employees."

* * *

The government prosecutor called Mr. Nat Webster to the stand.

"Mr. Webster. Were you employed at Scan-Man?"

"I *am* employed at Scan-Man."

"What is your position at Scan-Man?"

"I am chairman of the board of directors."

"Were you a director on Mr. Harrington's board?"

"I was a member of his board several years ago."

"Why didn't you continue on his board?"

"Officially, it was taking time away from me that I preferred to use in the lab."

"Is there an *unofficial* reason why you left the board?"

"Yes. Number one. The board wanted to inundate Europe with snow and then blame a 'foreign power' so the board could approach the government and initiate a plan to create the technology anew to combat the fictional foreign power. That scam was pegged at $41 billion that would go directly into the director's pockets. I wanted no part of it.

"Number two. The Searoc Beam can be refocused into a narrow beam, much like a laser beam. In our experiments on the ground, this beam has drilled a pencil-size hole through three inches of armor plate. When the beam is broadened slightly, it has melted an army tank into a lava flow. I was not interested in building military weapons."

"Were you involved with Scanner XII?"

"Very much so. I designed and built it. I launched it. I operated the Energizer that fired the Searoc Beam that created the Hole in the Night both times."

"It sounds to me like you are pretty much Mr. Scan-Man."

"Let's just say I have devoted my career to it."

"What is the main purpose of the Scanner XII satellite?"

"Scanner XII was designed to modify the weather."

"Has Scanner XII ever modified the weather?"

"Yes. Twice."

"Was one of those times on December 19 last year?"

"Yes."

"What happened?"

"I fired the Searoc Beam. This set a front in motion that was hovering over Greenland. That front began to move south."

"Then what happened?"

"A very active warm front from the Gulf of Mexico moved north and interacted with the cold front from Greenland."

65

"And?"

"This interaction caused a large cold front to move into New England and produced the now famous storm."

"Just what happened after you fired the Searoc Beam at Greenland last December 19?"

"I flew to Washington to report what the Scan-Man board was up to."

"Did you have a special relationship with the government?"

"I did. Early on, well before the launch in mid-December of Scanner XII, the President asked me to secretly monitor the director's activities in anticipation of their plan to carry out the proposed scam. You see, it was necessary to catch the board in the actual act."

"So you did disagree with Mr. Harrington."

"I did."

"Did Mr. Harrington ever threaten you?"

"Not that I recall."

"To your knowledge, did Mr. Harrington threaten any of the other members of his board?"

"Not to my knowledge."

"Mr. Stevenson has testified that Mr. Harrington threatened him with his life."

"Mr. Harrington has a powerful personality. He clashes with many people. It is very true that he wants his own way. I do not know what his relationship is with Mr. Stevenson."

"What has been your relationship with Mr. Harrington?"

"We pretty much operate independently. I've been fairly successful in running my end of the business in my own way."

"And what way is your way?"

"My main interest is weather. The company has always been successful in providing the world with accurate, detailed weather and climate information. I want to see that continue.

"There are weather events that trouble me, however. Violent weather has always been my interest. One of my goals is to moderate violent weather, such as tornadoes, hurricanes, extreme drought, flooding and precipitation. I believe all these extremes can be moderated.

"The former board under Mr. Harrington appeared to be only interested in making money. I feared the destruction of Scan-Man. My goal was to rid the company of its rotten apples. I assume that is what this trial is all about."

"That's not for me to say, Mr. Webster."

* * *

The police chief called Webster early one morning and asked him to stop by the station.

"I'm assigning three of my men to be with you 24-7," he told Webster. "They're reserve officers and just their presence with you should be some deterrent. Combine the shooting, your appearance in the media, and now the trial, your protection is all the more important."

"This may be a bit of overkill, but I appreciate it," Webster said.

"It might be excessive protection, but there's no point in taking chances while so much is going on with you. We're all under a lot of pressure from the press."

"How's this going to work for me at home and in the office?" Webster asked. "I don't have to sleep with each of them do I?"

"Whenever you're away from your home or office, in other words in public, one of them will be at your side. Otherwise, they will be in the general area outside your home or nearby."

"This is Officer McHenry," the chief said turning to a man sitting at the next desk. "He'll follow you, beginning now, in the cruiser. Replacements will take place every eight hours. You can just go about your regular activities as if nothing has changed. Ignore them. They'll keep a close eye on you. These men will give you as much privacy as they deem can be done safely."

"Well thanks, Chief. I appreciate all you've done."

* * *

"I was really impressed with Nat at the trial. I have to admit he was stellar," Maggie said. "I watched the expressions of the jurors during the cross examinations. I think they like Nat."

"Oh, Maggie, I'll be so, so glad when this thing's over. I'm going crazy with all that's going on. It just seems like the tension keeps building and building. Do you think things will ever return to normal?"

"What's your definition of 'normal' Ellen?"

"You're right. Normal is abnormal."

The women sipped orange juice, picked at their eggs and waved to the locals as they came and left the diner. Occasionally one would amble over and toss around some small talk about the local scene. Much of this casual conversation ended up in a *Bulletin* section titled "Heard Around Town." Once in a while Maggie heard something she recognized as pure gossip that had no news value whatsoever. When there was doubt, Maggie followed up these comments to check their validity.

When she erred on her job, the emails poured in criticizing her and the paper. It was always difficult to achieve a balance and make everyone happy. Local editors were often too close to their readers, socially.

All in all, Maggie loved the attention she received as editor of the *Bulletin*. She was free to admit it was an "ego trip."

Maggie turned back to Ellen. "Regarding the trial, one of the very interesting parts of the cross-examination of Stevenson was the mention of a 'hired gun.' Do you remember that Ellen?"

"I sure do."

"That might be significant," Maggie pondered. "Do you think there might be any connection between Harrington and these death threats?"

"How could there be? Harrington's in jail and out of Nat's way, thank God." Ellen looked troubled. "The chief called last night and asked Nat to stop by the station this morning. He mentioned something about a security detail."

Ellen suddenly jumped up from her seat, startling Maggie. "Nat!" she shouted, waving her arms. "Over here."

Webster saw Ellen and came over to the table, sporting a big grin.

"What are you doing here?" Ellen asked, breathless. "Here! Have a seat."

Webster answered her in a stage whisper. "I'm testing the effectiveness of my security guard that I picked up a few minutes ago. He's out there in an unmarked car. I'm supposed to ignore him."

"Why are you here?"

"I thought I'd stop by to see what kind of people hang around truck stops. I've heard a lot about the diner."

"How many years have you been in town?" Ellen asked.

"I know. I know. I don't get around much."

Ellen looked at Maggie. "He has a path worn between the house and the office -- that's it."

Jack noticed the stranger who joined the women and went over to the table.

"Jack. This is my boyfriend, Nat Webster." Ellen said.

"Son of a gun," Jack said. "I've sure heard a lot about you. Welcome to my fine establishment." Jack paused and smiled. "I saw this stranger slide into the booth with my girls here and I came over to protect them."

"Good to meet you, Jack. They're my girls too. And I thank you for your chivalry."

Maggie cut in. "Jack's our chef in shining armor."

"Can I get you a coffee or somethin', Mr. Webster?"

"Only if you call me Nat. Yes, please, Jack." Webster looked at the two plates the women were working on. "Let me have a couple poached eggs on toast and a side of bacon."

"Comin' right up, Nat."

"Why are you really here?" Ellen asked.

"Well," Nat said thoughtfully, "I feel pretty good today. I survived yesterday's cross-examination and I just felt like doing something different. I expected you two would be here at this early hour and decided it would be fun to surprise you."

"It worked. I'm glad you did." Ellen paused a moment. "Do you have any idea how long this trial will go on?"

"No. But I can't imagine it going on for much longer. It all seems so cut and dried to me."

"We were just talking about the hired gun that was mentioned in the Harrington and Stephenson questionings," Maggie said. "Do you think that is related to these death threats? By the way, how's your arm?"

"My arm is OK -- healing well. I don't know if my incident is related. Stevenson's comment was a surprise to me. I was never threatened by Harrington."

"Did you ever hear of this general they spoke of?" Maggie asked.

"Yes. General Ruben. He was on the President's original team during the investigation of Scan-Man. He was shot shortly after our first meeting."

"Was that ever investigated?"

"I don't know. The killing was reported in the *Post*, but I never read about an investigation.

Maggie continued. "To have this happen to a member of the President's team that was investigating Scan-Man, as well as Harrington, seems very suspicious -- almost like Harrington wanted to get rid of someone who might spill the beans to the President's team."

"Interesting. I'll mention that to my attorney," Webster said.

"I'd tell Chief Wilson of your suspicions also, Nat," Ellen added.

"You are both right. I need you two on my defense team."

* * *

Mabel was working on a wedding cake when Frank walked in with the eggs. She was humming to herself as she squeezed the icing bag, creating thirty swags around each edge of her three-tiered masterpiece.

"Business is pickin' up again," she said. "Got the third order this week!"

Frank hefted one of the egg baskets onto Mabel's counter.

"Not there, Buster. That's my workspace. Put 'em over there," she instructed, pointing.

Frank dutifully moved the baskets across the room.

Robby came over to Mabel's worktable. "Oh, Grammy. That's beautiful."

"Thank you Robby. And the icing bowl's over there if you want to clean it up."

"Oh, goody. Thank you Grammy."

Mabel turned to Frank. "'Member the girl who was gettin' married and cancelled her cake 'cause of the storm?"

Frank nodded.

"She called again. I guess her weddin' was cancelled too. She said she was sorry to cancel and asked if she could order again. So, the weddin' is back on. I told her not to worry about the other cake. Told her we had put it to good use. We had lots of company for Christmas dinner and ate it for dessert.

"She told me her family had a' awful winter. They thought they'd freeze to death after the electric went out. She said she heard that from a lot of people. The storm caught everybody by surprise – no time to stock up on stuff."

Frank began candling the eggs. Every once in a while he would toss one into the kitchen sink.

"What a waste," Mabel said every time Frank candled.

And every time Frank answered, "'Tis a waste, but most folks don't like red spots in their eggs."

Robby had icing on the end of his nose. "Mmmm. That was good."

* * *

Webster left the diner. They watched his car leave, followed by the cruiser. The girls continued their discussion.

"This armed guard is already a pain," Ellen began. "Wherever we go in public, he's not far behind -- restaurants, movies, you name it. We even have to buy his ticket to the movies. But for restaurants, anyway, he sits outside."

"How long will this go on?" Maggie asked.

"Who knows? Until the note sender turns himself in? That's not going to happen. I wish we could just go to some far away place for a few months."

"I think we all wish that occasionally," Maggie mused. "I'd like to know what, if anything, the police are doing about finding this guy. I know it must hard. What clues do they have?"

"From what I've heard, just a bullet and its casing."

"No fingerprints on those."

"The only advantage I can see," Ellen said, "is Nat is safe with the guard around all the time, and I should be happy with that. No one would dare try anything. So we're stuck with this guard forever?"

"I just don't know, Ellen. It's so sad."

* * *

"I'm glad you're here, Chief," Maggie said as she walked into the police station. "I need a few minutes of your valuable time."

"Any time, Mag," the chief chuckled.

"And don't call me 'Mag', you old bugger!"

"OK, Maggie my friend. Pull up a chair, put your feet up, and let's hear it."

"You've assigned a twenty-four-hour watch on Nat Webster, I hear. That makes sense since he's been threatened several times, he's a high-profile figure with front-page headlines every day, and he's been shot."

"Correct on every point," the chief acknowledged.

"From what little I think I know, you don't have much evidence."

"You are full of truths, Maggie."

"How about this, then? What are you doing to find the culprit who is harassing him so severely?"

"Excellent question. Unfortunately, not much."

"Can you be more specific?"

"Nothing."

"That's more than disappointing."

"I'm sure it is," the chief said, turning very serious. "Between you and me, I have nowhere to go. It's a waiting game -- a goddamned waiting game. Waiting for more evidence, or to catch the bastard in the act."

"So we have to just wait until Nat's attacked again, or killed?"

"And *that* may not result in catching the bugger."

"That is frightening."

"All the more reason to keep it to yourself. We are doing everything we can possibly do."

"Unfortunately, I see your point,' Maggie nodded. "I sure don't want Ellen to find this out. She might cave."

"In my years of police work I've learned sometimes it is best to do the best you can, quietly. I certainly don't want the bastard to know we are waiting for the next move."

"True."

"And, let me add." The chief leaned forward. "It is also *possible* the culprit will back off and forget whatever weird reason he had for going after Nat in the first place. It has been known to happen."

"If that's the case, how long would you continue with the twenty-four-hour guards? I realize it's very expensive for the town."

"I can't answer that now." The chief shook his head. "It's a wait and see -- a nerve-wracking wait and see."

* * *

"Good news, gentlemen," Selectman Bob Sivolesky began, "we have a request from the hotel to begin remodeling. Their new manager, Henry Crumm, dropped it off this afternoon."

"Didn't the other manager get killed?" Selectman Warren Coulter asked. "What was his name? Pizza? No. Pizzazz? No. Pazzita! I got it. Vito Pazzita. What a mind I have!"

"You are a virtual bibliographic encyclopedia, Warren," Chairman Sivolesky remarked. "Now, a little background for those present in this room. The Hollandson Motor Hotel had a collapse of their multi-story atrium in December because of the heavy snow. Also, because of the snow, hoards of people were stranded there for days; the electricity went out; no toilets worked, no running water and, in short, the place took more than a beating. Once everyone was out they shuttered the place. Now, only two months later, they want to fix it up again."

"I'm all for it," Roy Langer said. "The place is a great asset to the town. It pays good taxes and it brings in people who spend money in town."

"I'm surprised how fast they moved on this," said Coulter. "Usually, in cases like this, the property sits it out, sometimes for years, until insurance claims are settled."

"I heard those scientists who were there in December signed for a two-year commitment to bring the convention back," Langer commented. "They want to hold their summer meeting here! That's a laugh. Have your seen the place?"

"This is big bucks for the hotel and a big incentive to get it up and running again," Langer added.

"Can you believe it? The NSA convention is supposed to begin in July! Lots of luck," Sivolesky said.

"Sign it, Bob, and let's get it moving," Coulter urged.

* * *

Puff Chabus and Rev. Dick Masters stood across the street from a vacant storefront on Washington Street, Boston not far from the hubbub at the intersection of Summer Street.

"I think this is the perfect location," the Reverend said. "It's near all the souls I want to reach, from the down-and-outs to the department-store shoppers, from the street-walkers to the guys who buy their thrills."

Puff was horrified. "Richard! You must be kidding. I pictured you at the Park Street Church. You know what I mean? You'd be perfect there."

The Reverend looked down at his companion. "You are probably right, Puff. Perhaps I would fit in very well at an established church."

Puff put her arm around her man and pulled close to him. She looked up hopefully. "Yes, Richard. That is where you belong."

"But that's not what I want. That's not the congregation I seek. I want to help the desperate -- those who are at the bottom of society and can sink no further. They're the ones I need to find and show them the way out of the mess they slipped into."

"Doesn't the Salvation Army do that?"

"They do, my little lady, and they are very good at it. But I think my brand of preaching can fit in a niche that is needed here."

"Can we talk about this back at the condo?" Puff asked. "I need a stiff drink."

The Reverend was dependent on Puff Chabus. It was an uncomfortable situation for him but one in which many others in the ministry had learned to accept. Financial comfort was often dependent on the generosity of others. Simply put, she had the funds he needed to set up a suitable down-town chapel.

The two had met last Christmas Eve at the Hollandson Motor Hotel. A couple hundred people were stranded there because of the heavy snow accumulation. It was a desperate situation. Sanitary conditions were non-existent and food was scarce. There was no heat except for the fire that burned in the center of the hotel lobby.

Otherwise, the Reverend thought, that was a beautiful evening. A young Black girl, with a soft, angelic voice had begun to sing "Silent Night." This simple beginning had rallied many of the desperate souls who joined in. One carol after another followed. People moved in close to each other. Inhibitions evaporated and hands were held.

During this satisfying, emotional interlude, Rev. Dick, as he preferred to be called, had stepped forward, near the fire, and offered a prayer. Bowed heads and comforting words sealed the spirit of Christmas.

He remembered that Puff came over to him following his prayers. She introduced herself and they partnered. He was taken by Puff's vigor and enthusiasm. And he had to admit, she was a sexy little thing and appealed to his baser instincts.

Oh, Lord, he had thought. Please forgive me, but I am human and I have needs that have too long escaped me.

The emotion of the moment helped. Puff was soon sitting in his lap and he had his arms around her.

Puff Chabus had her needs as well. Just the day before Christmas Eve her husband had been killed in the horror of the collapsed hotel atrium. To make matters worse, his body couldn't be extricated. There was no equipment available to raise the steel beams that had fallen so decisively.

Christmas Eve progressed to midnight when someone ran though the lobby claiming it was like daytime outdoors. Puff and the Reverend joined the curious and witnessed the great light and the evaporation of the snow clouds.

The Rev. Dick fell to his knees, much to Puff's astonishment, afraid he had a heart attack. But no. He had his hands together, was looking up into the heavens and praying.

Puff didn't know what to think. The whole scene was so confusing, eerie, actually frightening. She sat beside him and put her arm around him and watched his profound concentration. She was in awe of the man.

Then the light suddenly went out. As their eyes became accustomed to the darkness again, stars appeared.

"Puff! We have just witnessed a direct sign," the Reverend said with powerful emotion, his arms raised, his voice shaking. "My calling to minister to the poor and the downtrodden has been confirmed. The light from heaven has shone down on me and on you. God's hand has been laid upon us. Oh, my God! I have read about this all my life. All my life I sought to have a blessing. I have sought to communicate directly with God. It has finally happened."

Puff had pulled away from him during this emotional outpouring. She looked at him as if he had transformed into an alien.

But then he stood and was silent, showing a broad smile. He held out his arms to Puff. After a brief hesitation, she went to him again and felt his comforting arm around her.

That was several months ago. The Reverend again had his arm around her.

"Of course, my little lamb," he said. "Let's return to the condo and you can have your drink."

* * *

78

Chandler Harrington was morose. He didn't understand why he was in prison. He was guilty of nothing. Nothing had transpired between him and the government. No contract was signed. No deal was completed. No money changed hands. He was innocent. There was a misunderstanding, his attorney confirmed. He would get him out of this. It was that bastard Webster's fault. It was Webster who convinced the others it was the director's plot. But Webster had the jump on him and had the first word.

Harrington shivered at the amount of money Webster was now grabbing. He had heard that Webster had taken his place at Scan-Man and had a new board of directors. He had thought he had Webster under his thumb.

But, people can turn on you quickly he knew. Take General Ruben for example. He turned on a dime, Harrington thought. A lot of good it did to have those photos of him screwing his secretary. But I got Ruben in the end.

Webster was always on his mind now. He had plenty of time to think about Webster and how he would get even. He smiled. He had the connections. He still had the power to get his way.

Relatively speaking, he had it easy, Harrington thought. He was in a minimum-security prison. He had white-collar privileges and that included his laptop. He still had communication with the world -- and his finances and the people he considered important to his well being.

Money is not a problem he told his attorney. "Get me out of here, whatever it costs."

Harrington thought of his parents again. They had lived long enough to see him as the head of Scan-Man. But since then, he had the power to demand a meeting with the President of the United States. He had actually met with the President and his men. He dealt directly with the President.

How proud mother and father would have been of their son. Harrington glowed with his parent's imagined pride.

* * *

Nat Webster had a late night at the office. He was exhausted and was looking forward to a good night's sleep. He and his escort, Murphy, left the Scan-Man building about ten.

"Good night George," he said to the security guard at the front desk.

Outside, they crossed the macadam to Webster's VW. It stood alone in the pale light of a full moon.

"What a beautiful night," Webster commented, looking up at the moon. "On a night like this I continue to marvel at man's ability to place an astronaut up there and get him home again."

The marveling was short-lived. A figure popped up from behind his vehicle. Both Webster and Murphy let out gasps and stopped short. Murphy reached for his weapon and Webster heard a muffled "putug!" Murphy crumpled to the pavement. Webster, puzzled, took a quick look down at the immobile Murphy and then back to the figure.

His heart immediately went into overtime. What the hell is this? he asked himself. What's going on?

"That should have been you, Mr. Webster!" said the figure. It was a woman's voice!

He stared at her but it wasn't bright enough to see any details. She looked ghostly.

The woman laughed and began a slow walk toward him. She was tall -- taller than him. She was slim. She had something over her face that blurred her features.

She walked closer. Webster's instinct was to run. But where could he go? There was no place to hide. If he ran, she could shoot him in the back.

As she continued her approach he watched her place her handgun back into its holster and snap the strap to secure it. She was now ten feet away and he was frozen in place. It was a stocking that covered her face. What the hell was happening? Who was this? She laughed again -- an evil laugh. Another shiver ran through him. His hands were dripping sweat. He was fixed on her face. He couldn't look away.

She came right up to him -- three feet away.

"Hit me!" she commanded, her voice harsh.

"What?" Webster replied, surprised.

"I said, hit me!" she said, louder.

"Who are you? What do you want?"

Another laugh, high and shrill.

She leaned into him, face to face, inches away and shouted, "Hit me, you coward!"

Webster was now shaking -- his body vibrating.

He slowly raised his arm as if to push this creature away from his face. As his arm came up, the woman raised hers and her hand crashed against the side of his face.

Webster's head swung to one side with the impact, and as it did, he felt another harsh crash against the other side of his face. It was not a woman's hand. There was nothing soft or feminine about it. Her hand was hard and masculine.

He instinctively brought an arm up to feel his face when the woman's knee came up and slammed into his groin. He bent forward in pain and something came up hard and caught him under the jaw that snapped his head back. His knees weakened and he fell.

He was curled on the macadam. He hurt all over. He groaned. He felt a sharp kick on his shoulder.

Oh my God, what is happening? Why?

The woman put her foot on Webster's shoulder rolled him onto his back. She straddled him and dropped her knees heavily onto his upper arms. She was still laughing and calling him names. She slapped his face back and forth. His head rolled from side to side. He had no strength to resist.

Finally it stopped. She put her face down to his and spoke with a snarl through the stocking. "You are dead meat, Mr. Webster. You are going to die, but it won't be tonight."

Another shrill laugh. "You are my mouse, Mr. Webster. I am the cat. You are my toy." Another chilling laugh.

Finally she pushed off, stood, and looked down at him. "You hurt? You're going to hurt even more. This is the beginning. I'll chase you down again. Good night, Mr. Mouse. Meeeowwwwww."

He heard her words, but distantly. He couldn't believe this was happening to him.

* * *

Webster was gently roused by the relief security-desk guard. She was just arriving for the midnight shift change. She saw Webster's VW and a couple of unidentified objects on the parking lot and investigated. She called 911.

"Can you hear me, Mr. Webster?" she asked as she hovered over him.

The female voice startled him and he gave a reflexive jerk thinking the evil one was still with him. But this voice was pleasant and soothing. It was not *that* woman.

"I don't know," he answered, shivering violently, his teeth clicking. He was very cold. He passed out again.

Now he heard another female voice. This one was familiar. It was Ellen. She had her face down next to his and she was sobbing. "Oh, Nat, Nat, Nat."

With some effort he opened his eyes and, through a haze, he saw her. He wanted to put his arm around her, but he couldn't move. He couldn't move anything. Everything hurt. He opened his mouth to say something but he just made an ugly sound.

He passed out again.

* * *

Webster spent twenty-four hours in the hospital. He slowly recovered, able to sit up in a chair and communicate intelligently. He had plenty of bruises. He asked for a mirror. He didn't recognize himself. His face was puffy and purple. Every muscle in his body ached. He had no wounds other than the pre-existing one in his right triceps.

Visitors were plentiful. Few were able to recognize him. Ellen never left his side. Wilson and Officer Commerwitz spent some time with him as well -- asking questions. The nightmare returned. He tried to answer the chief but his jaw hurt badly

"Officer Murphy will recover," the chief said. "He has a collapsed lung from the chest wound. Unfortunately he was not wearing a vest. It seems we underestimated the aggressiveness of your assailant.

"Murphy wasn't able to tell us much. Just that this figure jumped out from behind your car. Then, we figure, he was shot. He has no memory beyond seeing her appear. His weapon was on the ground beside him which means he made an attempt to protect you."

"I'm grateful," Webster said through his teeth. "I'm glad he's OK. Please pass along my condolences."

"Now," the chief continued, "What about you?"

"She beat me up. Pure and simple."

"That's it?"

"Oh, no. She said several times that she was going to kill me, but not now." Webster shivered.

"You couldn't see her face?"

"It was covered with a nylon or something."

"Did you hit her?"

"It's funny. Well, maybe not so funny," Webster began. "At the beginning she challenged me to hit her. I didn't. I had no reason to hit her, except, I guess I didn't think of Officer Murphy lying beside me.

"I was too shocked. First, by Murphy going down. Second, by her very strange appearance. Third, by her being a woman." Webster paused. "Not many women in my life have challenged me to hit them. I'm not a fighter. She obviously is. I've never hit a woman."

"No description?"

"Just that it was a woman. She was taller than me -- over six feet I'd say. Her figure was slim and athletic."

"Anything else?"

"I was frozen in place. She walked toward me with the gun in her hand. But at about ten feet away, she put it in the holster on her waist. Strange."

"Apparently she made an assessment of you and decided she could take you on," the chief added.

"I thought she might just want to talk. But she kept coming, hands at her sides, until she was looking down at me, uncomfortably close. Then she started saying 'Hit me'!"

"Maybe you should have."

"Maybe. But I wouldn't know how. She had a rough, threatening voice. I was ready to talk. But that didn't happen. She was fast and brutal -- obviously experienced."

"Was there another vehicle around?"

"I didn't see any. Only mine." Webster paused. "Another thing. Her hands. They were men's hands -- hard and bony and they hurt. She was not your everyday housewife."

Chief Wilson was pleased. He had some clues -- enough to get him started. He jotted them on a pad: Tall, thin female. Expert marksman. Probably used a silencer on her gun, according to Webster's description of the gunshot sound. Very athletic. Rough voice. She considered herself the cat and she even meowed. They found a single shell casing at the scene -- a .38 caliber.

He sent Commerwitz on a tour of all the shooting ranges and gun shops in eastern New England from Rhode Island to southern Maine to find a woman of this description. Looking for a tall woman who was into guns should certainly narrow the search.

* * *

Ellen hovered over Webster night and day. More wary escorts, now with bulletproof vests, were accompanying Webster.

Recovery was slow. His entire body ached despite the pain medication. He had difficulty talking through his swollen jaw. He was able to walk slowly around the house to keep his joints moving. His brain was still working normally, but images of the cat woman sometimes hindered his sleep.

Three days of boredom. Ellen went to work daily. He kept track of things by phone, and he had his laptop.

Webster had plenty of time to think about his attacker. Who would want him killed? Certainly not her. She could be a local person, but more likely she was from somewhere else. But if she was hired to kill, why was she delaying it? Two incidents so far: the shot through the window and then beat up in the parking lot. This was obviously an intimidation tactic. He remembered the chief telling him the intimidation factor might be the way the killer gets her kicks. Well, it was working.

Who was it that could hate him this much? Who had he so grossly offended? It was his nature never to offend anyone, if possible.

Ha! I have it! thought Webster. The Scan-Man directors. They were fired. They were accused of a crime and are on trial. But which director? Ed Randolph? Not likely for he was incommunicative. Peter Stevenson? No. He was a yes man and never took a step forward on his own. Chandler Harrington? There we go, baby! I hurt Harrington on December 19 when I disrupted his initial plan by creating the New England storm. I foiled him again when I appeared at the White House during his presentation.

But that's not all, Webster thought. At the trial there was talk of the assassination of General Ruben. He was part of the original Scan-Man presidential meeting that Harrington attended. Could Ruben have turned against Harrington? Could Harrington have ordered Ruben killed?

Webster called Chief Wilson. "I think I have a lead for you on who may be behind this plot to kill me."

"That's interesting. Where are you?"

"I'm at home licking my wounds. Come on over when you can. But watch it, I have a guard lurking around."

"Well," the chief said. "You haven't lost your good humor."

"Don't believe it for one second."

* * *

"In a way, Ellen, my forced home stay has made me more aware of what's going on in the world. I've spent an inordinate amount of time on the cable channels and reading the newspapers. I've been too Scan-Man focused -- a common problem among lab workers such as myself. I've just noticed

86

the vast amount of damage the December storm has done, not only to Hollandson, but to New England in general."

"I'm glad you're seeing this," Ellen agreed. "You were away for all of the storm. Now that you're here you can see the damage for yourself.

"People are suffering, Nat. Many have no insurance to rebuild or repair."

"I now realize that," Webster acknowledged. "But I also realize I may be able to do something about it."

"Oh?"

"I want to take the initiative here, before the trial produces a verdict that Scan-Man *must* pay for damages. In the next few days I will meet with the directors and propose setting aside a few billion dollars to be distributed throughout New England -- much like the plan with the Deepwater Horizon Oil Spill and the Gulf Coast states. I see this as a bit like that."

"You'll make a few friends."

"I realize some will look at this effort as distribution of guilt money and, in a way, it is. But Scan-Man has to maintain its squeaky-clean image as a responsible company."

"My hero," Ellen said, and kissed him.

* * *

"I have come to the conclusion that Chandler Harrington is behind this threat to my life," Webster told the chief. "I think he is funding this killer woman, although it may be her choice to play cat and mouse with me for a while."

"Do you have any proof it's Harrington?"

"No. But I can't think of anyone I've done more damage to."

"Harrington's in prison," the chief said. "They won't let him out on bail."

"I know that," Webster said. "But I'll bet you anything he's fully in touch with the outside world."

"Of course. He still has his laptop, but it's being closely monitored."

"Who monitors Harrington's laptop and who is monitoring the monitor?"

"I have a guy on it."

"I hope you're looking over this guy's shoulder."

"He's keeping a log on the activity."

"Has he been given any hot points?"

"We've told him what to look for. We're tracking his history of financial transactions," the chief said. "Where it gets hairy is if his attorney is laundering his money. Apparently the attorney has access to his accounts."

"Can you handle this type of surveillance?"

"I have people who can." The chief acted a bit snubbed, as if Webster doubted his snooping abilities.

* * *

Sasha and Helena sat side by side on bar stools next to a narrow table between them. Each had a martini. They sat facing the Boston skyline. They were both nude. They were hot and perspiration was beaded on their foreheads. Their hair was damp and unkempt. Both had new scratches, and small welts had appeared on their torsos. Their rule of combat was -- never assault the face or neck. All other body parts were fair game.

Surprisingly, to a casual observer, these women wore no tattoos in an era when tattoos were at the height of popularity.

"I saw you cleaning a pistol tonight," Helena said.

"You are one bright girl."

"It was dirty again?"

"It gets dirty every day."

"What do you do with it?"

"I shoot it."

"What do you shoot at?"

"My, you're inquisitive," Sasha remarked.

"I love you. I want to know more about you."

"You know everything about me -- except my guns."

"When are you going to teach me about guns?"

"Helena. We've been through this before. I will never teach you anything about guns. They are dangerous. It's enough for only one of us to know about them."

Helena pouted. "That makes me sad."

"Well, you're just going to have to be sad." Sasha paused. "Make me another martini, Helena. You do that very well. I can't make martinis."

"I can show you how," Helena said hopefully.

"I don't want to learn how. I have you and you are the expert."

"What do you do when I'm not here?"

"I find someone else to make me a martini."

"What do you shoot at?"

"Jesus Christ! Helena. I shoot at targets! There! Are you finally happy?" Sasha's voice was shrill.

Helena pouted, but went to the bar and made two more martinis.

"Guns make you happy," Helena bravely continued.

"Yes they do make me happy."

"I don't know any other girls who have guns."

"Shut your friggin' mouth. I don't want you to mention goddamn guns again -- or you're out of here. Get it?

"Do you get it!" Sasha repeated loudly and tossed her martini glass at Helena who ducked and the glass broke against the wall. "Oh! You piss me off sometimes."

"Yes, Sasha," she said meekly. "I get it. I'm sorry."

"Now pick up the mess and make me another drink."

* * *

General Armand Stringer, Chairman of the Joint Chiefs of Staff, was smiling at his top men -- smiling a little bit like the proverbial cat that ate the canary. This was an informal, social meeting. It was limited to six general officers that included the commanders of the Army, Navy, Marines, Air Force and the National Guard. This was a very rare, private gathering among competing forces. Each understood this meeting was unofficial and there was no need to record anything.

The common denominator in the group was their lifetime military careers. Each held the highest rank in their services. They were the cream of the military crop. But they were also well aware that they answered only to civilians, all of who were either elected or appointed and who came and went with elections and appointments. It wasn't easy for men of this rank to follow orders from civilians who might be gone tomorrow. It was torture to deal with a know-nothing newbie. To survive, to make it to the top, required an extraordinary ability to judge character and to know when to speak up and when to shut up.

"What I want to talk about is the capability of the new Searoc Beam that's built into the recently orbited Scanner XII satellite. It is an exciting piece of hardware.

"What interests me very much is the claimed ability of the Searoc Beam to pierce three inches of armor plate. And, I'm told, it can also turn a military tank into a puddle of molten steel.

"But that's only the beginning, gentlemen. The beam is operated remotely from the satellite. Very much like drones, the operator can zero in on a target and obliterate it.

90

But it can't be shot down like the drone because the beam originates in space.

"You can tell I'm a bit excited. And, because it's in space, it can zero in on other orbiting satellites and space gear, identify and destroy them. This is 21st Century Star Wars at its best. Only this is for real.

"How's it work? The Scanner XII satellite has to be in direct sight of the sun. An Energizer on board captures the energy in the sun's rays by way of a giant convex, collapsible (think focusable) titanium mirror. The mirror converts the rays into concentrated energy that's transferred to the Searoc Beam. Now think back to New England on Christmas Eve. Here the beam, expanded to the max, evaporated the cloud cover over the entire region in less than an hour.

"Remember when you were a kid and you used your dad's magnifying glass to burn a hole in a piece of paper, or set fire to a piece of wood? It's a bit more sophisticated than that, but you get the idea.

"The potential for this is limited only by the extent of our imaginations.

"There's one little problem. Nat Webster, the developer of this technology, and recently elected chairman of a new board of directors at Scan-Man, says he is against using this for military purposes. Webster looks at this as something worse than a nuclear bomb. Indeed. In the wrong hands it *would* be difficult to deal with.

"I want to hear your thoughts."

* * *

The *National Geographic* reports there are an average of one hundred thousand uncontrolled fires in the U.S. and they consume four- to five-million acres a year. Recently, this has increased to nearly nine million acres a year. Everything in the paths of these fires is consumed, including homes and people.

A wildfire can move at a rate of fourteen miles per hour, faster than most humans and animals in its path can run.

Firefighters call the conditions that are necessary for a fire, the fire triangle. There must be oxygen, fuel and a heat source to allow any fire. Oxygen, of course, is the neighboring air or atmosphere. The fuel is the forest undergrowth, fallen trees and the trees themselves. The heat source varies from a single match, a carelessly thrown cigarette, a smoldering campfire to, of course, a lightning strike. Even the sun can produce enough heat to spark a fire.

Dry weather and a lack of moisture turn green vegetation into tinder that is susceptible to natural fires. Still, four out of five fires are started by people.

Wildfires take place around the world, but they are most common in the western U.S. It is here that drought, and many thunderstorms, produce the lightning strikes that initiate these violent infernos. Once a fire is started, it is often worsened by the Santa Ana winds that can carry sparks across many miles.

* * *

In the spring of 2012, Colorado and New Mexico forest fires broke all records. After several years of relatively few fires, the western states were hit by a hot, dry summer of drought. Wildfires in Colorado alone that summer destroyed more than seven hundred homes and structures along the Front Range.

The drought was the result of a dry La Nina winter, tinder-dry forests, and the melting of a lighter than usual snowpack.

In all, more than fifteen hundred structures were lost to wildfires in the western states in 2012.

Smoky haze filled the air from the Wyoming border all the way south to Denver and into New Mexico. The smoke was trapped by cool air and calm winds.

The fires became a crisis situation as more and more homes succumbed to the flames. Fire apparatus and personnel were diverted from smaller fires in Wyoming and Utah to help with fires in their neighbor's states.

The media in the eastern states began to report the western crisis at the same time they were headlining the Scan-Man director's trial. The *Times* and *CNN* were two of the leaders in focusing attention on Scan-Man and Nat Webster in particular. They were suggesting that Scan-Man prove the value of its much-trumpeted weather-modification technology by moving moisture from the wet Gulf Coast to the West.

Pensacola, Florida, for example, had obscene amounts of precipitation. Within twenty-four hours, 13.11 inches of rain fell in Pensacola, part of the mid-June 2012 deluge that dropped as much as 20 to 27 inches on the Florida panhandle and coastal Alabama.

Other media picked up on the weather-modification subject as conditions in both the East and West worsened in their respective ways.

Nat Webster was urged by Ellen to accept the challenge.

"Nat," Ellen said. "It's been almost five months since we've used the Searoc Beam. This will be your vindication. I want to see you win this."

"You're right. The time is ripe."

Ellen was thrilled and nervous. "I'll get the crew together, study the weather patterns, and put together a plan. I already know we have several options."

"Excellent, " Webster said. "I'll call a board meeting and ask for their support."

* * *

Donya and Reed Lynch and their two adolescent children are Colorado residents. They live in a small community on a lake adjacent to the Pike National Forest. It is a beautiful location with majestic peaks, often snow-covered, rising to the west. They live in a handsome log home erected largely by themselves and their family some twenty years ago. A long porch runs along the front of the house that faces the lake and mountain views.

The interior is upscale rustic. The front door opens into a spacious, open living area bordered by bedrooms, a kitchen and utility rooms. A massive stone fireplace is the central focus. The mantel is a half log. It holds family photos. An antlered elk head is mounted above the mantel. More photos, paintings, sculptures, glassware, and several Native American tapestries grace the walls. Scatter rugs define the activity areas. A bookcase, floor to ceiling, is arranged with hardcover and paperback fiction and nonfiction, filling the space between two windows. The atmosphere is homey and comfortable.

Outside are a small barn, a tractor and a large corral. A small vegetable garden fits between the house and the barn. Beyond, stretching down to the edge of the lake is a pasture where two handsome quarter horses are grazing. Behind the barn is the edge of the forest.

The overall scene is picture-perfect Colorado -- except for one thing. The high-altitude Rocky Mountain air is thick with gray smoke.

The normally white-coated mountains were only thinly covered with snow this winter. The white had vanished well before the end of the season. There was far less runoff. The streams are trickles. The water has receded several feet from the edge of the lake. The grass around the house is brown and sparce. The vegetable garden is struggling. Fortunately, the family's well is artesian and it is deep. But having experienced drought in the past, they still use their water sparingly.

The one constant sound in the house today is the forest service reports of the mountain fires -- the worst since the Lynches have lived here. The fires are advancing toward their home. Thousands of experienced forest firefighters are attacking the blazes, but the fires now cover such a large area the number of firefighters are thin to unavailable in most places.

The Lynches see no cause for alarm at first, although forest fires are never an event to take casually. But now they can see the flames in the near distance and the smoke, blowing in their direction, is choking at times.

Today, the Forest Service is advising evacuation in areas nearby. The family begins to think about when, if and how they will evacuate should it come to that. Is it reasonable that they can stay and protect their life investment? The thought of deserting their home is frightening. They hear of others who had stayed behind, ignoring evacuation orders. Some succeeded in saving their homes. Others were found as charred bodies curled up in their basements.

They had read. They had heard. They knew what could happen to them. Reed says he will stay and Donya and the kids will leave with their most precious possessions. The horses will stay. But they will be freed to flee to the lake for safety. That's what Reed will do also if he stays behind.

Donya won't hear of it. We all go or we all stay. Reed agrees. But he won't take chances with his children.

They prepare for evacuation while they still have time and an available escape route. They know that the single-lane road could be overwhelmed with fire, and then there would be no choice.

The order finally comes to evacuate. The ranger comes to their door and is apologetic. "It's time to leave -- now!"

They depart amid tears and grief. They have no room for all they want to take. The dog is big and takes up a lot of valuable space, but he too is family.

Off they go, turning in their seats for one last look at home. They aren't alone on the road. Their neighbors are in front of them and behind. It is a stream of anguished refugees. Knowing they aren't alone is somewhat comforting. They wonder who, among their neighbors, will be staying behind. They can come up with no names. It's hard to consider how neighbors will react psychologically when decision time arrives.

There is no plan for where they are heading. It doesn't matter. Just get out. Wait no longer than you have to. Then rush back to see what is left of your life.

They finally find a motel that has a vacant room. It appears that all of Colorado has moved to motels. It is dismal. The single, small room is another harsh reality. They have their fire radio with them and they listen.

The kids like the swimming pool. They spend most of their time splashing and paddling. They make new friends and, through the kids, the adults meet each other. They commiserate. They dine together at nearby restaurants. Joviality is scarce. The main topic of conversation is the obvious. Nothing but speculation.

Four days pass before they receive word that they can return. It is high-tension time. Nerves are frayed. They don't want to think of the worst-case situation.

The long road to their home has been burned over. Trees that had fallen across the road have been bulldozed to the side. They pass house after house that is gone, fallen into the cellar, leaving only the chimney standing. Wisps of smoke still rise from the ashes.

They round the final bend, leaning forward in their seats. They see the blackened mountainsides rise before them, and then their house. All four of the Lynches immediately break out in tears. The tension is released all at once. The homestead is intact! It is probably the best day in their lives. Somehow, the forest behind the barn has not been burned. Reed credits the metal roofs for saving the buildings. Flying sparks, landing on dry shingles, are a common cause of fire.

They park the car next to the house and gather in a big hug of praise and gratefulness. Even the dog wants to be in the middle of the small group.

Another neighbor has the same good fortune. Others do not. The unfortunates are welcomed into the fortunate's homes for the first night at least. The phones are not working. The lines have been burned. They will have to travel elsewhere to make arrangements with insurance companies and other suppliers.

One of the families doesn't think they can live here any more. Too much is gone. More than the house itself are the scorched mountain views. It will be years before abundant new growth returns. They choose to move elsewhere and develop new memories.

* * *

Ellen was flying high. She wanted to run through the offices to the Control Room in her excitement. But she restrained herself. It's going to happen, she thought. It's going to finally happen.

Sam Polcari was at his station. He worked with Ellen and was a close assistant to Webster himself. He and Ellen were together last Christmas Eve when Webster was in D.C. With Webster using a remote, the three of them produced what became known as the Christmas Eve Miracle.

"Sam," she was bubbling with excitement. "We're going to do it. We're going to test our expertise and make an attempt to put out some fires in the West."

Sam spun around in his seat at the first mention of his name. "Say that again so I can believe what I think I heard."

"We're going to rev up the Searoc and demonstrate its fantastic abilities. Here's the plan."

From his keyboard, Sam used Scan-Man's satellite cameras to focus in on the western-state fires. The images, in real time, appeared on the huge wall screens before them. Smoke and haze was startlingly widespread over Colorado and New Mexico. There were other spots of fires in Wyoming and Utah, mostly along the Rocky Mountain shoulders and mountain approaches. The smoke from these fires clouded the skies with haze, and the rising heat compounded the sun's drying effect and dissipated any hint of rain clouds.

Ellen, on the other hand, scanned the East Coast from New England to the Gulf looking for clouds with enough moisture to withstand the transport and still be effective in dampening some of the fires. She settled in on the Gulf Coast that was covered with thunderclouds and heavily pregnant with moisture.

Weather generally moves from west to east in the northern hemisphere. Ideally, the damp weather of southwestern Canada and Washington State would be easier to budge to the south or southeast because of this general motion. But it had been dryer than usual in these areas as well, although the drought was nowhere near as severe as along the ridge of the Rockies.

"This will be a challenge, Sam. It's the Gulf States that are saturated at the moment, so that's our best bet for the wet blanket we need."

Sam turned his attention to Ellen's screen. He studied the weather-front activity between Florida and New Orleans. "The sun on the Gulf is sucking moisture up into those clouds along the shore. The clouds seem to be quite pregnant. Your indicators show them to be at eighty-four percent capacity and growing. They could work."

"Let's now consider the movement from east to west," Ellen said, forcing her scientific background to take control of her emotions. "We have a transport of about two thousand miles over a west-north-west track, following the sun. The jet stream is well above this on a pretty flat track of its own moving in an easterly direction along the Canadian border. There should be no interference. We will be creating our own jet stream traveling at about 300 mph at an altitude of 50,000 feet, with little atmospheric resistance, well above commercial air traffic."

"The Santa Ana winds are spurring the fires and blowing southeast," Sam said. "Santa Ana has little altitude except where it sweeps over the summits of the Rockies. We can stay south of the highest summits and come in from the west side and then let it rip on its own."

"Now, of course," Ellen said, "this is all theoretical. I sure don't want a repeat of December 19. Let's go over this once again."

Ellen and Sam re-studied all the data that had been collected in the past hour from the two meteorological satellites hovering miles above the fire area. It gave them a very clear picture of the weather activity, as well as the conditions in the Pacific that would, in the next few days, change the current conditions.

"I'm convinced this is as good as it's going to get," Sam said.

"I agree." Ellen added. "But do you see anything, anywhere that could interfere with our plan? I don't."

"We have to move within the next few hours, Sam said. "Every minute we're on hold brings on the possibility of something we have not anticipated."

"Good. All we need now is Nat's OK," Ellen said. "He's with the directors now."

* * *

Webster strode into the Control Room with a broad smile. He hadn't been there for several months. The last time was December 19, when Harrington and the old board of directors were looking down on him. That was the day he launched the very first use of his Searoc Beam -- and it worked!

Now, he saw the activity on the two wall screens. He studied them.

He spoke to both Polcari and Ellen. "I want to be absolutely certain we can nudge that front to our destination and, I want to be certain there is nothing in between that can interfere. What do you think?"

"If we fire the Searoc in the next hour," Ellen said, "we calculate it will take six hours for our Gulf clouds to arrive just to the west of Salt Lake City. We will be following the sun west so our energy for the Searoc will be maintained. We're going to run into some updrafts from the ground fires as we pass to the south them. We have to stay well below and south of the jet stream. Our water-laden front will rise on that heat and then drop again after we pass it. Our front will pause just west of Salt Lake City and then head east. We'll have a front that extends from the bottom of Montana to central Arizona. Precipitation will begin just before it reaches the fires. The precipitation will be heavy enough and cold enough to counteract the hot updraft. As it progresses, it will blanket the area and smother it. There will be enough rain to soak the ground cover."

"You sound very confident, Ellen," Webster said.

"I am confident. This will work. This *has* to work! We can't afford any embarrassment -- or worse."

Polcari spoke up. "We considered attempting to drop precipitation as our front moves west over the fires. But attempting two tasks simultaneously is risky until we have more experience. Ellen has pointed out the simplest and surest maneuvers."

"You said if we launch within the next hour," Webster considered, "how do conditions change as we move into the next six hours?"

Ellen answered. "Our wet front will move further east and then northeast -- further away from our target. Secondly, the clouds are near fully pregnant and as they continue their journey east they are losing more and more of their ammunition."

Polcari added. "Delaying may give time for other fronts to develop, or sneak up on us, and interfere with our goal."

"OK," Webster said, convinced they were ready. "I'm going to activate the Energizer and go through the checklist for the Searoc. Ellen, will you please call the directors in? I have asked them to watch this from the observation deck."

Webster took his station, after he saw that the directors were now in place above. (He had a brief and unpleasant recall of the December activation.) He acknowledged them, flicked a few switches, and watched the software run through the checklist.

All was in order. The Energizer's mirror was angled to the sun and it was receiving maximum energy. He kicked the Searoc Beam into action and examined the width of the wet front he had to move and he adjusted the focus to cover most of that front.

This is considerably different from December 19, Webster thought. There were so many unknowns back then. He grimaced. Hell. There are plenty of unknowns right now.

Ellen and Polcari were looking over his shoulder at the wall screen that showed the wet front. It ran from one hundred miles south into the Gulf, and then to the northern boundary of Alabama.

Webster activated the Searoc Beam and eased on the power. With the cloud cover over this area, the beam could not be seen from the ground. As Webster made adjustments, the three of them watched a great transformation take place. Gradually the front halted its eastbound transit. Then it began to move in reverse. There was nothing in its path to interfere. It was heading exactly as planned.

The cloud mass began to rise, slowly at first, then faster as it turned into a long stream of clouds. Up it went increasing to supersonic speed.

The crew let out a whoop and settled down to take turns making adjustments and watching the front race westward.

* * *

A weather front of any kind advancing east to west in the northern hemisphere will cause great consternation among the meteorologically literate. Because of the Earth's spin, winds travel west to east in the northern hemisphere and east to west in the southern hemisphere.

102

That consternation expressed itself on evening television weather broadcasts.

"Ladies and gentlemen," one broadcaster began, "global warming, it seems, has taken a new turn. The Gulf states are experiencing a strange weather phenomenon in which a large front has decided to reverse its direction. We are seeing on this satellite image a front moving from the east to west as if retreating.

"I have never seen such an event. My staff is researching just why this is happening and what the repercussions of it may be."

A similar reaction took place around the nation. No one had an answer.

"That is one problem with the modification of weather patterns," Webster commented when the broadcasts were brought to his attention. "I don't know what we can do about it. We can't announce in advance to the affected areas that we are doing this -- there just isn't the time. We have to act on the moment, when the conditions are favorable, to be successful."

Now six hours has passed. The front reached its turning point. The Searoc Beam had done its job. Mother Nature now took over and the front ran its natural course. The clouds dropped when the driving force of the Searoc was discontinued. As they dropped, they re-formed into more natural shapes, still bearing their burden of moisture. The operation did as planned, drenching the mountain areas with much needed precipitation. Most of the fires were extinguished within a few hours.

The "consternation" crowd had tracked the wet front as well. They noted that the front changed direction and put out the fires. Residents of the fire-affected states called this a miracle that, in many respects, it was.

The Scan-Man directors were ecstatic. They saw the Searoc activation and the initial movement of the rain clouds to the west. They saw the weather broadcasts and the unfortunate consternation of the broadcasters as natural events were turned upside down. They saw the video clips of the rain falling on the gleeful, soot-covered firefighters at the very edge of the raging fire front. They watched the evening news footage of the joyful residents whose homes, in the direct path of the advancing flames, had been saved.

"This has been the highlight of my life," said Susan Morales. "Nat, you have done a stellar job. We all congratulate you and say how proud we are to be representatives of the company."

Webster saw his chance to take advantage of his success. He called the *Times* and the *CNN* cable channel to return for another interview. There was no hesitation.

It was a short session under the eye of the television camera and the two reporters.

"This was the third use of the Searoc Beam," Webster began. "There was much controversy over the first two events. The present one was conducted, I might add, after being challenged by your editors. In so many words, I was told by the media to put up or shut up.

"What I believe I have proven is that weather modification can be beneficial to mankind without causing death and disaster.

"This entire event is a matter of record. Meteorologists nationwide recorded the whole show. Further death and disaster has been avoided as a result of using the Searoc Beam."

Webster felt very good. His dreams were finally becoming the reality.

* * *

The following day, Webster met with the directors again.

"Gentlemen and lady," Webster began. "I'm about to present you with a plan for Scan-Man to spend $5 billion on goodwill."

A gasp was heard around the table, followed by "Great!" The comment was from Susan Morales.

"I am pleased to say that Scan-Man has survived the mistakes of the previous board as well as the terrible winter we inadvertently created. I am proud of our company and everything it does.

"But we still need to go further." Webster continued. "As a major international company we have responsibilities that go well beyond the run-of-the-mill. We have to be able to justify what we do. We have already apologized to the nation for the winter storm. But we must do more than that. I want us to pay financially for the damages we have caused.

"I am suggesting we set up a $5 billion Recovery Fund for the New England region, beginning in our own backyard of Hollandson. I want to hire an independent, well-respected financial person to manage and distribute the money.

"I want to point out that, if we are going to do this, we must do it quickly before the media embarrasses us into doing it. I'd like to take the initiative before this happens. As a responsible company, we should pay for damages we have caused.

"By the way, I am sure you know we can easily afford to do this. You are all familiar with our books.

"So I move to set aside a sum of $5 billion for the purpose of a Recovery Fund for New England, the details of which can be drawn up later."

Susan Morales seconded the motion.

"Discussion?" Webster asked.

"A $5 billion bonus to our stockholders would be appreciated far more, I am sure," Scott Padilla commented.

"I'm sure it would," Webster answered. "But if we give them such a bonus, the media might come down on us for lining our own pockets while ignoring those for whom we have caused great damage, I wouldn't want to be in your director's seat Mr. Padilla."

Peter Posednik cut in. "If I may say so, Mr. Webster, we have already been embarrassed by your apology for Scan-Man's actions, for *your* screw up on December 19. Now you want to blow $5 billion of our assets. That would be another of your blunders. How many more will there be?"

"Thank you for your honesty, Mr. Posednik."

"I want to apologize to you, Nat, for Mr. Posednik's outrageous behavior," said Susan Morales. "I am familiar with the company's financial situation and I think it is in our best interests to create this Recovery Fund. We have had an excellent reputation worldwide for about twenty years. This would boost that reputation further. It will give us good press. But, most of all, it is the right thing to do, as they say."

A round of applause followed.

"Thank you Ms. Morales. Any more comments?"

"Move the question!"

"All those in favor of the motion say aye."

All but one voted in favor -- a great vote of confidence for Webster.

"All those opposed say nay."

Mr. Posednick was alone with a nay.

"Thank you all," Webster said. "I will have a draft of the details put together. In the meantime I ask each of to search through your inventory of potential outside candidates and come up with a suitable person to manage the fund."

* * *

Fifteen minutes later, Susan called Webster and asked to see him.

"Congratulations on winning that handsome Recovery Fund vote, she began. "We should get great press for that."

There was something about Susan that antagonized him. In spite of her good looks and eagerness to please, she irked him. Maybe it was her aggressiveness.

"What can I do for you, Susan?" He didn't offer her a chair.

"You mentioned going outside the company to find an administrator for the Recovery Fund."

"I did."

She seated herself opposite his desk and continued. "As you know I'm a CPA and have a solid background in banking and finance. Why not use someone close to home to administer our own funds? It's going to be a big job and I'd like to offer my services as part of my director's duties."

"That's very kind of you, Susan. But this is one event I want the company to stay clear of. We cannot afford to be accused of misusing these funds. With a publicly announced outside expert, we can divorce ourselves from any apparent fraud."

"Well. I'm just trying to be as helpful as I can. You know I'm always on your side when it comes to a board vote."

"I've noticed that and I appreciate it."

"May I ask you a personal question?" She smiled and deftly leaned forward, allowing the V-neck of her blouse to droop and expose her braless breasts.

"Try me," Webster said, gallantly trying to avoid the obvious, intended view.

"I know you're not married and I'm aware Ms. Bloodworth is a friend of yours, but do you ever share your free time with other women?"

It was a simple question, but it was wrapped in sexual innuendo and tied with a bright red ribbon.

"That's an interesting way to put it, Susan." He answered politely. "I'm flattered. But I am quite content. I am not dating other women."

Susan Morales stood and smiled, composing herself. "Please excuse me then. I thought we might just have a chance to go out for a drink, let's say, to chitchat informally about how I might be more fully engaged as a director. I'm just a single woman looking for a little company now and then."

"I understand. It's very nice of you to ask."

Susan turned and Webster watched her stylish figure cross the room. She turned and smiled at him once again as she went through the door.

Webster shook his head and realized he was still a regular guy who on occasion had lustful thoughts. He was glad he was happy with Ellen.

* * *

They finished their run and sat down in the diner.

"Mornin' Black an' White. The regular?"

"Always the regular, Jack. Thanks."

"You girls hear about what Scan-Man did the other night?" Jack was uncharacteristically enthusiastic. "They put them forest fires out in the mountains out West. Can you believe it? Their beam thing swooped right in there and put 'em out like nothin'."

"I did see something about that," Ellen said, keeping what she knew to herself.

"I couldn't believe it. What a rig that thing must be!"

"I agree," said Maggie.

"What are they gonna to think of next?"

"It's going to please a lot people out there," Maggie added. "And, of course, there are many who lost everything. It's a shame."

"Yeah. Like here durin' the snowstorm," Jack said grimly.

"You're right. A similar thing."

"OK. The regular for both of you comin' up."

"I have good news, Maggie. The Scan-Man directors approved a $5 billion Recovery Fund for the New England region. Isn't that great?"

"Wow. That's wonderful. Think everyone *here* will rejoice when they hear that news. You know that Hollandson has already been gathering figures on snow damage around town. When's it going to be official?"

"A news release is going out very soon."

The food arrived and they began their usual picking at it. Other thoughts tumbled in their heads.

Maggie spoke first. "You certainly had the weather people on edge the other day. Everyone was fooled by moving that storm from east to west."

"It was a relatively quick decision, Maggie. I didn't have time to warn you. The fires were so dreadful with the burning of houses and people dying, Nat wanted to move fast."

"So this was really your first attempt to use your technology this way?"

"Yes it was, and it couldn't have worked better." Ellen paused. "What really bothered Nat was not being able to warn the meteorological world that this event was man made. Unfortunately, it caused a lot of stress for those in the know. He's not yet worked out a way to give an effective advance warning for these events. We expect that weather catastrophes, such as hurricanes and tornadoes, will have to be dealt with at a moment's notice also.

109

"Nat's so excited about this success. However, he's getting mixed press because of the confusion we caused. We expect it's the nature of weather manipulation. It'll always be controversial."

"My personal opinion," Maggie said, "is when you keep people informed in advance of these events, the more they will be appreciated."

As they were talking, Angie, one of the regulars at the diner, came over to their table.

"Sorry to interrupt. I know you work at Scan-Man, Miss Bloodworth. I just want to thank you for taking care of those fires out West. My sister-in-law lives in Fort Collins and her house was in danger and now it's saved. She had already given up on saving it. But when she learned what happened she couldn't believe her good luck. Please pass our thanks along to whoever's responsible over there."

"Why thank you, Angie. It's great to hear your feedback on that. I sure will pass it along."

Angie turned to Maggie. "I wish you would write some details in the *Bulletin* about how they did that, Maggie."

"I'd like to. I'm very excited about it myself," Maggie said. "But what might mean more to our readers, Angie, is for you to write a letter to the editor telling your story. I'll be very happy to publish it."

"I've never written to a newspaper, but there's always a first time. Thanks."

* * *

"Well, folks, the March 31 deadline is here and the numbers are in," Selectman Bob Sivolesky announced to fifty or so residents that crowded the room for this particular event.

"We got more than two-hundred estimates of property damage from the December snowstorm. These quotes range from a few hundred dollars to more than a million dollars."

Gasp. Murmur. Oh! Egad!

"The bottom line is a total of two point three million bucks. The highest estimate was for the replacement of the hotel atrium."

Sivolesky looked at the expectant faces around the room. "Are there any questions?"

A hand shot up. "We've been led to believe that the town is going to reimburse us for our expenses. Is that true?"

"What was it that led you to that conclusion?" Sivolesky asked.

"Well, why would you have us go to all the trouble of getting estimates if there wasn't some hope of getting money?"

Sivolesky responded. "You're going to have to get estimates anyway if you're going to repair your property, aren't you?

"Maybe. Maybe not."

"What do you mean?"

"If I fixed it up myself I mightn't spend as much as I would if you was going to do it."

That comment brought a lot of laughter.

Langer spoke up. "We'll take a real close look at *your* estimate, Charlie."

More laughter.

Sivolesky continued. "Obviously we as selectmen want to help our citizens reconstruct however we can. Our first step here was to get a feeling of just what the total damages were. We now have that. Our next step is to find the money to satisfy all or part of the need."

"It's Scan-Man's fault," someone shouted out. "They've got plenty of money."

"There's also federal disaster relief programs," Langer added. "There are also low-interest loans that are available."

"But it's Scan-Man's fault."

"That has not yet been determined," Langer said.

"Of course it has."

"We will see."

Sivolesky continued. "Unless someone has some creative ideas to fund this recovery, this meeting is closed. Our board will get to work looking into finding some money."

Maggie itched to tell the group that Scan-Man had just voted recovery fund money. But she kept quiet. Official information would be available very soon.

* * *

The *Times* was the first to announce the Recovery Fund, followed quickly by all the daily papers in New England. The headlines were variations of "$5B N.E. Recovery Fund Announced."

The reports were extensive, covering details of the fund and its management. The director would be Jason Goodhue, a well-known entrepreneur, art collector and philanthropist who was based in Boston. Goodhue's reputation, the papers said, was blemish free.

The stories reported what was known about Scan-Man's history and its latest venture into weather modification, including the extinguishing of forest fires in the West.

They also delved into the current trial proceedings of Webster and the members of the former board of directors.

The surprising part of the *Times* story was the inclusion of the details on the threats and the two attacks on Webster's life. These details were dredged up from the police logs, hospital records and unnamed witnesses.

The Hollandson citizenry hung on every detail about this revelation. A large percentage of the readers worked at Scan-Man. Most were unaware of the reported details about their company and chairman.

Emotions ranged from "that poor guy," to "it serves him right after causing that snowstorm."

Maggie was thoroughly embarrassed by the *Times* article. Her readers were asking how the *Times* got hold of this story before the *Bulletin* -- after all, Webster was a local celebrity and Scan-Man employed most of the town.

Maggie attempted an explanation in an editorial. The *Bulletin* was a weekly paper, published every Thursday. It could not, and should not, compete with daily papers. Scan-Man, although its headquarters was physically in Hollandson, was a company of international interest providing international services. Thus, there was a fine line in this case of what was local and what was of wider interest.

There were explanations Maggie did not say in her editorial. The *Bulletin* had not been invited to attend the press conferences to which the Times and CNN were privy. In addition, Nat Webster was a friend. To report unbiased news of this personal nature (death threats and attacks) might be questioned by her readers had she attempted. It might also have been embarrassing to Webster himself.

During their breakfast following the appearance of the *Times* article, Maggie and Ellen discussed this.

"I'm embarrassed also, Maggie," Ellen explained. "I understand the spot you're in. Nat didn't think to include the *Bulletin*. He was not thinking local."

"I don't blame him, Ellen. I'm thinking of the death threat and the attacks. I would never even think to invade your privacy and write about that. Then again, perhaps I should have asked Nat if he'd mind if I wrote about it. But then, what if I didn't know Nat? Would I have written everything I could find out about his problems? Maybe. This is every editor's problem. A local editor is often too close to the people she writes about. The are definite boundaries."

"Do you want to be invited to Nat's press conferences?" Ellen pursued.

"If it's a very local subject, such at Hollandson's benefits from the Recovery Fund, yes. One part of the fund benefits is strictly local."

* * *

The McCulloughs were shocked. They had just received a letter from Marsha Randolph.

I have had a long time to think about how much I love Robert and how I want to give him a good home and a good schooling. He would do well down here in Florida. It is summer all year. The ocean is nearby and there are several children from nice families living right here in the high-rise. We even have a recreation room right here next to my penthouse. There are all kinds of things to do there. Videos, TV, game boards. He will love it.

I will be travelling north sometime soon and will stop by to pick Robert up. Don't worry about his clothes and things. We'll get a new wardrobe suitable for life down here.

Cheerio. See you then.

P.S. I'll give him a call soon to talk about things.

Frank and Mabel were devastated.

"What can we do?" Mabel asked. "We're not anythin' legal. We don't even have any papers on the deal we made with Mrs. Randolph. Nothin' legal." Mabel began crying.

Frank came over beside her and put his arm around her. "You're right. There's nothin' we can do. She's the mother and she can do what she wants."

"What if Robby doesn't want to go?"

"He's underage. He's got no say."

"Oh, this is such a mess," Mable sobbed. "I'll miss him terrible."

"Me too. He's like a son. He's fit in here at the farm like a new chick in the henhouse. He tries so hard at the chores, and he loves the animals."

Mabel added. "He's always polite. He studies hard and gets good marks. I don't think he'll like it in Florida."

"Well, we have to be careful," Frank said. "We don't want to turn him against his mother. That wouldn't be right."

"Let's just tell him that whatever happens, he is always welcome here."

"That's good, Frank. We'll always have a room for him no matter what."

"That's what we'll tell him."

Mabel looked at Frank. "Do we have to show Robby the letter?"

"I guess we do if his mother is gonna call. We have to prepare him. We don't want him fightin' off his ma."

"We don't."

"We'll tell him he should go with his mom, but if it doesn't work out he can come back to the farm."

"Somethin' sad about that, Mabel. That's what we told our own kids years ago. 'If things don't work out, you're always welcome back at the farm.' Well. I guess things worked out for them, and we should be happy about that. That's what you're supposed to do with your kids. Get 'em ready for the world and then let go of 'em."

"Do you think Robby would ever come back?"

"It's hard to tell, Mabel. It's very hard to tell."

115

"Yup. Sometimes they do and sometimes they don't."

"Oh! Frank. Hold me. I'm gonna miss our Robby terrible."

* * *

"I can't help it," Puff said. "The idea of a chapel in that area scares me."

They were in Puff Chabus' expensive penthouse condo on Summer Street in Boston. Their suite was on the top floor of the Zenix Tower. They had a magnificent view of the Financial District and Boston Harbor. Puff loved her fancy living area and the amenities that came along with it. She could afford it. She had her successful deceased husband's multi-million dollar portfolio to pay for it all.

Puff was wearing one of her many her short cocktail dresses, each of which were cut low at the neckline showing the crowns of her well-endowed breasts. This dress was pink and it accentuated her petite stature -- like a little girl's. She relished the turned heads she attracted from both women and men. She wore white stockings and tiny white spike heels.

"But, my little lamb," Rev. Dick Masters gently argued, "this is where my followers live. These people need me."

"I need you too, Richard. I need you here."

"And I need you also. I need your financial help."

"And how much financial help is that?"

"Just a few thousand."

"What for?"

"To rent that storefront and upgrade it as a chapel."

"Richard!" Puff exclaimed. "I would give you *many* thousands for a traditional church with a tall steeple, with seating for a thousand and a large organ, an entryway with tall, fluted columns, and a chancel for a large choir and a pulpit. Something simple. I'm not looking for a glass cathedral, although that would be nice."

"Here we go again," Rev. Dick reminded her. "We've been together for almost four months now, and it's the same argument over and over. We're good together in bed, but that's not what my real life is all about. I'm afraid we're not meant for each other. We have too many differences. It was a terrible mistake for us to get together in the first place."

Puff leaped into the Reverend's lap. "I need your love, Reverend Richard," she said passionately. "Love me and I'll give you anything you want. Just don't expect me to hang around your little chapel."

The Reverend picked up his little lamb and carried her to the bed. "I think the best place for you is here anyway. Frankly, your loveliness would scare away my people. This is where I need you most."

* * *

It was several days before the McCulloughs showed Robby the letter from his mother. They had kept delaying it. It had been a torturous decision.

"Will Robby understand?" Mabel had asked. "Should we get a lawyer? Can this go to court? How will it affect Robby? Maybe we just hold the letter and wait for the mother's phone call."

"I don't know any answers, Mabel. If we wait for the phone call, the shock might be too much for Robby and he'll want to know why we didn't tell him.

"And lawyers?" Frank asked continued. "Lawyers will get things all mixed up."

The day arrived. Robby came home from school, had his snack and finished his chores. Frank and Mabel sat down at the kitchen table with him and showed Robby his mother's letter.

At age nine, Robby had trouble translating his mother's script and needed help. But, even before he had finished the letter, he knew what it was about and broke into tears.

"I don't want to go!" he cried. "She can't take me away. I like it here with you, Grampy and Grammy."

Mabel tried to explain to him that there was no legal way that he could stay. He was a minor and his mother wanted him with her. Unfortunately that was all there was to it.

"I don't understand," Robby said. "She doesn't like me anyway."

"Don't say that, Robby," Mabel continued. "She said she loved you. Things might be different now. You might like it in Florida. There's no snow."

"I like snow. I don't want to live in a tall building. I want animals and a barn and fields to run around in."

"We want you to stay with us, but she has her rights as a mother," Mabel explained.

"Don't I have rights?" Robby argued. "At school they say kids have rights."

"I just don't know about that," Mabel sighed. "All I know is we love you and you are always welcome here. We don't want to come between you and your mother. We don't want to argue with her. You are her son and for the time being, maybe you belong with her."

* * *

Nat Webster felt vulnerable to the woman who called herself a cat. The more he thought about her, the more he visualized her attacking him again. He had to find some escape.

118

He appealed to Ellen. "Baby, I have to get out of here and move to someplace secure. As much as I like the hominess of this house with the Billings, my presence here has put, not only you, but them in danger. I'm going to move into a secure condo somewhere until this whole mess is over. I want you to go with me, but I know how you're so close to Maggie."

"I don't want to sound like a soap opera, but I'll follow you to the ends of the earth."

"I don't want to sound like that either, and I hope I don't have to go to the ends of the earth."

They hugged and nuzzled.

"I assume this is a temporary situation," Ellen said. "I'm hoping that our lives can soon return to at least a token of what they used to be. This may be silly of me to suggest, but Scan-Man must have an area at headquarters that we can temporarily use as living quarters.

"Think of this," she continued. "What could be more secure than not having to commute? By staying in the building, you have the security that is already built in. Because this is only temporary, I hope, we can put up with it. What do you think?"

Webster considered. "I think you hit on it. There are rooms adjoining my office. These could be vacated, secured, and we could move in. The building has a cafeteria and all the necessities of life. But I still have a creepy feeling about the vicious woman who's trailing me. I really don't think any place is safe from her. Your idea is worth a try. I'll set it up tomorrow, Baby. I'll also stop by and see the chief so he can reassign the guards.

"What bothers me, Ellen, is it takes you away from your daily run with Maggie. That's a big thing for you."

"It is. But I can still run with her each morning. I think, darling, you are the one who's imprisoned."

The phone call came after the McCulloughs and Robby were in bed. Frank, half asleep, and irritated at the persistent ring, trudged down the stairs to where they kept their phone in the kitchen.

"I want to talk with Robert," The woman's voice said.

"Who is this?"

"This is Robert's mother. I want to talk with Robert."

"He's abed and asleep for a couple hours already. I don't want to waken him."

"Mr. McCullough," Marsha Randolph said sternly. "Don't make this difficult. Wake my son and let me speak with him."

Frank paused, holding his temper. "You can give me a message now or you can call Robby after he gets home from school at three tomorrow."

"You are asking for trouble, you old bugger. I'm coming after Robert next Wednesday. I'll deal with you then."

The phone clicked and the dial tone came on. Frank looked at the mouthpiece. His hand was shaking.

Mabel met him as he was going back upstairs. "Who was that, Frank?"

"Robby's mother. She's coming to get him next Wednesday."

"Oh, Frank," she sobbed.

* * *

Jack's diner was abuzz this morning with reactions to media reports on the Recovery Fund. Maggie and Ellen were in their corner booth taking note of it all.

"This is the best news I've heard since my wife told me she was pregnant," Bud Kelly, road superintendent, exclaimed. "After ten years of patching up my equipment, it looks like my nightmares are over."

Kelly was hovering over Maggie and Ellen's booth. "You're right, Bud," Ellen said. "Nat tells me he's taking care of his own first, right here in town. While your plows and trucks don't exactly fit the Recovery Fund definition of storm damages, Scan-Man recognizes the need for new equipment."

"That's the difference between government money and Scan-Man money," Maggie added. "Scan-Man can dole it out as they see fit."

Selectman Bob Sivolesky could be heard from the other end of the diner. "Great news!" he shouted.

Kelly left and Jack went over to the women's booth with his pot of coffee. He poured without asking. "The town's pretty happy, Ellen. It was good to meet Mr. Webster the other day. Wish we could see him oftener."

"As you know, Jack, he's got a lot on his plate, as they say." Ellen thought for a second. "Nat tries to keep the media at arm's length. Whenever he's in public, the media just fall all over him. He's really a private guy, Jack."

"Well, maybe we can see him again sooner than later."

"I'll see what I can do," Ellen concluded.

"We miss you guys at the house," Maggie said after Jack left. "It was so nice just to knock on your door and visit."

"We miss you too," Ellen said with some emotion. "It's terrible living in the Scan-Man office. We put his VW in one of the garages so this crazy woman won't know Nat is there."

"They have to find her soon," Maggie said. "Chief Wilson has sent out an APB using the information Nat gave him."

"APB?"

"Sorry. It's an All Points Bulletin. It goes out to all police units in the area."

* * *

Nat Webster was well liked as a manager throughout Scan-Man. Although his leadership was not necessarily by consensus, he encouraged all personnel to contribute ideas on any subject that could be beneficial to the company. Financial rewards were given for concrete plans that were adopted.

Among his closest advisors were those in what he called his Brain Trust. These were his creative types. When Webster had a particularly nagging problem, he called them together to try for a solution.

"As most of you already know," Webster began, "Texas has been experiencing droughts, wildfires and extreme heat. The most severe of these droughts encompasses seventy-eight percent of the state. Climatologists called 2011 the worst one-year drought in the history of the state.

"The impacts are, of course, on agriculture, water supplies and wildfires.

"Ninety-four percent of the Texas rangeland and pastures are non-producing. Hay has to be brought in from neighboring states, and cattle herds are being culled because of the water shortage. Only eight percent of the corn crop is useable. Newly planted cotton has been abandoned.

"Precipitation in Texas for the year 2011 was a mere 15.18 inches -- a record low.

"So much for the ugly facts," Webster continued. "The question now is: What can we do about this drought -- if anything?"

Ellen spoke up. "The most obvious solution is to bring rain to the region as we did in Colorado and New Mexico. However, there are problems with this. The Southwest is a huge area. The volume of water needed to even begin to solve the drought is just as huge. Finding and transporting a single storm front will be difficult and will not remedy all the problem areas. But, perhaps, a series of small, pregnant fronts could begin to remedy one area of the state at a time."

"That is a possibility," Webster answered. "But, first of all, we need to locate and corral a series of small, pregnant fronts without depriving those areas of *their* precipitation needs."

This discussion electrified Ellen's creativity. She loved her job as head meteorologist. Her mind soared into the complicated swirling, whirling activity that takes place in the atmosphere every second of every minute of every day above the heads of all humanity. It was a beauty she relished, that few beneath it can understand, despite the fact it directly impacts us every day.

Ellen had to tread lightly because of her relationship with Webster. Her peers all knew of their bond and because of this, perhaps, she had insider information that gave her an advantage over her peers.

Ellen handled it well. She was up front with her fellow workers. She was not a power grabber.

Sam Polcari had another suggestion. "Let's look at the stem of the problems -- El Nino and La Nina. I wonder if it is possible to manipulate them. Do we know what causes these opposite effects and why they shift from one to the other?"

"We *do* know what causes the effects of both El Nino and La Nina," Webster answered. "They encompass the entire Pacific Ocean. It's the interchange between the atmosphere and the ocean water.

"We also believe the extremes in weather we have been experiencing in recent years worldwide are affected by the increasing extremes of El Nino and La Nina. We believe now the two are affected by the man-made Greenhouse Effect.

"Look at the contrast here. Ocean surface temperatures off the west coast of South America are usually cool, ranging from sixty to seventy degrees Fahrenheit. Whereas, in the central and western Pacific the temperature of the ocean surface often exceeds eighty degrees.

"The warm, western Pacific water expands to cover the tropics during El Nino. During La Nina, the easterly trade winds increase in strength and upwells cold water along the equator and the west coast of South America. This drops the water temperature at the equator by as much as seven degrees below normal.

"The oscillations between these warm and cold conditions usually take three to four years and they each create different climatic effects, desirable and undesirable, on different parts of the planet.

"So, to answer Sam's question, how desirable is it for us to influence the entire Pacific Ocean in order to satisfy the thirst of the U.S.? Probably not. Modifying El Nino for the benefit of the U.S. would, quite likely, inversely affect other parts of the planet."

"So we're back to square one," Polcari said.

"Maybe," Webster answered. "Square one may be where we should be. The problem, I think, boils down to utilizing the extremes: flood vs. drought and how they can benefit each other. The Searoc Beam may be a tool for moderating almost any weather extreme, including the extremes of El Nino and La Nina.

"As we continue to experiment with our new and exciting technology, I believe we can exert a moderating effect on weather throughout the planet."

* * *

Neither Frank nor Mabel mentioned the previous night's phone call to Robby. They had no sleep that night. It took a long time for Frank to stop shaking.

The McCulloughs decided to visit Robby's school since Mrs. Randolph would be taking him away, and they felt they should let the school know of the change.

Robby had already taken the bus to school. It was now late morning. They took out the old Chevy and drove it the two miles to the Hollandson Elementary School. The children were at recess as the couple walked across the parking lot. Some of the children stopped playing to watch the old couple, one in bib overalls and a straw hat, the other in a long dress with a colorful apron. They waved to the children but none of them returned the wave. Instead, the children ran deeper into the play yard.

They passed through the big front doors and into the entryway. The couple was taken aback by the size and beauty of the interior.

"Some different when we went to school, eh Mabel?"

A young woman noticed them looking around.

"May I help you?"

"Yes. Thank you," Mabel said. "We want to talk to someone about Robby."

"Robby?" the woman looked puzzled.

"Yes."

"What's his last name?"

"Randolph. He lives with us."

"Oh, yes," the woman said with a smile. "I know Robby. A very nice boy. Let me take you to the principal's office. Follow me."

After an introduction, the principal invited them into her office where they were seated.

"What can I do for you? Are you Robby's grandparents?"

125

"No," Mabel answered. "Robby lives with us."

"How are you related?"

"We're not related. When Robby's mother left for Florida, she said Robby could stay with us."

"For a week or so?"

"No. We believed it was forever."

The principal shuffled in her chair. "We'd better back up a little. First of all why are you here?"

"Robby's mother is coming to get him. She wants to take him to Florida with her, but Robby doesn't want to go."

"Will you excuse me a minute? I have someone I want to join this meeting."

The principal disappeared. It was several minutes before she returned.

"Mr. & Mrs. McCullough," the principal said. "This is Mary, our guidance counselor. She knows Robby. She met his parents some years ago."

"Do you want to tell me your story?" the counselor began?

"It's a very long story," Mabel said. "An' actually we only came here to tell you Robby will be leaving school to go away with his mother next week."

"Why is Robby living with you?"

"After the house fire, and after Mr. Randolph went crazy, Mrs. Randolph said she wanted to move to Florida alone. She asked if we'd like to take Robby. You see, it was durin' the snowstorm that the Randolphs moved into our place because their place burned down. Mr. Randolph was very sick mentally and we couldn't get him to a hospital. Oh, it was awful. One man died tryin' to get to our place. We had eight or ten people at our place until the snow melted. Robby was there too and he loved it. He helped with the chores and learned to milk a cow.

126

"When the snow got low enough, they took Mr. Randolph away to a care center. Mrs. Randolph gave us money that we put into Robby's education fund and she went to Florida. She now lives in a tall buildin' where she wants Robby to live now.

"She's comin' to take Robby away next Wednesday. We came in today to tell you Mrs. Randolph is takin' him out of school."

"That is quite a story, Mrs. McCullough," the counselor said. "Robby seems to be a well-adjusted boy. He's happy and is well liked. But there was an incident just last week when he just didn't seem himself. He was very quiet and withdrawn. His teacher brought it to our attention. We talked with Robby and he said something like, 'My mother is taking me away.' He just shrugged his shoulders. We didn't think too much of it and he seemed a little better the next day.

"I expect Mrs. Randolph will come in, she'll sign Robert out and all will be fine."

"I hope you're right, Ma'am," Mabel said cautiously. "We don't want to cause any trouble."

"Thank you for coming in. It's been nice meeting you."

"Very nice people," Mabel said as they drove back to the farm. "I'm glad we told them everything. It'll help them when they meet Mrs. Randolph."

"Don't count on it," Frank mumbled.

* * *

Nat Webster's original concept of weather modification was to homogenize weather to rid the planet of its extremes. No longer would there be hurricanes, tornadoes,

127

drought, heat waves and floods. These would be moderated with the help of his Solar Energizer and the Searoc Beam.

But as his thought process matured, he learned that homogenization was not only impractical, it was undesirable. Where one interest group wants sunshine, another group wants rain. Where one wants to ski, another wants to play golf. The conclusion was, you can't satisfy both interests at the same time in the same geographic area. So we have some liking Florida in the winter, and other liking Colorado in the winter.

What about weather no one likes? Webster saw no benefit to a tornado. What was the benefit of a drought? How does a hurricane benefit anyone? Perhaps something could be developed to moderate these.

Flooding rivers, historically, have served to irrigate farmland and spread nutrients from the river. But then cities were developed along the banks because the rivers served as transportation routes. Mills were built to run waterwheels. Houses were built along the waterways so workers could be close to their jobs. What happened during the spring floods then? Man's creations were endangered.

So, man built dams and flood-control gates to tame the rivers. That worked just fine until heavier than usual snow and or rain came and the rivers rose above normal flood stage. Then, in order to save their towns and businesses, sandbags were needed to build even higher walls to contain the river.

Webster was well aware that man never gives up trying to control Mother Nature. And usually man fails. He had considered that he might also be among those who fail in their attempts to control natural forces.

However, his thought was that he was doing it differently. He had used the Searoc Beam successfully on three occasions, one of which backfired because of his neglect, but it

128

had worked to move a large weather front. He was proud that he had smothered forest fires that had raged uncontrolled in the West for months.

Now he faced the persistent drought in Texas. Could he move another rain front to Texas the way he did in Colorado and New Mexico?

* * *

Marsha Randolph appeared at the McCullough farm on Wednesday as promised. With her was a police officer.

"I'm here to pick up Robert," Marsha announced when Frank answered the door.

Frank was surprised at the sight of the officer. "Come on in, ah, both of you."

They came into the kitchen where Mabel was taking an apple pie out of the oven, while another sat on the counter cooling. The aroma was intoxicating.

"Pull up a chair folks and make yourself at home," Mabel said, straightening up and gesturing. "How about some coffee and fresh apple pie?"

"We're not here to eat," Marsha said sharply. "We're here to pick up Robert and leave."

"Frank," Mabel said. "Why don't you take them out to the barn." Then to the others she said, "Robby's doing his chores."

"I don't care to go a filthy barn," Marsha said. "You go get him."

"He should be milking Henrietta about now," Frank said. "You don't want to interrupt that." Frank looked at the officer. "Let's you and me go out and see Robby."

"Why not?" the officer said. He nodded at Marsha and followed Frank out the door.

"You a friend of Marsha's?" Frank asked as they crossed the driveway.

"No. I'm a family counselor for the town."

"What do you do?"

"I investigate complaints of child abuse."

They entered the barn. Robby was sitting beside Henrietta along with the cat. They could hear the rhythmic beat of the milk hitting the side of the milk pail.

"Hi, Grampy," Robby said without pausing. "I'm doing much better today."

"I can hear that," Frank said. "Good for you."

Robby turned for the first time and saw the stranger. He stopped milking and got up from the stool.

"This is Mr. ..." Frank began.

"Morgan," the officer said.

Robby smiled and put his hand out to shake and the officer reciprocated. "Nice to meet you Mr. Morgan."

"Mr. Morgan and your mother are here," Frank began.

Robby's smile immediately disappeared. "I don't want to go," he said emphatically.

The officer said nothing.

"I don't want to go, Mr. Morgan," Robby repeated. "I like it here with Grampy and Grammy."

The officer gave Frank a puzzled look. "Are you related?"

"No. That's just what Robby calls us."

"Why don't you want to go with your mother, Robby?" the officer asked.

"She doesn't want me, and sometimes she is mean to me."

Frank told Mr. Morgan the story Mabel had told the school.

"Very interesting," the officer said. "But she is your mother, after all." He paused thoughtfully. "Has your mother ever beaten you?"

"No," Robby said.

"How is she mean to you?"

"I don't know," Robby said. "I just think she doesn't want me. She isn't nice, like Grampy and Grammy."

Mr. Morgan turned to Frank. "Mrs. Randolph asked you to care for Robby, ah, Robert, gave you money for care and left him here?"

"And now she wants him back," Frank answered.

"I believe Robert has to be returned to his mother, at least for the time being. It appears there was no physical abuse. It is quite natural for many children to find life more exciting in a different environment. We can only hope that Robert can readjust with his mother."

"We understand," Frank said.

Robby, of course, understood everything that was said and began sobbing.

Frank put his arm around Robby. "The man is right. You must go with your mother. Maybe you can visit us now and then. That'd be wonderful."

The three of them returned to the house over Robby's objections that he hadn't finished milking Henrietta. Frank said that was all right and he would finish.

When they entered the house, Mrs. Randolph ran across the room and hugged Robby.

"Oh, my darling Robert," she said. "I missed you so much."

She pulled away from Robby and looked him in the face. Tears ran in rivulets down his cheeks.

"I don't want to go, Mother. I like it here on the farm."

"You'll like it in Florida too," replied Mrs. Randolph. "You'll have lots of toys and new friends. We'll have parties and go on vacations and . . ."

"I don't want to go, Mother," he said more firmly. "I will run away."

"OK. Let's get out of here," Mrs. Randolph said sternly. "We'll discuss this later."

She picked Robby up. He struggled, beating her shoulders with his hands.

"Put me down, Mother!" Robby screamed.

"Will you please help me with this child?" she shouted at the officer.

"I think you should put the child down," Mr. Morgan said calmly.

"Are you with me or against me, Mr. Morgan?" Mrs. Randolph shouted, struggling with the boy.

"Put me down, Mother! Put me down. I won't go."

"Mrs. Randolph," the officer repeated more firmly. "Please put the child down."

She held Robby sideways now, losing her grip and Robby pushed against her. She moved quickly toward the door but as she did, Robby slipped out of her arms and got his feet on the floor. She still had hold of one arm.

"You little brat," Mrs. Randolph said, and slapped Robby across his face.

Both she and Robby stopped struggling, shocked at the slap that was now turning into a red blotch on the boy's cheek. Robby escaped and ran to Mrs. McCullough. "Grammy!"

Mr. Morgan acted fast. "Mrs. Randolph, you are under arrest for assaulting a child. You will come with me. The boy will stay here for the time being."

Mrs. Randolph screamed, "No you won't, you sonofabitch. He's my child and I'm taking him with me."

Mr. Morgan grabbed Mrs. Randolph's arm and clipped on a handcuff. He deftly took the other hand and cuffed it behind her. He put his arm through Mrs. Randolph's and held her.

"With your permission," Morgan said, "I will leave Robert here temporarily. I'm taking Mrs. Randolph to the police station."

"Yes," the McCulloughs nodded, quite shaken by the turn of events.

Robby was now between the McCulloughs. The three of them watched as Mr. Morgan led Mrs. Randolph out the door to his van.

They were left in silence, the three of them sitting on the couch.

"Robby," Mabel began. "I don't know what to say about this. We're just glad you're here with us. It's all very sad -- very, very sad. It really hurts me to see your mother like that. I don't know what will happen next. I guess we'll just have to wait and see."

"Grammy?"

"Yes, Robby?"

"Thank you for having me here. I love you both." There was a long pause as they looked at each other. Then ... "Can I go out and finish milking Henrietta?"

Frank and Mabel burst out laughing. "Of course you can, Robby."

Now Robby laughed. "Are you going to help me Grampy?"

"I sure am. Let's get at it."

Off they went to the barn, hand in hand.

Mabel was left in the company of a big grin.

* * *

Sam Polcari opened the 'Brain Trust' forum.

"We believe we have something, Nat. Our goal was to create rain clouds where there were none by using the Searoc Beam. We believed we could draw water up into clouds much the same as Mother Nature. The Searoc Beam we thought could act like the sun, let's say, on the Gulf of Mexico, the Pacific Ocean or the Great Lakes. We could then move these sponges to the drought location.

"We tested our theory during the last few days, and it worked like a charm. Specifically, we applied the beam to the Gulf water surface. The application covered a seven-mile diameter area. Within just thirty minutes enough evaporation took place to form a modest cumulonimbus. It was like we dropped a giant hose onto the water and sucked it up. While the water vapor was cooling, we transported the cloud to an area in Texas just above the Mexican border. By this time the vapor had turned into tiny droplets and, probably for the first time in years, a rain shower took place in southwest Texas."

"It was a thrill," Ellen added. "We tuned in to a local TV broadcast and listened to the meteorologist trying to explain the phenom to her listeners. Sam did a great job."

"Therefore," Polcari continued, "as Ellen suggested yesterday, we should be able to create a bunch of these cumulonimbuses and move them to strategic locations in Texas. Maybe in the process, we can learn how to create a nimbostratus to cover a larger geographical area."

Webster listened intently. He never even heard the other ideas presented. What Polcari suggested was exactly what he wanted.

"Thank you everyone," Webster ended the meeting. "Please put these ideas in writing for the record.

"And, Sam. Work with Ellen and come up with a plan for, shall we say a 'wet run' in Texas."

A few chuckles followed.

134

* * *

Nat Webster was a member of the National Scientific Association (NSA), which held its last annual conference in December at the Hollandson Motor Hotel. Webster had been scheduled to be one of NSA's featured speakers, but he bowed out when he became so involved in the launching of Scanner XII.

A reporter for the association's *NSA Today* had scheduled an in-depth interview with Webster during that conference but that too was scrubbed -- until today.

Marion Lee was a lively, personable, middle-aged woman. They met in a small room at Scan-Man.

Webster asked the first questions. "Tell me about yourself Ms. Lee."

"I'm likely to be of no interest to you, Mr. Webster. I'm just a long-time writer/reporter for the NSA."

"Everyone has something interesting about them," Webster pursued. "What do you do when you're not reporting?"

Marion showed her embarrassment with a blush. "This has never happened to me. I don't know what to say. I'm married, I have children, I write, I read, I have a psychology background and I love to interview people."

"I imagine most of the people you interview are scientific types."

"True, like you."

"And you find us interesting."

"Of course. I think your pursuits are far more interesting than mine -- at least that's what I believe after studying the obvious in preparation for meeting you."

"Thank you for indulging my inquisitiveness. I like to know something about those who probe my life. I like your personality. We'll get along."

"My interest in you is your creativity," Marion said, "How did you get into this business of satellites and weather modification? Did you play with rockets when you were a child?"

"I've always been a dreamer. I built things I could imagine with my Erector Set, but I rarely followed directions. If I felt the metal parts needed to be bent, I bent them. That's a no-no according to the directions. I built model airplanes. My gas-engine models I flew in a circle at the end of long wires. I built some to my own design but those weren't very successful in flight.

"I once had an old vacuum-tube radio -- the one that preceded the transistor model. It was the kind that took thirty seconds or a minute to warm up before it worked. My challenge was to take it apart, lay the parts out on a piece of plywood and solder them together again with wires so I could watch them work. Most of that was a failure also, but I enjoyed the effort of trying.

"And, of course, I read fantasy comic books about flights to other planets.

"When the Internet was developed, I spent a lot of time on any number of sites studying the technology of satellites -- particularly weather satellites rather than, let's say military or communication satellites. I was enthralled at the detailed data the technology picked up from Earth -- temperatures, humidity and the like."

"I was surprised when I learned you went to a liberal arts college," Mrs. Lee said.

"That is baffling, isn't it? I never dreamed of MIT or Stanford or Northeastern. Boston University was my school, and I enrolled in the School of Liberal Arts -- now called something else.

"I guess you'd say I am self-educated in my scientific pursuits."

"How were you able to get so far in technology with no formal education in the subject?"

"Dumb luck, I guess. I knew how to start a business, and how to hire people who had better skills than me in the areas where I needed it."

"But that takes money."

"It does. But I had ideas that attracted that money and people who knew how to use that money most effectively. All I did was pull the right strings.

"Your modesty is unbecoming, Mr. Webster. You and I know the hell you went through along the way pursuing your dreams."

"You're right. I loved working in the laboratory designing, assembling and experimenting. I disliked meetings. I still dislike meetings, and being on the board of directors. But, the old saw of doing what you have to do to make it work is what I did in the end."

"How did you come up with the ideas of the Energizer and the Searoc?"

"Among my childhood toys were magnifying glasses. As perhaps with many children, I learned early on that I could create a powerful beam simply by focusing the sun through one of these. The glass multiplied the power of the sun many fold, enough to ignite a piece of paper, a sliver of wood and even a campfire.

"It wasn't until I was in college, yes liberal arts, that I experimented with a collapsable, concave food drainer. It worked like a satellite dish and focused the sun's rays to a center point. From there I built a ten-foot diameter dish with a highly polished silver coating of aluminum. At the focus point, I attached a heat receptor that I devised. It created a point of heat of about three thousand degrees."

"Excuse me. What is a heat receptor?"

"It's a group of specialized cells that respond to sensory stimulation, in this case, heat."

"You designed this?"

"I did. It was the predecessor of the Solar Energizer I use today. "

"I'm amazed."

"Please don't be. It's the next step that was difficult -- the exchange of the heat into energy and transferring that energy into the Searoc for use as a Searoc Beam.

"The energy is transferred from the receptor to the Searoc receiver much like a laser beam. It's a direct shot so the two units have to be within sight of each other. The Searoc receptor, attached to the Scanner XII satellite, accepts the energy and stores it temporarily in a sophisticated battery.

"The Searoc Beam is focusable, from a pinpoint to about a 300-square mile area when shown on the surface of the Earth. When focused to a pinpoint, the energy level is at its highest. It is able to penetrate three inches of armor plate. Increase the focus to ten feet and it will melt an army tank in three minutes. The wider the focus, the less the energy drawn from the energizer, and therefore the longer the charge lasts. Wide focus was used to diffuse the snow clouds that covered New England last December."

"So, now you have hinted at weather modification. Tell me about its capabilities regarding weather."

"With the successes I've had in New England, and more recently in the Rocky Mountains with the fires, I am encouraged to accept other challenges.

"I want to deal with alleviating drought in cases where long periods of minimal rain is harming agriculture. By the same token I want to alleviate heavy rainfall that leads to severe flooding.

"More tricky is moderating tornadoes. They pop up here and there with great rapidity and can spread over a wide area. Generally, it is not practical to manage tornados individually. I believe we have to focus on their concentration area and deal with the general atmospheric conditions -- killing them all at the same time. This has not yet proven itself, but then the tornado season is not yet here."

"How do you come up with these wonderful ideas?"

"Daydreaming helps activate the right hemisphere of the brain. I deal with a world of fantasy and reality. I believe you have to fantasize before you can realize. If you can't imagine something, you will never materialize it. For me, daydreaming can be like a volcano with spurts of images bursting from the brain. There is a lifetime of images, words, people, thoughts, names, games, feelings, sensations, senses and ideas stored in that marvelous three-pound chunk of muscle, wires, nodes, cells and blood.

"The brain can't be managed. It has a life of its own. Your experience in life trains it, but most of the information stored in it has been gathered by itself. All those memories you have stored during a lifetime are still there. Some are more difficult to recall than others. Most of the stored information was collected unconsciously. Some are recalled from an outside stimulus. Think apple pie. You can probably recall its aroma without the pie anywhere near. Think of a loved one you have lost. That pain of loss can return in a flash.

"You asked about ideas. Invention is simply a recombination of ideas. Think of the Model-T. Look at how that has developed into today's automobile. Look at any object from years ago and look at it today. Creativity is the opening of new possibilities."

"Your ideas are very stimulating," Mrs. Lee said. "I suppose I can relate this to writing. You begin with a blank page. You know what the subject is and you begin typing as the ideas flow. The original ideas develop in succeeding sentences and paragraphs and pages. Isn't that a similar progression to the Model-T?"

"It is," Webster answered. "Both words and things are derived from ideas that are brain generated."

"Thank you. Now, may I get a little personal? I'd like to know a little about your family life. Do you mind?"

"My initial inclination is to say, 'Yes, I do mind.' But try me and we'll see what happens."

"Are you married?"

"No."

"Were you ever married?"

"Yes."

"Do you have children?"

"No."

"Do you have a partner?"

"If you mean do I have someone about whom I care a lot, I can answer 'Yes.'"

"What do you do outside of work?"

"Not much. My work is my life. My partner works with me also."

"You mean you don't travel for pleasure; you don't have cookouts; you don't go out to eat; you don't go on picnics?"

"We do some of those things and my partner does more of that than I do. Frankly, any woman who takes an interest in me has to take a major interest in the company. I am thrilled by my job. I hope she is thrilled by it as well, although I can understand why she is not as into it as I am."

"Most people would think of you as a bore."

"Remember, there are no boring subjects, just boring people. I think boredom results from poor presentation. Some people speak in a monotone. Others speak with verve and excitement. But all this is neither here nor there. Do you have any other questions?"

"Yes. You have had death threats. How are you coping?"

"An ugly subject. I am not coping well. Death threats are one thing, being beat to a pulp by a woman and having her say she is going to kill me -- eventually, was one of my less happy days. The major problem is, I don't know why she is after me. All I have are my suspicions. But this has nothing to do with NSA."

"On the contrary. Everyone in the association knows you and your accomplishments. As fellow members they care for your well being."

"That may be, but it doesn't get me out of this situation."

"May I be forward and tell you what I think?"

"Thank you. I'd appreciate it."

"There has been little or no publicity about your death threats. I would call the media together and make this a federal case. Right now you are just limping along and no one will know about this until you are dead.

"Also," Marion continued, "get yourself a good detective. He or she can be more effective than the police. You say you have your suspicions? Trace phone calls. Keep on top of it. You're sitting around like a duck at a target shoot."

"You *are* an unusual reporter. And you say you are not interesting. Don't you believe it!

* * *

Four young women sat in a corner of the company cafeteria. They had their heads together, laughing and giggling, sometimes loudly, but most of the time quietly, intimately, among themselves. They were interns, taking time off from under-graduate colleges to work at Scan-Man and do practical, on-job training for their respective school science and technology curricula.

They had just chatted with Nat Webster during his walk-through. Each of them had been near the man several times as they delivered packages to his office or listened to him speak at company functions. Some of them were fortunate enough to work side-by-side with him in the company laboratory.

"Oh, God. He's so handsome," one of them remarked.

"I know," said another. "He's a walking Adonis straight out of my Greek mythology course."

"Can you just imagine what it would be like to be wrapped in that hunk's arms?"

"It'd be heavenly. I can just feel him now."

"I wet my pants just thinking about him."

"Me too."

"Oh. Don't talk like that. I can't stand it."

That brought the giggles again.

"Did you see how he looked at you, Lois?"

"What do you mean?"

"I mean I think he wants you."

"Get outta here!"

"I'm serious. I'll bet if you put the heat on, he'd give."

"Get outta here!"

"Really! The way he looked at you with those gorgeous eyes. I bet he'd go for you in a minute."

"You really think so?"

"If you did it right."

"I don't think he would. He's not that kind of guy."

"All guys are the same when it comes to sex, you know."

"Not Mr. Webster. He's the real thing. But I'd let him hug me -- anytime."

"He's already got a girlfriend. What would he want with any of us?"

"For one thing, we're younger, softer and virginal."

"Don't you think he'd want someone experienced?"

"No way. Men like to teach women."

"Like what?"

"All kinds of things."

"Oh, well. We can dream."

"He's a man I could easily love -- handsome, smart, rich."

"I can't stand thinking about him. I shiver all over."

"Lois. You're too much."

"I'm afraid the next time I see him alone I'll do something stupid."

"Showing your love to this man can't be stupid."

* * *

Ellen was usually up before Webster to join Maggie on their daily run. As she left their Scan-Man living quarters, she saw something splashed in red across the hall wall.

In huge red letters, it read:

"YOU WILL DIE, MOUSE!"

She screamed and ran to Nat. She jumped onto the bed, causing him to sit up immediately.

"Nat! She's in the building. She's written all over the wall! She's in this building! I can't believe it. How did she get in? Where was Security? Oh, Nat!"

Webster was groggy. "Oh, damn, damn, damn!"

"What are we going to do? How can we get away?"

"Calm down, Baby. I have to think this through. You go do your run with Maggie. I'll be OK."

"I'm not going anywhere. I'm here with you. Nat, I'm scared to death. I can't stand it! We've tried everything and it keeps happening. Now she's at our very door!"

Webster called Security. "Have we had any untagged visitors during the night?"

"I've been here all night, sir. Only employees in and out last night and this morning."

"Is your door the only entrance to the building?"

"Yes, sir. Everyone goes in and out of this here door."

"Thank you."

* * *

"Have you made any progress on my case, Chief?" Webster asked.

"Nothing."

"You're still tracing Harrington's laptop activity?"

"You're interfering with my job, Nat."

"It's a simple question."

"We are."

"Any good information?"

"Not yet."

"Paul! For godssake. My life is at stake! What have you been doing to find this person?"

"Nat! For chrisakes! Calm down! What do you expect us to do? What do we have for leads? A tall, thin woman, a bullet and shell casing, and, we have your hunches. As far as tracing calls is concerned, Harrington is on trial. He's in jail. He's not making any calls."

"I've got another clue for you. She was in my building last night. She's scrawled her threat on our hall wall this morning. We are scared witless. *Your* security guard didn't see anything. My security last night didn't check in any strangers. So much for the safety we thought we had in this building!"

"It sounds to me like this person, this 'she', is one of your employees," the chief offered. "Either that, or this she has an accomplice who did the scrawling. I want to see that wall."

* * *

"This is pretty outrageous," the chief said, looking at the scrawl on the wall."

"It is outrageous all right. It's right outside my door."

"Again, I think this is an inside job, Nat. You've told me that no strangers have passed through your doors."

"I can't possibly think of any of our employees who might have this much hate in them -- especially against me. I don't know that I've made any enemies."

"I need some more clues, Nat. You're going to have to put some more thought into who you might have done wrong to. I'm going back to my office and think this out. I'll get back to you."

"Well I hope to hell you can do a lot more than just think about it," Webster said sarcastically.

"I can only do my best, Nat."

* * *

"Things are getting too close to us, Nat," Ellen began. "I hate to say this, but I think you should leave town until these threats blow over."

"How can I do that? I have a company to manage. I have other obligations. Besides, I don't want to leave you."

Ellen thought. "What if you went to Washington like you did before? You won't be in isolation. You can run the company from anywhere. You have directors, and I can help you. We have all the technology of the 21st century."

"Touch computer screens don't feature the touch I need with you."

"Very funny. But I'm serious, Nat. The move wouldn't be for long."

"I'll think about it."

* * *

Two days later Lois, the intern, is given a FedEx package to take to Webster's office. When she sees his name on the label a shock passes through her. She is going to have to face her ideal man, the man she has planted in her garden of dreams.

Is she presentable? She quickly looks herself over. She rushes to the restroom, brushes her hair, straightens her skirt and tucks in her blouse. She is shaking. Her friends have made such a big deal over this man. She now has Mr. Webster built up in her mind as her dream lover. She isn't sure she can even walk into his office.

She'd better get going. This is a rush package. Mr. Webster will be looking for it, waiting for it.

She knocks, hears his baritone answer, and enters. She is trembling. She is frozen in place. The door closes behind her. Her teeth are chattering. There he is, behind his desk. Now he is looking at me! He is smiling at me.

"You have my package? Lois is it?"

"Yyyyesss," Mr. Webster." She can't look him in the face.

Webster stands and walks toward her.

He looks at her strangely. "Are you all right, Lois?"

"Yes sir."

"Look at you. You're quaking like an aspen. Come over here and sit down for a minute."

He puts his arm around her shoulder and guides her to a chair beside his desk and facing him. "Please. Sit down."

Ohhh, he's touching me, Lois thinks, reveling in the experience. He's so big and strong.

"Thank you, sir."

Webster looks down at her, studies her. She is a lovely girl, he thinks. He has seen her around the campus here and there. "Wait. Let me get you some water."

Lois watches him cross the room to a sideboard that has a carafe on a tray. He pours. Her imagination is running wild. Am I in a movie scene? Am I dreaming or is this real? He's waiting on me?

Webster returns and hands her the cup of water. "Try this. It's only sparkling water."

Lois takes the cup and feels her hand brush against his. Her hand is shaking. This is so embarrassing. He is still watching her closely.

Why is this girl so upset? Webster thinks. I hope she doesn't faint on me.

She brings the cup to her lips. She spills a couple drops on her skirt, looks down and tries to brush them away, but spills a few more drops when she tips her hand.

Still shaking, she reaches out and tries to return the half-full cup to Webster's desk.

"It's OK, Lois. It's only water. Finish it up. It'll do you good."

147

Lois puts the cup to her lips and empties it with several sips.

"That's the way." He smiles at her, reaches out and takes the empty cup.

"I'm nervous, Mr. Webster."

"About what? About me?" He laughs. It's a beautiful laugh. "Please, Lois. You can call me Nat. I try to be informal. I like a relaxed atmosphere."

Lois can't help herself. The emotion can no longer be contained. It wells up in her and she begins to cry softly. She feels a tear run down her cheek. She is mortified. She is making a fool of herself. She is stupid.

He hands her a tissue. "I don't like to see you so upset."

"I'm sorry, Mr. Webster. I can't help it." Lois blurts out. "I'm in love with you." She looks up into his face. "I've had dreams about you for a long time. I'm sorry. I just can't help myself."

Webster stands and holds his arms out to her. "Come to me, Lois."

Is this it? she thinks. She stands obediently and takes two steps toward him. He gently puts his arms around her. He feels her shaking. He cuddles her, holds her tightly. Her cheek is against the middle of his chest. He sways gently. Finally, she puts her arms around him. Slowly, very slowly, her shaking subsides. She is relaxing, and she stops crying. She feels his heart beat against her. Oh, this is so comforting. Let me stay here forever, she thinks.

Webster feels the girl's emotion subside. He releases her and motions for her to sit again. "Do you feel better now, Lois?"

"Yes, sir. I feel wonderful." She is now in a full, radiant smile, white teeth gleaming. This is a different girl, not the one that walked in the door.

148

"Very good." He smiles at her. "You look so much better now. Why don't you stay a little longer while I open the package you brought me?"

Lois watches his every move. She notices his facial muscles and jaw as he works. His hands are big, but they are gentle. This man is magnificent in every way, she thinks. He loves me. The way he holds me so tight. I know he loves me.

The package is opened and the contents taken out. It is a book. He is looking at the front cover, then the back cover. She can't read the title. He opens the book and looks through a few pages, then shuts the book and sets it aside. She sees the title, 'Thermodynamics.' Oh, my God, she thinks. That is my subject!

He turns to her with the book in his hand. "I am excited to receive this," he says. "This is the first time I've seen it printed and bound."

"Did you write it?" Lois asks.

"I did. This is my attempt to spread my ideas beyond the boundaries of the company."

"I noticed the title," Lois says. "I studied a little on thermodynamics last semester. That must be related to the Searoc Beam."

Webster is surprised. "You're right. Exactly. How perceptive of you."

"Thank you. I've been following Scan-Man's progress with the Searoc on the Internet."

"Do you have any thoughts on it?"

"Nothing world-shaking. Just that I think the Searoc would be useful if it could be used at ground level, maybe like mobile TV trucks send and receive signals."

"Hmm. Tell me more."

"I can see the Solar Energizer mounted on the top of a truck taking in the energy beam sent from Scanner XII. The converted energy is then transferred to the Searoc and the beam could be directed up into the atmosphere rather than down from the satellite." Lois is out of breath.

"Lois. I'm amazed. Pardon me. I just didn't expect this insight from an intern. This is very unusual."

"Thank you." She smiles back at Webster. She feels so good now, so relaxed and so mature all of a sudden.

Webster pauses in thought. "Would you be interested in writing a paper on your thoughts relative to what you have just told me?"

Lois sits up straight, fully attentive. "Wow, Mr. Webster. I would really like to do that. I can't promise anything startling."

"Lois. Have confidence in yourself. Believe in yourself. You can never tell how the nugget of an idea will develop."

"I am very excited about this."

"I'm glad to hear it. I look forward to seeing the results."

Webster stood.

Lois stood. "Thank you for calming me down. I feel so foolish."

"Don't feel foolish. It's my pleasure to have you with me. I enjoyed holding you."

"You did?" She is astounded at this statement.

"Lois. You are a nice woman. I like you. I hope you become a great success in life -- maybe even at Scan-Man."

He called me a 'woman', she thought. I *am* a woman! He knows I'm a woman.

"You said you loved me a couple minutes ago," Webster says. "Thank you for that. We all need to be loved. I hope that I passed along a little of my love to you."

Lois nods, studying his rugged face and penetrating blue eyes.

He takes her hand. Her heart immediately skips into a faster rhythm. He gently pulls her close to him and takes her into his arms. She feels ever so wonderful.

Webster slowly, ever so gently, releases her. "Thank you for delivering the package, Lois. Especially for sharing your insight on our technology.

"Move on with confidence. You are a beautiful woman, Lois. You have a full life ahead of you. I hope you find a partner you can really love and who will love and respect you in return."

He ushers her to the door and opens it. "Goodbye, Lois. Again, I look forward to seeing your paper."

Lois is thrilled far beyond her expectations. Her head swirls with new thoughts. He called her a woman. She has never thought of herself as a woman. He gave her his love, she thought, a love that she had never expected or experienced. He gave her confidence. He encouraged her to excel beyond her own expectations. She will thrive on this. Her meeting with Mr. Webster is something personal, she decides. It will be between them alone. She will *not* share her revelation with the girls.

She thinks of her friends and how they had goaded her into seducing Mr. Webster. She smiles broadly, titters to herself. It is me who was seduced, she realizes. I was seduced *mentally,* and I loved it.

* * *

The trial ended. The jury had deliberated for eight hours. Chandler Harrington was found guilty on all charges. Peter Stevenson guilty on one charge. Nathaniel Webster was found not guilty on all charges.

The judge gave Harrington ten years and Stevenson a single year.

Webster was a free man. A wave of relief passed over him. Finally, something had happened that released some of the pressure. He was in a daze.

Maggie and Ellen left their courtroom front-row seats and ran to Webster. He felt arms around him and kisses on his cheeks. More hugs followed. He put his arms around the women. He felt loved.

"We have to celebrate," Webster said. "Let's get out of this place. I need a Guinness."

Webster was filled with enthusiasm. "Where's Phil? Let's pick him up and drive up to Newburyport. It's a beautiful day. How about Michael's Harborside? I want to sit out on the deck and look at the Merrimack. I don't want to think of anything but the river, the boats and how good it is to be free."

Maggie called ahead to tell Phil the news. They picked him up and headed north. It was indeed a nice spring day, just slightly on the cool side. The four of them were for the time being, chattering, bantering overgrown kids.

In less than an hour they were seated at a table on the lower deck of the restaurant. They reveled in the gentle breezes blowing over the Merrimack River and through their hair.

"I want to make the toast," Phil said. The others looked to Phil and raised their glasses. "To our good friend, Nat Webster. May this be the beginning of the end of a host of problems that have plagued you and Ellen. We love you Nat."

"Thank you, Phil," Webster began. "I could not have survived this nasty trial without your wonderful support."

He leaned over to Ellen. "You, Baby, are the best. I love you."

Ellen nodded. "Thank you," she said looking down in embarrassment. Looking up again, she said, "I've been waiting a long time for this day, although in reality it's only been a few weeks. Add the terrible winter to that and it's been nearly six months since Nat and I have gone away together.

"I want to propose that the four of us take a three-day weekend and head for Kennebunkport and stay at the inn we liked so much. It's been almost a year since we've been there, and you know how I love B&Bs."

They each nodded.

"Nat," Ellen continued. "You've been working too hard. You need to take more breaks. We all need more breaks. What do you say, Maggie?"

"I don't think Phil will disagree." She looked at him.

"I'll go away anytime," Phil said. "New England is waiting for us."

"Nat?" Ellen looked at him questioningly.

"Me? Sure. I can work around my schedule."

"Everybody. Did you hear that?" Ellen said. "You're my witnesses."

* * *

"I am very dissatisfied with the chief's work," Webster told Ellen when they returned to her house. "It's been bothering me for a while. We are weeks into this threat business and we are nowhere. Even the chief admits it."

"What's the alternative?"

"I'm glad you asked. I have an acquaintance who is a detective and operates in Boston. I met him at an NSA meeting a couple years ago. He's a crazy guy in a lot of ways, but he has an unblemished track record. I googled him yesterday. He's worked on some notorious, high-profile cases that ended in convictions."

"What do you mean by 'crazy'?"

"He's a risk-taker. He likes fast, noisy bikes. He's a bachelor and dates celebrities. He hob-nobs in high society and therefore gets a lot of their business. He knows everyone who's worth knowing -- at least in Boston. His many contacts and his ability to keep his mouth shut about his clients make him someone you can trust."

"He sounds very interesting," Ellen said. "I can hardly wait to meet him."

"Be careful. He's going to like you."

"What's his name?"

"Odie Gallop."

"You're kidding."

"That's his name."

"With a name like that, he must be good."

"Let's find out," Webster concluded.

* * *

"Odie. This is Nat Webster. We met at ..."

"How could I ever forget you?" Gallop interrupted. "We met at the NSA meeting two years ago July."

Webster couldn't help but respond with a hearty laugh. "I can't believe it! You're the man I need."

"We talked about an interesting new high-tech thing you were working on -- the Searoc, I think."

"That's it, Odie."

"I've been keeping up with your activities. Very interesting, Nat. But why would a busy bugger like you be calling me?"

"I need help," Webster confessed. "I'm being chased by a woman who wants to kill me for a reason I don't know. She has already beat me up once and shot me another time. It seems she just wants to play cat and mouse. In fact, she calls me the mouse and herself the cat."

"Interesting. This sounds like some of girls I've dated," Odie said with a laugh.

"Believe me, Odie. This is no one I'd consider dating," Webster answered. "Frankly, she scares the devil out of me. Our local police haven't been able to do anything."

"I assume you're still at headquarters in Hollandson. I want see you this afternoon."

"I'll be here."

* * *

Webster received a hand-delivered letter from the Department of the Army. In brief, the letter expressed an interest in experimenting with the Searoc Beam. The Army wanted to set up a date for a meeting to discuss the issue.

This was a problem for Webster. First of all he did not want the Searoc Beam used for military purposes. On several occasions he had made this point to the media. But not surprisingly, the military had a mind of its own.

Secondly, at this time, there was only one Searoc Beam and that was being used for weather purposes. He certainly would not share it.

If the Army wanted to own and manage its own Searoc Beam and its technology, this might have consequences he had never considered.

With that thought in mind, he likened the Searoc Beam, at least in part, to the drones currently in use in the Middle East. And, there was a report that drones may be considered for use within the boundaries of the United States -- for drug trafficking, for instance.

Webster just could not get his mind around the possibility of a command center for Searoc Beams set up in Hollandson, similar to one in Houston used for guiding drones.

Sometimes Nat Webster felt like Alfred Nobel, the inventor of dynamite, who was rumored to regret having invented it. It may be as a result that Nobel created in his will the "Peace Prize." It would be awarded to the person who "shall have done the most or the best work for fraternity between nations..."

Does the world need another weapon capable of mass destruction?

To Webster, that was a very easy question to answer. To the military? That was easy for the military to answer also. However, the answers were quite likely as different as green and orange.

Webster knew who would win if there was a confrontation. This was going to take some thought. He had to know the answer himself and how he was going to handle it before he set a meeting date.

This was such a major issue that he would have to bring it before the board of directors. There were eleven men and one woman who had been on the board for less than five months. How were they going to react?

One driving decision for them was money -- money for the stockholders. To receive a contract to produce one or more satellites, solar energizers and Searocs would bring billions of dollars into the company coffers and increase the value of the company by two fold or more.

How can I ask the directors to reject that potential offer? Webster thought. How can I ask them, especially if the Army would get its own way eventually?

Am I a foolish idealist? Probably.

* * *

"It's good to see you again, Odie," Webster said. "I did a quick Google on you. Congratulations on your sleuthing successes with the high and mighty. You sure know how to keep the media's attention."

"You're no wall flower yourself, Nat. You keep everyone guessing on which way the wind blows." Gallop paused with a chuckle at his pun. "Give me a rundown on this woman. She sounds dangerous. I want we can trip her up."

"Initiative is what we need. Our police chief, Paul Wilson, is frustrated and in over his head. If you take on this project I'm sure he'll be glad to get me off his back."

"Be gentle, Nat. Small-town cops are rarely trained for tracking down assassins."

"You're right. He's a nice guy and he says he's done his best."

"OK. What do we have?"

"This all started several months ago," Webster began. "I received several death-threat letters in the mail. Frankly, I didn't pay much attention to them until I was shot. It's amazing how a bullet can wake you up.

"I was sitting at my desk at home when a bullet came through the window and my right biceps. I called the police in and they found the bullet and the shell casing.

"The chief later assigned a twenty-four-hour guard to keep watch on me -- maybe you noticed the police cruiser outside when you arrived. He justified the guard because of the trial I was involved in, the negative press I was getting because of my weather activities, and because I was shot.

"It was soon after the guard was assigned that I was beat up. We were leaving this building after dark, about ten. The guard was shot and I was beat up by this woman who called me 'mouse' and herself 'cat'. I couldn't identify her because she had what looked like a nylon stocking over her face. I was in the hospital for twenty-four hours. These bruises on my face are what is left of her efforts. She said I was going to die.

"Then, we woke up yesterday morning to find the wall outside our living quarters here scrawled with another
157

threat. So she must have been in this building. This put the greatest fear into my girlfriend, Ellen, and myself because of how near this has come to us.

"Oh. A couple other things," Webster remembered. "We're looking for a woman. She is taller than I am -- perhaps 6-foot-1 or -2 and she's athletic. Her hands are bony and hard. I felt a sustained use of them on my face. The chief thinks she is a marksman, and her gun may use a silencer. So that's it briefly. I expect the chief can give you more details."

"Very interesting," Gallop commented. "It's quite unusual to have a woman playing this role."

"Why do you think she's doing this? Have you ever handled anything like this?"

"Yes. A number of times, but not with a woman. These thugs get some kind thrill out of it -- often sexual. They are usually masochists who achieve an orgasmic climax by hurting and being hurt by someone they see as powerful or superior. They will continue to hurt or torture their victim as long as they feel the thrill. After that, the victim is no longer necessary and they deal the final blow that often results in death."

"Is there any way to judge where I am along that timeline?"

"Unfortunately, no," Gallop said. "The faster we find this culprit the better."

Gallop thought for a moment. "You say you have no idea why this woman is after you."

"As a matter of fact I do have an idea. I suspect she is on Chandler Harrington's payroll. He was the former chairman of Scan-Man. He has every reason to hate me. I just put him in jail for ten years."

Webster gave Gallop the full background on Harrington and their relationship.

"I followed the trial. This is beginning to make sense."

"That's good news," Webster said with a smile.

"I think it's time we both visit the chief for an introduction, and for me to get a rundown from him."

"I'll give him a call now."

* * *

"I want you to know, Chief, that hiring Detective Gallop to help with this investigation is nothing against you personally. I'm getting the hint that my life is in imminent danger and calling Odie in can't help but move things along."

"Frankly, Nat, I'm relieved. This is beyond what my department is trained to handle.

"Mr. Gallop," the chief continued, "I am aware of your reputation and am honored to be able to work with you on this."

"Thank you for the kind words, Chief," Gallop began. "Now, give me a rundown of what your department has learned about this woman."

"Nothing beyond what Nat has said he told you," the chief said. "I have Officer Commerwitz checking all the firing ranges and gun shops in the area for any information on a tall, thin, athletic woman who is an expert marksman.

"Nat believes Harrington may be the person who has hired this woman. He has just been convicted of scamming the government and will be spending ten years behind bars in a minimum-security prison.

"We know Harrington has a laptop and we have a man monitoring its use. He's keeping a log that is open for your use, Mr. Gallop."

"Good start," Gallop said. "I want to see that log."

"I've also sent out an APB with a description of the woman," the chief said. "But, she may be a lot closer than we

159

have anticipated. After seeing the latest threat on the wall, I think she may be a Scan-Man employee."

"That may be," Gallop said, getting up from his chair. "Thank you for the information and your insight. Let me see that log now and meet the chap who is maintaining it."

"Sure," the chief said. "He's in the next room."

* * *

"Well, sir, we're following an image of Harrington's laptop screen," the logging officer began. "I am printing out all his activity in real time. Unfortunately, I can't get into his hard drive where all the good stuff is."

"Who's he been communicating with?"

"He does e-mails with his attorney, Benjamin Miles, in Boston. It appears Miles has been managing his funds for years. There's an account at Chase with a hundred grand in it. It seems to be used by Miles for bill paying and legal fees. Here's a printout of his transactions. This account is fed from a blind source we can't trace, probably something offshore. You can see here fifty grand being deposited and then that same fifty transferred to a private account somewhere. We just don't have the wherewithal to trace these things."

"Very interesting. Who else?"

"There's a lot of e-mails with someone called Sasha. They use code words. Look at these printouts. Harrington is very insistent that Sasha chase the mouse, and drag the chase out. My guess is for psychological torture. Interesting. He tells her fifty grand has been deposited to her account. This verifies the transaction I just showed you."

"You could be right," Gallop said. "Anyone else?"

"Not that I've found."

"OK. Thank you. I'm taking these printouts with me. Good work. Keep at it. Let the chief know if there's anything significant."

Gallop turned to the chief. "Has Officer Commerwitz had any success in checking out the firing ranges and gun shops?"

"Not yet. He'll be starting in Boston tomorrow."

"Too bad he didn't begin there in the first place," Gallop rebuked. "He should be able to do Boston in a half day. I suspect he'll find something. You've got my cell number. Don't hesitate to call."

* * *

"Nat," Gallop began. "You said you were having someone go through the personnel files looking for female employees six feet and taller. Any results."

"Yes. They gave me seventeen that fit our description along with their mug shots. We were able to trim that down to ten by looking at their weight and other features."

"I want you to accompany me, Nat, to point out each of these ten to see if any fit your description."

"When do you want to do that?"

"Right now," Gallop said. "It's early afternoon. Most of them should be here, unless they're on another shift. I want you to shake the hands of the most likely candidates."

* * *

It was five o'clock when they finished. Webster shook hands with all of them. Two of the ten were not available. One of those was Mildred McCoy. Thursday was her day off.

161

"None of those we met today, Odie, had hands that could compare with the ones that met my face. I'm doing my monthly walkthrough tomorrow. I'll be sure to see Mildred."

"Very interesting, Nat. You have my cell phone number. I'm never without it."

* * *

Once a month Nat Webster did a walk-through of selected departments of the company, so that at the end of the year, he would have visited most of the Scan-Man offices and departments and shaken hands with the employees. This was a task he enjoyed, begun soon after he had offices and departments to walk through. He enjoyed meeting the employees, speaking with them, and listening to whatever they had to say.

Very few employees dealt with the general public. The dress code was relaxed and employees were free to wander. There were game rooms, cafeterias with hot meals, fast food and candy machines and, in fair weather, there were outdoor gardens for simple enjoyment or meditation. Downtown Hollandson and the Sudbury River were each within a fifteen-minute walk.

Webster melded easily with the young people Scan-Man employed. Maybe that had to do with their high level of respect and admiration for him. He never talked down to the twenty-somethings. After all, he was a young turk when he helped found the company. The young were his hope for the future. They each had their separate personalities and goals. They were brought up on technology he had helped develop. At age thirty-nine, Nat Webster was the 'old man', the guru of the space technology industry.

Along the way, he shook as many hands as he could. Occasionally someone had something to say and he listen intently. He gave an answer if he knew it. Otherwise, he said he would check it out and get back to the person.

As he walked through the shipping department, where trucks arrived and departed, and boxes and equipment of all sizes were received, he noticed a particularly tall, thin woman. He studied her from a distance at first, unable to see anything recognizable. She wore no makeup, but you could tell by her features she might have been pretty at one time. Her hair was tied up in a plaid kerchief. He went over to her. She was a few inches taller than he was, maybe six foot two or three. She looked down on him with a pleasant smile but said nothing. She acted distant, or even drugged. He felt strange when he shook her hand. It was muscular, boney, masculine -- like no other had he had shaken during his walk.

He forced out a "How are you today?"

"Fine, thanks," was all she said. She never looked him in the eyes, but then many employees never looked directly at him. Her voice was not the gravelly one he remembered. Still, he couldn't help but wonder about her.

Before he left the shipping department he heard one of the large garage doors open. It struck him that, of course there were other entrances to the buildings -- entrances that had no regular security. Shipping materials were coming and going, mostly during the day, but sometimes at night. A non-employee might easily slip in unnoticed, especially during a very busy time.

* * *

It was Friday morning when Mabel received a phone call from Massachusetts Health & Human Services. The woman said she would like to visit to talk about consideration of the McCulloughs as foster care parents. Mabel agreed, with some dread.

163

Robby was in school when Mrs. O'Flaherty arrived just before lunch.

"I took the opportunity to stop by Robby's school," Mrs. O'Flaherty said. "I met with the guidance counselor and also with Robby. I must say he is a charming boy. He appears very happy also."

"Thank you, ma'am," Mabel said. Frank nodded.

"My job is to screen you for consideration of making this a semi-permanent home for the boy. I'd like to ask you some personal questions.

"OK."

"How old are you and your husband?"

"I'm 81 and Frank is 83."

"Do you have children of your own?"

"We do. We have three boys."

"Do they live locally?"

"No. They are here and there around the country."

"How long have you known Robby?"

"Since he was born. His family lived next door until their house burned down in December."

"Why is Robby living with you now?"

"His mother, Marsha Randolph, asked us to care for him when she moved to Florida. Her husband is in a hospital. He went crazy."

"How did Robby's mother come to ask you to look after him?"

"When their house burned down, the Randolphs and their friends moved in with us. It was durin' the big snow-storm and they were stuck here for almost two weeks until we was dug out."

"My! How many people did you have here?"

"Ten people."

"How did you manage without food and electricity?"

164

"That was no problem. We have gas lamps and a generator. We raise and preserve all our food and keep it in the freezer. We're what I guess you call self-deficient."

"I think you mean self-sufficient."

"Yes. Self-sufficient," Mabel agreed.

"And what does Robby think of this farm?"

"He says he loves it. He's learned how to milk the cow and feed the chickens and collect the eggs. He has regular chores. Robby also gets good marks in school. He's a smart boy."

"What do you do for a living -- how do you earn money?"

"We both have Social Security and Frank works part time at the landfill. I make wedding cakes and we sell a lot of eggs and some milk from Henrietta. We have a good-sized bank account. We don't spend much."

"What about Robby's expenses?"

"He doesn't cost much. I make most of his clothes but we buy special clothes for school. Mrs. Randolph sends us money for Robby sometimes, but we have a special savings down at the bank and put all that away for his college education."

"That all sounds wonderful, but I'm concerned about one thing."

"What's that?"

"Your age."

"What about it?"

"What happens when either of you die?"

"What happens when anyone dies? We are just like any grandparents who take care of their grandchildren. We hope to live long enough to send the kids off into the world on their own. Robby's nine now, almost ten, and we expect to easily live ten or more years. Our parents lived into their nineties."

"Thank you, Mrs. McCullough. You and your husband are remarkable people. Can you give me that tour now?"

"Frank. Why don't you take her out to the barn and I'll show the house when you get back."

An hour later Mrs. O'Flaherty was gone.

"What do you think, Frank?"

"She's a real nice woman."

* * *

That night when they were alone again, Webster told Ellen about the tall woman he saw in the shipping department.

"It felt very strange," he said. "I made a point of shaking her hand. It was strong, more muscular than you'd expect of a woman."

"Like mine?" Ellen said offering her right hand.

Webster took her hand and gripped it in a handshake. "No. Her hand was hard." He smiled. "Yours is firm, but definitely feminine."

"What's her name?"

"Mildred."

"I'm going to check this out for myself," Ellen said with determination. "I could only hope that your female friend would be that easy to find."

"Be careful," Webster said. "Odie is checking her out also. She's a suspect and we don't want to screw it up."

"Hands like that in shipping may not be unusual if you're handling boxes and heavy objects all the time. That's a hard place to work sometimes. Are there other women in shipping?"

"Oh yes."

"Did you shake their hands?"

"I did, but they weren't six-feet tall."

166

"Another thing," Ellen said. "Of course if that is her, she's already in the building and she could have written on our wall."

"You're right."

"Oh, darn," Ellen said, raising her finger as if lecturing. "Did you remember to check for traces of red paint on her hands?"

"I didn't think of that," Webster added. "But don't you think a smart death-threat artist would wash her hands?"

"So where does that leave us?" Ellen asked. "It leaves me ready to go to shipping to meet this female -- tomorrow."

* * *

"Odie. I met Mildred today," Webster reported. "She definitely has the height and -- those hard, bony hands."

"Very interesting. I'll take it from here, Nat."

* * *

"I've decided to fight the military, Ellen."

"My wonderful idealist. Going against the tide again."

"One way to overcome a potential vote against me by the directors is to buy back the outstanding stock and dissolve the board of directors. But that's not very practical unless we had an extra $100 billion sitting around in a bank, and I've just given away $5 billion of whatever we *do* have for the Relief Fund. Off hand, I don't know how much cash we have, and I don't know how much stock we have outstanding."

"I hope you're talking tongue-in-cheek."

"I am. I should be thinking of other ways to win the directors over to my way of thinking."

"I have to give you credit," Ellen said. "You don't think small." Ellen chuckled to herself. "Have you considered buying out the military?"

"Ha, ha. Very funny."

"Have you thought of buying off the directors?"

"That's just as ha ha."

"But if I do any of the above," Webster reasoned, "the military is bound to have the last word."

"Of course," Ellen said. "The argument will always come down to national security. In the name of national security, we need the Searoc Beam to protect our citizens."

"So you're saying I cannot win. Period."

"Nat. It seems that way. The military, the President, the Congress, the Senate can say the Searoc is too important an item for a single company to control."

"Yes. I guess you're right."

"Can you imagine one company controlling the atomic bomb? But, on the other hand," Ellen reasoned, "look at how NASA has reluctantly rid itself of the Space Shuttle in the name of cost savings. Public companies are now in the shuttle business."

"Ellen. You're brilliant! The companies are taking over because the taxpayers don't want to pay NASA's expenses. Private companies can do it less expensively than the government."

"But is that true for military weapons?" Ellen asked. "Look at the drones. They're made privately but who operates them? The U.S. Air Force, with remote pilots."

"Right again. The Searoc is most similar to the drone, or as the Air Force calls them 'unmanned aerial vehicles'. Both are unmanned, both are operated remotely, with a real-time observation, from miles away. But, there is one obvious difference. The Searoc can't be shot down."

"So where are we?" Ellen asked.

"Instead of a win-win situation, I'd call it a lose-win. My idealism goes down the drain while Scan-Man stands to earn another few billions. Every single chairman of every single corporation in America would laugh heartily at a chairman that would vote against the prospect we are looking at."

"So, Mr. Chairman," Ellen asked. "When do you make your decision?"

"My decision may not rest on my losing or winning. It may rest on how effectively we negotiate."

* * *

Ellen visited the shipping department early Monday morning. She brought an excuse with her -- a small box to be mailed to her mother in St Louis. This was only the second time since she worked at Scan-Man that she had visited this area of the huge building. She didn't know any of the workers, but Webster said she should ask for Tony who was in charge.

"Is Tony here?" she asked the first person she met.

"He's in his office, ma'am, right over there."

Ellen scanned the area as she crossed the platform to Tony's office. "Tony?"

"I'm Tony. How can I help you?"

"I have this little package I'd like to mail." Ellen showed it to him.

"No problem. First class?"

"Please."

"Insured?"

"No. Just regular."

"OK. It's done."

Tony's office was behind a large picture window that had a view of the entire area.

"Excuse me. You're Ellen, aren't you, a friend of Mr. Webster's?"

169

"Why yes." Ellen was surprised. "Mr. Webster's a nice guy. He comes by to see me about once a month on his walk-through."

"Oh, Tony," Ellen said. "Do you have a rather tall woman who works down here? She's probably a couple inches taller than me."

"Oh, yeah. That'd be Mildred. Mildred McCoy. She works half time three days a week -- Tuesday, Wednesday and Friday. A nice lady. Hard worker. Been here two or three years. Quite a character though. She rides a motorcycle."

"Gosh," Tony continued. "There sure is a lot of interest in Mildred."

"What do you mean?"

"Well, Mr. Webster was here on Friday. You are here today. And Mr. Gallop was here a few minutes ago asking about her, but he told me not to mention our talk to anyone. But I figured it was OK to mention it to you because you're a friend of Mr. Webster's."

"I think it's very important that you *do not* mention any of this to anyone, Tony. I'll be back tomorrow to meet Mildred."

Hmmm, she thought. Mildred McCoy rides a motorcycle.

* * *

The jet streams are ribbons of air currents that circle the Earth and move from west to east in the northern hemisphere. They are responsible for moving daily weather patterns in and out of where we live and work.

There are two main jet streams. The strongest are the *polar* jets. They are at varying altitudes of 23,000 to 39,000 feet above sea level and they flow over the middle to northern

170

latitudes of North America. The higher and weaker ones are the *subtropical* jets located at 33,000 to 52,000 feet.

The speed of a jet stream can vary considerably. Depending on its temperature gradient, it can travel at sixty mph and in some cases it's been recorded at close to two hundred and fifty mph. Commercial aircraft often take advantage of the jet stream current by joining it and thereby increasing fuel efficiency on a west to east course.

Jet streams are caused by Earth rotation and by the sun heating the atmosphere. These meandering rivers of air act as boundaries for differing atmospheric characteristics. The polar stream drags behind it cold air from the north, and pushes along the warmer air it meets. When cold air meets warmer air it produces a weather change. This you see every day on the TV weather report. And when a subtropical stream of warm air moves north into the colder air it too produces a weather change. The atmosphere is constantly filled with air in motion thereby giving us changes in the weather and fresh air to breathe.

Scan-Man had plans to make good use of the jet streams. The Searoc beam, according to Nat Webster, had the capability of both straightening and deepening the troughs in a jet stream. As those dips and humps in the stream are straightened, weather is moderated. Extreme winters in the northern hemisphere could be moderated by creating a barrier that fences in the polar stream to the north or by cooling extreme summer heat by drawing the polar jet south.

* * *

Ellen returned to shipping the next morning. She stopped to see Tony briefly. Tony pointed out the tall lady. She was packing boxes. Ellen's spine tingled.

171

She then determinedly walked across the floor to Mildred. "Hi," Ellen said, putting out her hand. "My name's Ellen." Mildred took her hand. Ellen could feel its bony, masculine strength. Then, carefully watching Mildred's eyes, eyes that avoided hers, she said, "I'm Nat Webster's girlfriend."

No unusual reaction. Drats, Ellen thought. Mildred simply smiled and said, "He's a nice man. Can I help you with something?"

Ellen was embarrassed now. "Oh. No. I just wanted to meet you. I met Tony and the others yesterday. I just wanted to see you because you were out yesterday."

"Yes," Mildred said. "I only work part time."

"Well. Nice to meet you. See you later."

* * *

"I've been thinking," Webster said. They had gone to bed for the night and were reading. "I'm going to ask the chief for a license to carry a gun."

"Nat Webster with a gun?" Ellen chided him. "You'd let a woman kill you long before you'd kill her! You're putty in the hands of a woman. You would never hit one, never mind kill her. If anyone gets a gun, it will be me. I'll go see the chief."

"No," Webster reconsidered. "I think if I saw her coming toward me with a gun, I would pull mine out and shoot it."

"No you wouldn't, because she'd have shot you already. Just remember Murphy. He didn't get a chance to shoot. I'm going to get a gun," Ellen insisted. "And I'm going to keep an eye on *you*."

"Why isn't that like Murphy?" Webster asked.

"She won't suspect me."

"Oh?"

"I wouldn't go for my gun until she concentrated on you," Ellen reasoned.

"What do you mean by that?"

"I don't know. I just feel it better for me to have a gun than not to have a gun. I'll use the gun on her."

"I have a feeling you would. I can see you now, Annie Oakley."

"Let me tell you something you don't know about me," Ellen said. "My daddy taught me how to shoot. We used to go out to the dump and shoot rats, bottles and targets."

"How come you don't have a gun now?"

"You of all people ask me that, you pacifist! Times have changed for us Black folk, Massa," Ellen mimicked. "The nooses have been pretty much put away. We Black folk have laws on our side now, Massa."

"OK. OK. So I hate guns."

"Since you won't protect yourself, I will." Ellen was determined. "We don't need those useless guards around the place anyway."

"Now can I get back to my murder story? I'm trying to relax."

"Yes, Massa." Ellen tee heed.

"Cut that out!"

They returned to their reading.

"Ooooo," Ellen said. "I just love this bed. It's so soft and sexy. You sink way down into it. Put the book away, Nat. I need company."

Webster pulled the covers over him and sunk into the softness and the two rolled together face to face.

"This is nice," Webster admitted.

"Hey, Massa," Ellen whispered. "Want to make love to a little Black girl?"

"Never mind that stuff. I want to make love to the woman I love, you goofy girl!"

173

* * *

Gallop had been on the job only a few days when he gave his first report to Nat and Ellen.

"Yesterday Nat and I checked out the tall women in the company. Only one had the bony hands Nat remembers so well. I talked confidentially with Tony in shipping and found out Ms. McCoy rides a bike, like I do. Tony showed it to me. She keeps it under the stairwell next to the loading dock. Did you ever see her bike? It's Ducati Superbike 11999cc. It's expensive and its customized -- all black. It makes my Harley Dyna look like crap. I attached a GPS tracking device to its frame.

"I was waiting in the shadows on my bike when she pushed hers out the door at the end of her shift. What a transition! She had changed her clothes into a black jumpsuit, a full helmet and running shoes.

"I followed her, in spite of the GPS. I think it was her bike that lured me. I kept asking myself how could a part-time box packer afford such a machine?

"I didn't follow her very long. That quiet, apparently shy, box packer is either an adept rider or she's a goddamned fool. She surprised the hell out of me once we were on Rte. 2. She must have noticed me. She gunned that machine, zigzagging in and out of the traffic and left me far behind. I'm a risk-taker. But Mildred? Whoah!

"So old hotshot, Odie Gallop, swallowed his pride and drove legally, following her traced route on my device. I had another surprise when she pulled into the shipping dock at the Zenix Tower on Summer Street in Boston. This place is a posh collection of expensive condos.

"Very conveniently, I knew the Towers manager. In fact, I dated her a few times. For some strange reason we're still on pretty good terms and, after a promise of a late-evening drink downtown, she shared some confidential information with me.

"The big news is, Mildred is known as Sasha at the Towers. Ring a bell with you? Harrington has been communicating with a Sasha on his laptop.

"This is where it gets very interesting," Gallop continued. "Sasha's condo is half of the Tower's huge penthouse. Her monthly fee is direct deposited from a blind source and the amount is about ten times what Mildred makes a month at Scan-Man.

"Does this mean that our Mildred is the Sasha that Harrington is funding?" Gallop asked rhetorically. "Does this confirm that Mildred, with the bony hands, is being paid by Harrington to terrorize you? I don't know, but it sure seems likely."

"How can this be?" Ellen asked. "Why would she work for peanuts when she obviously lives so well otherwise?"

"The answer may be Harrington." Gallop said and added, "Consider this. Mildred may just be a distraction for us. There's nothing I've seen that indicates she's responsible for the threats. Our leads now are bony hands and, perhaps, another person by the name of Sasha."

"I suppose it's possible there is another Sasha that Harrington is working with," Webster pondered, "although that name isn't very common."

"I have a lot more work to do on this," Gallop said. "It's puzzling. If she is the Mildred/Sasha we're looking for, it is Harrington that supports her. My friend at the Tower didn't care where the money came from to pay for that living style -- as long as it continued.

"As I talked with her, I wondered even more if we were talking about the same woman who works here. Her condo file contained her photo. She is stunningly beautiful when she puts it all together. Her Scan-Man photo, and in person, makes her look like Ms. Drab. It's shocking contrast."

"I find all of this astounding," Webster said.

"What I find *more* astounding, Nat, the lack of motion-detector video cameras in the Scan-Man buildings. You are a giant company and you're very vulnerable without video security. With your permission, I'd like to work with your people immediately and install cameras in critical locations. Think what we might have learned about the most recent threat had a camera been in the area."

"It's embarrassing. You certainly have my permission to go ahead with that."

* * *

The first item on Ellen's agenda the next day was to see Chief Wilson.

"Hi, Ellen," the chief said. "What a surprise to see you here."

"Hi, Paul. I'm on a mission."

"Uh, oh. What kind of mission?"

"Two things. I want to get a license to carry a concealed weapon and, I want retire your round-the-clock men. I think it's a waste of taxpayer money."

"What do you want the gun for?"

"I think the term is "for protection of person and property."

"So you want to be Nat's guard."

"Something like that."

"Does Nat know?"

"He does. I told him how when I was a kid, my daddy used to take me out to the dump shooting rats and things. Actually I was pretty good. But I've never had a gun of my own and have never wanted one -- until now."

176

"I certainly think a gun can be justified."

"Thank you."

"Now, about the guards. Are you sure you want to do this?"

"We're sure. I plan to be with Nat whenever he goes out."

"You're pretty gutsy."

"It appears he likes my company better than the guys. But I hope they won't be offended."

"They may be. They'll miss the overtime. We'll have to see. You may have to come in and apologize personally," the chief joked.

"No. They'll have to understand."

"Now, regarding the permit. That's no problem. I'll fingerprint you and snap your mug and write out a permit. Do you know what kind of gun you want?"

"Something small and deadly accurate."

"Want to try a few out on the range?" the chief suggested. "We can't use the dump any more."

"Yes. Thanks. I'd really appreciate that."

The chief gave Ellen the personal treatment. He followed her through the fingerprinting and photo and then wrote out the license to carry in Massachusetts.

"Now remember," the chief reminded her, "this permit is only good in Massachusetts. Leave it home if you go out of state."

"Gotcha."

"Want to go to the range tomorrow morning? Meet here about seven?"

"Sure."

"I'll get two or three samples from our archive."

"This is awfully nice of you, Paul. I feel special."

"Well, you and Nat are special."

"You stupid idiot! Put that thing down!"

Sasha was startled when she walked into the condo and found Helena in the middle of the room pointing a gun at her. She stopped dead, afraid to move.

Helena was giggling. "I like this." She giggled again.

"I said, put it down!"

"It's a nice toy, Sasha. Now I see why you like it. I like the way it feels."

"Take you finger off the trigger."

"What's a trigger?"

Helena was about fifteen feet away. The gun was wavering around, but it was generally pointed at Sasha.

Sasha cleaned her gun every night. She said it was her toy. It was a plaything. Helena saw nothing wrong with that. All she was doing was playing with it like they did on TV.

"That thing is loaded, you idiot! Stop pointing it at me!"

Helena just giggled. "Why can't I?"

"OK, you little idiot. You asked for it."

Sasha suddenly stepped forward to push the gun barrel to one side. Her rapid movement startled Helena and that reaction caused a reflex that pulled the trigger.

The bullet hit Sasha at an angle, in the right cheekbone, directly under the eye. It ripped away the right side of her facial tissue and underlying cheekbone. Her right eyeball fell out and was dangling next to her nose. The bullet did not enter her head. It was a severe glancing blow that rattled her brain into unconsciousness.

It all took place in an instant. Helena looked at Sasha in horror. She screamed, dropped the gun, and saw her lover fall to the floor in slow motion. She couldn't move at first.

She was frozen in place. She didn't know what happened. She just kept screaming.

Sasha lay motionless, twisted awkwardly. Her wound was exposed from where she lay. Blood was oozing steadily out of her ghastly wound and onto the white carpeting. She was breathing. Her chest was rising and falling rapidly.

Helena was shaking violently. The sight of the person she had made love to was too ugly to imagine. Her screaming gradually subsided. She realized she had made a terrible mistake. She had to leave. She had to get out of there quickly.

When Sasha wakes up, Helena thought, she will be very angry at me. I have to go. I did something awful bad. I was not a good person. I hurt her.

Helena left the condo in a hurry. She had to leave before Sasha woke up. She went out the door and directly to the elevator.

It was a beautiful night in Boston. A bright red moon was just rising out of the harbor. Its light reflected off the windows of the skyscrapers. The sound of the traffic was just audible. It was a perfect night to sit in front of a picture window and admire the view.

Two freshly mixed martinis, one with an olive, the other with an onion, were left sitting on the table in front of Sasha's window.

* * *

"We think we have something, Mr. Gallop," Chief Wilson announced on the phone.

"I'm all ears," Gallop said.

"It's the surveillance of Harrington's laptop. I have a printout in front of me. Since he's been in prison, he's been in contact with his attorney Miles, a woman named Sasha, and a number of other people. But it's this Sasha who has the most hits. We think it's his wife."

"There's a problem with this, Chief," Gallop answered. "Nat tells me Harrington has no wife. And we don't think he has a girlfriend. This Sasha we've learned is an alias. Her real name is Mildred McCoy, a Scan-Man employee, and she lives in a condo in Boston."

* * *

Puff Chabus has just taken the elevator to her floor in the Zenix Tower. As she steps off the elevator she hears what sounds like a gunshot. It is loud. Then she hears a number of screams as she continues down the hallway to her condo suite.

She unlocks her door and is about to enter when she hears a noise and sees a woman, frantic, sobbing, run out of the neighboring suite and dash to the elevator. Then the woman is gone. Everything is quiet.

Puff notices the woman left the door to her suite ajar in her haste.

Curious, as always, Puff closes her door and cautiously takes the few steps down the hall to her neighbor's door. She knocks. No answer. "Hello?" No response. Very carefully, she eases it open and peers around into the room. What she sees horrifies her, and she lets out a scream.

She runs back to her condo and calls the front desk.

"Something terrible has happened in suite 2120. I think someone has been shot. Yes. This is Puff Chabus in 2125."

Puff is shaking. She hangs up and returns to her doorway waiting for someone to arrive. Time passes. It seems to be forever. The gruesome image is planted in her mind. Regardless, she is still curious and wants to return to the scene, but she holds back. She can't do it.

180

Finally, the Tower security arrives, two of them, a man and a woman. Puff goes out to the hall to meet them. They ignore her and enter the room through the open door. Moments later, after an excited exchange between them, they return to the hallway and make a call to the police.

"Need EMTs. Victim female. Been shot. Still breathing. Half her face blown off."

They finally acknowledge Puff.

"You the one who called this in?"

"Yes."

"Did you see anything?"

"Yes."

"Please tell us what you saw."

"Nothing. Just this woman on the floor, her face all bloody, you know?"

"We know that. How did you find her?"

"Well. I just got off the elevator and I heard this loud bang that sounded like a gun, you know what I mean? I was going into my suite here when I saw this woman. She was very distressed, crying and all that stuff. Know what I mean?"

"Yes? What else?" Notes were scribbled on a pad.

"She ran out of that room to the elevator and was gone."

"Can you describe this person?"

"The first thing I noticed was her long blond hair that came nearly to her waist, you know? She was a lot taller than me, almost six feet I guess. She wasn't skinny. She was medium build. I never saw her face, only the back of her. I don't think she saw me. She was crying and sobbing."

"Then what?"

"She left the door open. I went to the doorway and that was when I saw the person on the floor. Oh, it was horrible!" Puff covered her face with her hands. "I came back and called the front desk."

* * *

Mildred didn't show up for work. Tony called her but there was no answer. He called again the next day and the day after. She had always been dependable. Maybe she got hurt on her motorcycle.

Tony thought about Mildred. What was it about her? Mr. Webster had shaken her hand on his last walkthrough. And then Ellen also talked with her. Mr. Gallop asked about her. And now she's gone!

As he wondered, he thought back over the years. When Mr. Harrington was boss, he used to praise Mildred for her work. Tony didn't think Mildred's work was *that* great. Surely no better than anyone else in shipping.

And what about me? Tony thought. Why didn't Mr. Harrington ever praise me for all I do?

Sure is funny how people come and go, Tony thought. Now he had to hire and train a replacement.

* * *

Ellen nudged Maggie with her elbow. "Look who I see. Isn't that Redford the chopper pilot?"

Maggie turned and looked behind her. She saw the man. It was him all right. It was the short handlebar mustache, military hat and handsome, square-jawed face that stood him out from the crowd.

He turned in their direction, scanning the diner. He looked, looked harder and then a smile broke out as he recognized them.

Maggie quickly turned back.

"Uh oh. He's coming over," Ellen said warily.

"Ignore him," Maggie gulped. "Maybe he'll go away."

182

He waved as he came, his eyes focused on them.

"Hey! Here are my honeys," Redford said. "Where have you broads been? I missed you."

The women looked down, embarrassed by his loud greeting amid their friends.

He was at their table now. He looked down at each of them. "You gonna invite me in?"

Maggie looked up. "Sure, Captain. Have a seat."

Redford slid in beside Maggie and looked back and forth trying to read the women's cautious welcome.

"Hey! We been through the war together," he said cheerily. "We're buddies. Where's your comrade spirit?"

"We're just fine," Maggie said quietly, "But you don't have to announce it to everyone here."

"Oh, I get it," Redford said with glee, "I embarrass you little cuties."

Maggie nodded her head to Ellen. "He's still the same old macho lady-killer, Ellen."

"So." Ellen said, "What's brings the lady-killer to our turf, Captain?"

Still buoyant, Redford continued. "I've got the day off so I'm just bumming around lookin' for a little excitement."

"I hope you don't think we're going to satisfy your need," Ellen said.

Redford looked at her surprised. "Hey, girls. Truce. I'm not looking for a lay for godssake. I like you two. I just want to be friends." An innocent expression crossed his not-so-innocent face.

Maggie had a change of heart. "OK. OK. Truce. Here comes Jack. Have some breakfast with us."

"Hi, Black an' White," Jack said. "Is this flyboy givin' you any grief?"

"You know each other?" Ellen said, surprised.

"Sure. The captain's in here now and then with a pretty girl under his arm."

"Jack, Jack, Jack!" Redford protested. "Give a guy a little privacy."

Jack laughed. "Ask the girls here. You don't visit the Truck Stop for privacy."

Jack's comment lightened up the atmosphere at the table.

"How's it goin', Cap?" Jack asked.

"Still the same old, same old," Redford said. "Flyin' and ... you know."

"How do you all know the captain?"

"We flew together during the snowstorm," Ellen said. "Actually, he did a fantastic job flying through terrible weather into Boston."

"Oh, yeah," Jack said. "I heard about that. Didn't you girls jump out of the plane?"

Maggie laughed. "We sure did. We had to do something drastic to get away from this lecher."

Redford leaned back and gave a laugh that resounded all over the diner. "Ain't these babes somethin' Jack?" he said in full voice.

Every head in the diner was now turned toward the table in the corner.

Jack looked up addressed the audience. "It's OK folks. No one's hurt. Just havin' a little fun here." Then in a lowered voice. "You want somethin' to eat, Cap?"

"Just a coffee, Jack. Thanks." Redford settled down.

"OK. I'll be right back."

"So what's going on in Hollandson these days?"

"A lot," Maggie answered. "Probably the thing you're most interested in is the hotel. They're starting to rebuild."

"Why would I be interested in the hotel?" Redford asked.

"Well, it's always been the most active place, socially, in the town. Surely you've patronized the place."

"Yeah. Once in a while. It's the only place to dance in town. They have nice bars. And their atrium is terrific."

"You haven't been there since this winter I can see."

"How do you know that?"

"Because the place has been closed since December. The snowstorm collapsed the atrium."

"That's a shame." Redford was serious. "Where do you go to dance now?"

It was Ellen's turn to laugh. "You don't know our men. We haven't danced since the last wedding we went to."

"That's also a shame."

"They're remodeling the place as we speak and hope to open it sometime in the fall," Maggie explained.

Redford's coffee came. He drank it quickly without comment. Maggie suspected he was somehow hurt -- maybe the pilot did have feelings.

"Tell us a little about yourself, Captain. We know nothing about you except that you tend to come on strong and bold."

"There's really nothing to tell. I'm career Army. I'm not married. I live to fly. I fly in air shows and even do stunts. I was the first to do a roll in the H-21. As a result I almost killed myself. The H-21 was never built to stunt -- but that's what made it more exciting."

"We can believe that, the way you volunteered to take us to Boston and how you managed your chopper in those high winds. We were truly amazed at your expertise."

Ellen's flattery seemed to bring Redford to life again.

"I also like women," Redford smiled.

"You're kidding," Ellen feigned surprise. "How about that, Maggie? Would you have ever guessed?"

They laughed. "Tell us more about your women."

185

"What's to tell?" he shrugged. "I just wish I could find an unattached woman like one of you."

"Now look who's flattering!" Ellen said.

"I'm serious. I never run into women like you. A woman like you two could bring stability to my life." Redford *was* serious.

There was a long pause. All three avoided each other's looks.

Finally, Ellen spoke. "I don't know what to tell you. Sometimes it's just luck. Probably most of the time it's looking in the *right* places. You know the song, 'Lookin' for Love in All the Wrong Places'? Where do you look for love, Captain?"

"Probably in all the wrong places. I know. I come on strong and that leaves girls like you with a bad impression. But that's me, the way I was brought up. You can't teach an old dog new tricks and all that stuff."

"You know?" Maggie said. "If I were single and got to know you beyond all your bluff and hot air, I might be interested in dating you. Deep down, I think you might be a lot of fun. As someone once said about Bill Clinton, 'I bet he'd be fun at a party.'"

"Thanks. Compare me to Bill Clinton. Maybe I should run for President."

"You'd have a problem with that."

"How so?"

"You'd have to give up flying and quit the Army."

All three laughed.

"Captain. It's been fun, but we have to get on our way," Maggie said.

They slid out of the booth and shook each other's hand, avoiding the hug Redford attempted to give.

"So long, girls. I'll pay the tab. Hang loose."

* * *

"Yes. We have a woman that fits that description," said the man at Boston Gun & Rifle Club. "Yeah. She's the best marksman we have in the club. The guys are insanely jealous of her standings. She goes by the name of Sasha."

Officer Commerwitz was ecstatic. "How about an address?"

"No problem. She's at the Zenix Tower on Summer Street, downtown."

"You don't happen to have a mug shot."

"She in trouble of some kind?"

"Not that I know of," Commerwitz said.

"Here we go."

"Would you mind photocopying that?"

"This might be invasion of privacy."

"Let me worry about that."

"Here you go. Good luck."

Commerwitz went out to the cruiser and checked in.

"Chief. I've got a photo and an address of the only person I've found who meets the description."

"What's the name?"

"Sasha. No last name."

"That's the one we want. Good job, Commerwitz."

* * *

Why the hell doesn't she answer my messages? Chandler Harrington thought. He'd been aggressively e-mailing Sasha for two days. His messages weren't being bounced back as undeliverable so the address must still be valid. He was puzzled. He had always been able to depend on her. He had paid her nearly a half million dollars over the years so he had good reason to make sure she was dependable.

What could have happened to her? Was she caught? Did she fall off her motorcycle? Harrington could not imagine. There was no reason at all for him to suspect her turning on him.

Harrington was anxious to know what the delay was for eliminating the mouse. Yes, he encouraged her to play cat/mouse with Webster, but now was the time. If she had gotten Webster it would have appeared on TV. He watched every news program. He would have seen the story if Webster had been erased.

Oh, Christ, he thought. Why have I always been surrounded by incompetents? It was not my destiny. My parents brought me up right. They were always proud of me. They taught me how to manage people -- how to sway them to my way of thinking.

But people failed me -- all of them. And now Mildred! She was so smart, so sly, so cool, so... yes, so wicked. Her cover was Scan-Man. That was the front to protect her. Everyone there thought she was wonderful. Yet one call from me, and a mere $50K transferred into her bank account, from the Scan-Man coffers of course, and I was rid of the competition. God she was smart.

Well, I'll keep trying.

* * *

"Mr. Gallop," the chief said. "We've got something important."

"What's that?"

"Harrington's Sasha hasn't answered her e-mails for two days. Harrington is frantic."

"What's he saying?"

"He's wondering what's taking so long to kill the mouse."

188

"You didn't answer did you?"

"No. I didn't know how to respond. This is why I called you."

"So Harrington's waiting for an answer from Sasha?"

"Right."

""I'll be right over," Gallop said. "Thanks for calling."

* * *

"I don't know, Mr. Webster," Tony explained. "Mildred just stopped coming in. She's not answering her phone. It's not like her. She is very dependable and hardly ever misses work."

"OK, Tony. Thanks for the info. I'll take if from here."

Webster called Gallop. "Tony in shipping reports that Mildred has not showed up for work for a few days and she's not answering her phone. He says it's uncharacteristic of her."

"The crazy woman probably fell off her bike. I'll give my friend at the Tower a call."

* * *

"Darleen. What do you know about Sasha?"

"Oh my God, Odie. She shot herself and is in the hospital now."

"Very interesting. Suicide?"

"No. It appears she was just cleaning her gun. She's a gun nut, I understand."

"Where is she now?"

"Mass General." Darleen changed the subject. "Hey, Odie! I'm still waiting for my night out with you. You promised."

"Believe me. I'm very grateful for all your information. I'm in the middle of case right now. But I haven't forgotten you."

"I'll be waiting, Odie."

* * *

"You can speak to him if you want," the nurse said, "but you won't get much response."

Ed Randolph was sitting outside in the flower garden by himself at the nursing home. The garden was in full bloom and the scent was pleasant.

A woman walked up to him. "Mr. Randolph?"

He turned his head and looked up at her.

"My name is Mrs. O'Flaherty. I'm with Massachusetts Health & Human Services."

"My name is Ed Randolph. I'm president of Scan-Man."

She put out her hand to take his, but it remained in his lap.

She sat in a chair next to him.

"How are you today, Mr. Randolph?"

"I'm fine."

"When did you last work at Scan-Man, Mr. Randolph?"

"This morning."

Mrs. O'Flaherty confirmed the nurse's warning.

"Do you have a family, Mr. Randolph?"

"I don't know."

"Do you have a son named Robert?"

He turned and looked at Mrs. O'Flaherty as if he recognized the name.

"A little boy named Robert?" she repeated.

He continued to look at her. Something was tickling his memory but he still said nothing.

"What is your wife's name, Mr. Randolph?"

"I don't know."

"What is your son's name?"

"I don't know."

Mrs. O'Flaherty stood. "It's nice to meet you Mr. Randolph. I'm going to go now."

"Goodbye."

* * *

Gallop arrived at the police department and looked at Harrington's inquiries to Sasha.

"OK. This is what I want you to do," Gallop said. "Reply to Harrington and say, 'Sorry. The cat's been busy.' That's it. Then wait for a reply. Call me when you get it."

* * *

Nat Webster felt he was in a moral bind. He did not want the military to have the Searoc technology. But, he believed they would get it in the end regardless of how he felt.

Did this mean he had to give in to the military? Was this a black or white question? Was there a middle ground?

In the letter they said they wanted to *experiment* with the Searoc Beam. They didn't say they wanted the technology. But, of course, if the experiment worked to their satisfaction, they would want full control of the technology.

It was a very bad decision on my part, Webster thought, to ever have mentioned to the original directors that the Searoc Beam had military potential. Once Chandler Harrington heard that, his eyes lit up with dollar signs.

Webster's early lab and field experiments tested every use imagined at the time for the Searoc. Even though the beam could penetrate three inches of armor plate, and could melt an Army tank, there were many non-military applications for a beam that could generate this amount of heat, environmentally friendly and -- at no cost!

One of those uses was in mining ores such as copper, gold and iron. Initial tests showed that once raw ore had been removed from the earth and dumped into a vat, the beam, focused on the vat, drew the metals out of the ore in liquid form and into a settling chamber. There the various metals were separated, resulting in on-location metal processing.

It was the heat of the Searoc Beam that, in effect, smelted the ore. Applying extreme heat to the ore is, in effect, the opposite of the natural process in which it was created.

Webster composed an answer to the military saying he was willing to proceed with initial talks. He said he was willing to host the talks at Scan-Man headquarters and offered some dates and times at which a meeting would be convenient.

* * *

The story ran top left on the front page of the *Times*. An editorial was also run that praised Nat Webster for his choice of Jason Goodhue as manager of the Scan-Man Recovery Fund.

Goodhue, a Maine native and an attorney, was also an experienced claims officer for the victims of the September 11, 2001 terror attacks.

Webster stated that all claims were to be administered through Goodhue's office. The claims must be certified damages that occurred as a result of the December snowstorm. A claim that has been certified by an independent arbiter will obligate the Recovery Fund to make payment. Therefore, there will be little or no delay in paying claims. Scan-Man had already deposited $5 billion into an escrow account.

Word spread rapidly through Hollandson. Those who had already submitted claims to the selectmen wanted to know what they had to do next.

Speaking with one resident over coffee in the diner, Bob Sivolesky said, "You can thank your selectmen for getting you kick-started. It's now up to you to get your claims into the Recovery office. We can't do it for you. Do it now and you'll be ahead of the rest of the crowd."

Anticipating a quick response to its claim, the Hollandson Motor Hotel doubled the size of its work force and ordered the manufacture and delivery of the replacement atrium expedited. "You're just copying the original plans, with one steel reinforcement change," the construction engineer told the manufacturer. "There should be no design and engineering hold up. We need it now, if not sooner."

Mary Ann Magnolia's garage had collapsed under the snow and damaged her car. Hers was probably the first postmarked letter the Recovery Fund received. Her claim was for $5,475.

Bud Kelly shuffled his documents for claims on his trucks and plows. "What do I do with my stuff?" he asked Warren Coulter in the selectmen's office. "My stuff isn't directly related to the storm, but I heard Scan-Man was doing something special for the town."

"I think you're right," Coulter said. "I'll speak to Maggie and see what she knows."

Coulter called Maggie. "You're right, Warren. I'll check it out with Nat."

Maggie called Webster. "You're right, Maggie. I should have clarified that before."

193

"The selectmen already have all the claims for the town," Maggie told Webster. "If I remember correctly it came to $2.3 million. That includes the hotel and the town trucks, the two biggest items, and a couple dozen private home damages."

"I'll give Bob Sivolesky a call," Webster said. "I want all Hollandson claims to come directly to me."

"That's awfully good of you, Nat. Is there anything I can do to help the process?"

"I don't think so. If anything, you can make it clear in the *Bulletin* that all Hollandson claims go through the selectmen. All others go through the Recovery Fund."

"Gotcha. Speak to you later. Bye."

Noting the sudden urgency, Webster immediately had his assistant call the selectmen's office. Bob had returned from coffee.

"Bob, this is Nat Webster."

"Ah, Mr. Webster. What a pleasure. What can I do for you today?"

"I understand you have all the claims for damage in Hollandson."

"We do."

"As you may know, I'm handling the town differently than the rest of the region. I want to do something special for the town. You people have handled your responsibility well in keeping Scan-Man plowed and its roads and lots in good condition."

"You have *our* thanks, Mr. Webster for employing our residents and being such a good neighbor."

Webster laughed. "A good old mutual admiration society, isn't it? And that's just fine.

"Regarding these claims, I want them all sent directly to me. I understand you are in need of a couple new trucks, some plows, and maybe other equipment. Is it true the claims to date, including the truck and things come to about $2.3 mill?"

"That's true."

"Have you ever visited our offices, Bob?"

"No, I guess I haven't."

"When you get your claims together, give me a call and we'll have lunch over here and I'll give you a tour of the company."

"That sounds like a plan, Mr. Webster."

"And Bob? Please call me Nat."

Now Sivolesky laughed. "I will Nat. And I look forward to the free lunch and tour."

Bob thought for a minute. Oh, my God. I've just told people to send their claims to the Recovery Office. Now, who did I tell this to?

He got on the phone.

* * *

Marsha Randolph lives alone in her penthouse in Naples after the disastrous visit to Hollandson. She had visited her husband at the rest home and he didn't recognize her.

God! What a burden Ed is, she thought. He's still young. He's going to be costing me big time for the rest of my life. There must be something I can do. Some alternative.

She had also just dealt with her son, Robert, and the damnable state agency. What a hell of a bunch. What do they know about taking care of kids? Kids need discipline. That was one of Ed's problems. He and Alberta just played with Robert. I was the one who had to discipline him.

That little brat, she thought. The McCulloughs can keep him. Good luck taking care of him at their age. At least he isn't her burden any more. They can have him. He's their responsibility now. And there're not getting any more money from me. They want him they can pay for him.

I'm finally by myself. I can do what I want, when I want. I have no strings. I have plenty of money. I am the envy of my new friends here, she thought as she looked out the wide picture window at the Gulf of Mexico.

It was then Marsha crumpled onto her soft Fleming & Howard sofa and sobbed.

* * *

"I can't say I'm thrilled with it," Webster said.

"Well, I am," Ellen insisted. "I went out to the range with the chief this morning and it was like I always had the gun. My aim was just like when I was with my daddy. I wish you'd been there. I was deadly."

"Annie Oakley."

"Don't make fun of it, my sweet. Just hope I never have to use it."

"It's small."

"But accurate."

"How are you going to carry it?"

"On my hip."

"What? Like a six-gun cowgirl?"

"No. No. Look at this." Ellen reached into a plastic shopping bag and pulled out a small pink leather pouch with an attached narrow black leather belt. She put it around her waist and cinched it. She slipped the gun into the pouch and dropped the flap over it. "How about that?" she said proudly.

"It's different. I've never seen anything like it."

"I tried a body holster under my bra strap but I didn't need three lumps on my body. Also, it was too difficult to get at in a hurry.

"I thought of carrying it in my purse, but that was too awkward as well. Besides, I might leave the purse somewhere.

"Then I thought of *you* carrying it on your hip where I could reach it. But finally I said why bother at all with all this gun stuff? Let him wear a rubber mask. Nat. If you had a bunch of masks, you could travel around as a whole variety of different characters."

"OK. OK. Very funny," Webster gave in. "I'll get used to pink. You're not going to wear it in the building, I hope. It's for when we leave the building together, right?"

"Right. Now we should get something for you in matching pink." Ellen laughed.

Webster laughed and they hugged each other.

* * *

Helena raised her hand to her mouth and gasped. She was watching the TV news.

". . . and she had half her face blown off by a bullet. She was taken to Mass General Hospital where she is listed in critical condition. The woman was found on the penthouse floor of the Zenix Tower on Summer Street. A resident of a condo on the same floor discovered the victim. She notified the hotel security who called the police. Police found the weapon nearby and have taken fingerprints. The victim is believed to have a roommate by the name of Helena. If anyone knows anything about the victim or the roommate, you are asked to contact the police . . ."

"What's the matter, child?"

Helena raised her arm toward her mother and said, "Shush!" She leaned forward to hear better, holding back her sobs.

197

Her mother heard the broadcaster use the word 'Helena' and she too focused on the story. She then turned to her daughter.

"What's going on here, Helena?"

Helena ignored her.

"Listen to me, child. What is going on? Somethin's wrong with you."

Helena began to cry.

"Have you done somethin' bad, child? Do you know what this is about?"

"I don't know, Momma." Her voice was shaking.

"You *do* know somethin', don't you?" She moved across the couch and put her arm around her daughter. "You tell me now. It's OK. You can tell Momma."

It took a few minutes for Helena to calm down and breathe regularly.

"Momma," she said tentatively. "Momma. I ... I did something awful bad. I was not a good person. I hurt her bad."

Her mother's grip around her daughter tightened. "What did you do, child? Did you go and shoot somebody?"

She looked at her daughter. Helena was bent forward on the couch crying, her head in her hands, turning her head back and forth as if to deny something.

"Oh, my child. Your Momma's here. Don't you worry, child. Your Momma's here."

It was then that Helena spilled out the story the only way she knew how -- haltingly and imperfectly.

"Don't you worry, child. You're here with Momma. You're safe. No need to worry."

Helena had gone directly from the accident scene to her mother's apartment.

"Oh, Momma," Helena had told her. "My roommate kicked me out and I have nowhere to go."

"Where are your things?" her mother asked.

"I left them. I don't want them any more."

"Well that was stupid! What are you going to wear here? My clothes won't fit you."

"I don't know," Helena cried, confused.

* * *

Harrington was happy again. Sasha finally responded to his emails.

"Sorry. The cat's been busy," was Sasha's reply.

Harrington responded: "You had the coach worried. I want some action from my quarterback."

Harrington leaned back in his chair with satisfaction. He grinned and rubbed his hands together. Finally I get that bastard. And I also get Scan-Man. It will wither like a leaf without Webster. This is a double whammy. I have won in the end. It will be fun to watch my former empire crumble.

* * *

The Scan-Man Recovery Fund was working smoothly. Jason Goodhue was receiving good press. There were very few complaints. By far, most requests were reasonable.

Webster approved the hotel request of $1.2 million for replacement of the atrium. The new plans included additional strengthening so that it would not rip away from the hotel structure regardless of the weight of snow.

The most satisfied residents of Hollandson were those who replaced fallen garage roofs and collapsed porches. The monies they received rebuilt the structures to a far better standard than they were when they were new. Standards had been upgraded over the years to their benefit.

Bud Kelly was beaming. Nat Webster personally approved his request for equipment. He was now looking at trucks that far exceeded the quality of the others. They were also more fuel-efficient. The plows, salt and sand spreaders, and a new front-end loader completed the inventory. Not only did these not cost the town money, but the sale of the old equipment went back into the town general budget.

Throughout New England, Scan-Man was generous almost to a fault. A bridge in Vermont that had been washed out by a flood was being replaced, but would take a couple of years to complete. That one item cost double that of the atrium.

Nat Webster smiled. He was very pleased to have at least one event in his busy life go well.

* * *

"I've already given hotel security all the information I know," Puff Chabus said. "Why do I have to do it again?"

"We will ask the questions, ma'am," the police officer said.

"What if I say no?"

"We'll give you a ride down to the station. You'll look cute behind bars in a dingy cell."

Grimly. "What do you want to know?"

"Tell us everything you know, from the beginning."

Puff repeated the story she had told hotel security.

" . . . And that's all I know."

"Then you don't know the other woman who was in the room," the officer said.

"I never saw her before, you know what I mean? I'd surely recognize her long blond hair."

* * *

It was now later that night. The police were gone and the hallway outside Puff's suite had been very quiet -- until she heard the elevator door open.

Intensely curious, Puff cautiously opened her door enough to see a young woman, the same woman, with the long blonde hair. The woman unlocked the door but didn't enter the room. She hesitated, reached her hand in and flicked on the light, then leaned her body in around the door without entering.

What should I do? Puff thought. This is probably the killer! I have to see her face.

With only her head still outside the door, Puff bravely said, "Can I help you?"

The woman started and quickly drew back out into the hall and turned to Puff. She was attractive and young, but she looked timid and her eyes showed she was frightened. It was as if she didn't know whether to enter the room to escape Puff or run for the elevator.

Puff took one step out into the hall, but kept one hand on her door. The woman, far taller, eyed Puff and apparently felt she didn't present any danger.

"Hi," she said, smiling, giving Puff a little-girl embarrassed wave of the hand.

"Hi," Puff returned. "Can I help you?" she repeated.

"I'm looking for my friend," the woman said.

Whoa, Puff thought. What's going on with this girl? Is she nuts?

"Who is your friend?"

"Sasha. She lives here."

"She's gone now," Puff said.

"Do you know where she went?"

"I don't. What's your name?"

"Helena. I'm Sasha's girlfriend."

201

Oh, my God, Puff thought. She's just like a child.

"That's a pretty name Helena. What's your last name?"

"I don't have a last name. So does Sasha. She doesn't have a last name too."

This girl is obviously mentally deprived, Puff thought. Why am I doing this?

"Where do you live, Helena?"

"I used to live here, but now I'm with my Momma."

"Where does your momma live?"

"Oh. I don't know." She looked down at her feet. "I only know how to get there."

Puff took a wild last chance to get more information. "Maybe you'd let me visit sometime. We could be friends."

"Sasha doesn't let me have friends."

"Can I get you something to drink?"

"I'm not supposed to talk to strangers. I'm goin' home to Momma now."

She abruptly turned to the elevator that was still waiting and the long blond hair disappeared.

Puff shrugged. As she turned to go back into her rooms she noticed Helena had left the door ajar and -- the key was still in the door.

What should she do? Would Helena return to retrieve her key? Should she shut the door and take the key? Should she just leave things the way they were?

Curiosity once again overtook her. She just had to get a closer look at that suite.

Puff Chabus had read enough mystery stories to know about fingerprints. She quickly returned to her own condo and went to her dresser in the bedroom. Here she retrieved a pair of long dress gloves and pulled them on.

She crossed the hall, removed and pocketed the key. Inside her neighbor's suite, uninvited, felt very creepy. The

202

first thing she noticed was the carpet. There was no trace of blood where she had seen the victim a few days before. She made a sweeping look around the main room. Physically, it was a mirror image of her suite but the decor was startlingly different. The wall of photographs and the bold headline above them was overwhelming. She was drawn to them. The photos were stunning. The subjects were beautiful nudes, many in embarrassing poses. Helena was everywhere. And Puff guessed the other woman must be Sasha. She had to consciously pull herself away.

On one side of the room, near the bedrooms, was a writing desk and phone. She glanced over the papers and shuffled through some bills and unopened mail. These were addressed to a Mildred McCoy at a post office box downtown. Who was Mildred McCoy? Near the phone was a pad of paper and on it were two penciled words. "Webster" and "mouse."

Coincidence or what? Puff's heart skipped a beat. She tore the top sheet off the pad and took one of the bills with the name and post office address on it.

Webster, she thought. Nat Webster? Hmm.

Puff made a quick walk through the bedrooms. She tempered her curiosity to look through drawers and closets. Instead, she left, pulled the door locked behind her and returned to her suite.

* * *

"Maggie? This is Puff Chabus. You may not remember me, but my husband was the president of the National Scientific Association, you know, that met in the hotel last December."

"I sure do remember you, Puff. What are you up to these days?"

"I'm living in Boston. I have a condo in the Zenix Tower on Summer Street."

"That sounds nice," Maggie said. "Some difference from Hollandson."

"It is, but it has its down side, if you know what I mean."

"What *do* you mean, Puff?"

"You may have heard about the shooting in this tower that took place a few nights ago. It was on the evening news."

"Yes. I did see that. Pretty gruesome."

"Well, I'm calling about something that may just be a coincidence. I happen to live across the hall from the condo where that woman was shot."

"Ooo. Not so good," Maggie said.

"I had the opportunity to go into that suite and came across a piece of paper by the phone that had two words hand-written on it. One word was 'Webster' and the other was 'mouse.'"

"Yes?"

"I just wondered if this meant anything to you."

"Of course 'Webster' means something to me. But that doesn't mean it is Nat Webster. 'Mouse' makes no sense to me."

"I was just curious," Puff said, disappointed.

"It would make more sense if you had found that info in Hollandson. But in Boston? That's pretty far afield."

"I guess you're right. Just a coincidence."

"Well, thanks for calling, Puff. Is everything else OK with you?"

"Same old, same old," Puff concluded. "Thanks anyway, Maggie."

* * *

"Why are people looking at us?" Ellen asked.

"It's probably your pink holster and belt," Webster joked.

"I'm a fashion setter, Nat. You watch. A few months from now women everywhere, and some men, will be wearing these things, without the gun, of course. What are you eating tonight, my Sweet?"

Webster and Ellen tried to eat out at least twice a week. Neither of them enjoyed cooking. They figured if they didn't eat out they would simply fade away to starvation.

Tonight they were at a bistro in Concord on Rte. 2A. It was a small, cozy place and the menu was short -- just what Webster liked.

Ellen leaned in the other direction. The bigger the menu, the better. She was the one who most often decided on the restaurant, so that included the long menu. This is where Webster often resorted to "Me too," or relied on Ellen's suggestion when the waiter asked.

"I'm going with the seafood salad," Ellen said.

"That never fills me up. Why don't you have something else?"

"Very funny. Why don't you have the house burger with mushrooms, onions, and all the other stuff they pile onto it?"

"Great idea."

"You are the world's laziest person," Ellen rebuked. "Why can't you make up your own mind?"

"I guess it's just not important to me," Webster said. "I go out to eat to enjoy you and the atmosphere of my surroundings. I don't care what I eat."

The restaurant was full tonight with no sign of a free table soon. They noticed a couple about their age that had been standing at the door for several minutes.

"Let's invite them to sit with us," Webster said. With that he raised his arm and gestured to them. The couple looked at each other, nodded, and joined them. Webster stood and introduced. They all sat.

Pete and Mary were bikers. "We bike all over the country on a three-wheel Honda Golden Wing. There's nothing like the open road with the wind in our faces."

"We've never done that," Ellen said. "I'd probably kill myself on a bike."

"It takes a lot of self-control. The Honda's so big and powerful that it rides very comfortably at all speeds."

"Are you from this area?" Webster asked.

"We're from Fort Collins, Colorado. We're on a three-week trip. We had to get away from the smoke and fires."

"What's that like?" Ellen asked.

"We weren't ever threatened, but that damned smoke kept pushing east. We've been keeping track of it. I guess the fires are mostly out now. A lot of homes were lost. It's very sad."

"I can only imagine," Webster added.

"Did you read about how the fires were put out?" Pete asked.

"Well, I know they used thousands of firefighters," Ellen said.

"No. I mean this thunderstorm came out of nowhere and soaked most of the fires. I guess it was a mystery to everyone. One day the fires are blazing all over the Rockies, and the next thing, this storm comes out of nowhere and puts them out."

"It's tough to predict Mother Nature sometimes," Ellen said.

"You people are lucky on the East Coast. You don't have the droughts we have."

"But we don't have the wide-open spaces and snow-covered mountains that you have," Webster countered.

"Ever been out West?"

"Oh, yeah. We love driving through Colorado. The Million-Dollar Highway is one of our favorite rides," Ellen added.

"It's a great country. We like your White Mountains also. They're so much more accessible than the Rockies. We do a little hiking up there. We just came down from the Kancamagus Highway. That's a good ride."

"It sure is."

And so the conversation went as Nat and Ellen enjoyed their new friends.

* * *

Chief Wilson cheered when his laptop tracker told him Harrington responded again. He called Gallop with the news.

Harrington had responded: "You had the coach worried. I want some action from my quarterback."

"Here's what I want you to answer," Gallop said. "'The cat has to play with the mouse before she kills it.'"

"Call me again when you get a reply," he told the chief.

* * *

It bothered Ellen when Scan-Man caused turmoil throughout the meteorological community. Typical was when they moved rain clouds from east to west in the attempt to extinguish the forest fires in the Rocky Mountains.

A similar situation occurred a short time later when rain clouds were moved from the Gulf of Mexico into Texas to help relieve the drought.

Each of these events went counter to the ways of Mother Nature. In fact, Ellen reasoned, every action Scan-Man had ever taken with the Searoc beam was counter to nature. No wonder meteorologists across the country were bent out of shape. NOAA was getting a bit feisty over the Scan-Man activity as well.

Ellen wanted the company to get into the loop so their activities could be forecast to the general public. No one was against what Scan-Man was doing -- so far. The problem was Scan-Man never announced its intentions.

Ellen's solution was very simple.

Scan-Man beamed, 24-7, a constant stream of weather data to thousands of their subscribing clients. Why couldn't Scan-Man's weather modification intensions be incorporated into this data stream of information?

The first test of this procedure came with the arrival of tornado season.

* * *

The Jacobwitz family lives in a relatively new suburban development on the southwest side of Joplin, Missouri. They have seen their share of nearby tornadoes over the years in this flat, lush, green countryside. They are a family living the good life with two young children. The area around the Joplin city limits has a population of some 49,000. It is a peaceful settlement, studded with tall, leafy trees, manicured lawns, and single-story homes with attached garages -- a typical middle-class city.

It is May 22, 2011, at 2 PM. One of Scan-Man's geostationary satellites, some 22,000 miles above, records a large collection of cloud lines over southeastern Kansas west of Joplin. By 5 PM spotters observe translucent tendrils extending downward from a low, black thundercloud. This is followed by a dark blob that drops from the clouds. It is more than a half-mile wide as it reaches the ground.

On it moves to the east hitting power lines, resulting in explosions and fireworks from transformers. Then it begins to flatten houses. The 210-mile per hour circular wind sucks up everything it touches -- roofs, house contents, cars, boats and trees. The area broadens to three-quarters of a mile and eventually to a full mile in width, yet it is only moving forward at about ten miles per hour.

It obliterates a section of Main Street Joplin. It chews through a dozen residential blocks. It disintegrates the Joplin High School. In the heavy rains, parking lots become ponds of floating debris.

Tornadoes usually leave their unique calling cards. We begin to see slivers of wood penetrating macadam and blades of grass planted in walls of wood.

McDonald's, Home Depot and Wal-Mart remain only as piles of cinderblock and trash.

At the end of the day, twenty percent of Joplin, 7,000 homes, are destroyed. It took only thirty minutes. Some 161 people die and about 1,200 are injured.

The suburbs affected are nothing but rubble and tree stubble as far as the eye can see.

The Jacobwitz family survives. They had heard the National Weather Service warning broadcast from Springfield, Missouri. They made use of their underground shelter for the first time and experienced the nerve-jarring thunder of the destruction just inches over their heads.

When they finally lift the doors and emerge into the silent new world, they see nothing but wreckage all the way to the horizon. Very gradually others emerge, and amid tears of loss and prayers of gratefulness that they have survived, they hug each other. The shock of the experience leaves them dumb. They are not able to think about what should be done -- until they hear a call of distress from the wreckage of a nearby pile of lumber and brick.

Banding together with a single mission, they go with neighbors from one collapsed house to another, listening, calling to possible survivors, carefully digging them out and aiding them however they can until professional help arrives.

This activity helps them temporarily forget their personal grief as they cope with the greater needs of their injured neighbors.

It is many hours before outside help does arrive. One of the firehouses has been hit and the emergency equipment is badly damaged.

The roads are impassible, littered with phone poles and sections of houses, fallen trees and crumpled vehicles. Even if they had a car that was operable, there was no way to get out.

They wait for a front-end loader to clear these passages. Meanwhile it is wait, wait, pray and wait and help others the best way they are able.

* * *

They were at the diner. It was two days after Maggie heard it that she casually mentioned Puff's unusual call to Ellen.

"Maggie!" Ellen sat up, startled. "Those words are *very* significant. Nat is the 'mouse'. The woman who is after him calls herself the 'cat'.

"I'm sorry, Ellen," Maggie apologized. "I should have told you sooner."

"Do you have Puff's number?"

"No. I don't, Ellen. But wait. She said she had a condo in the Zenix Tower in Boston."

"Zenix?"

"Yes. She said it was on Summer Street."

"I have to go now, Maggie." Ellen rose from the table. I have to tell Nat. I have no idea what all this means."

Maggie was left alone in the booth.

Jack saw Ellen run out of the diner and came over to Maggie. "You two have a fight again?" he laughed.

"No. I gave her some news and she had to get to Nat quickly."

"I guess so," Jack said. "She seemed pretty upset."

* * *

How tornadoes form, grow and die is not yet fully understood. As soon as researchers come up with one theory, another problem arises that counteracts the first.

There are two basic factors that contribute to the creation of *every* storm. One is warm, moist air from the south. The other is cool, dry air from the north. When these two contrasting systems meet, instability is created in the atmosphere.

This instability begins when the warm, moist air rises and condenses as it reaches the cool, dry air above. The result is the formation of a thundercloud.

With a tornado, as the warm, moist air rises it creates a change in wind direction and speed. The rising air within the updraft tilts the rotating air from the horizontal to the vertical. This area of rotation can be as large as two to six miles in diameter. The tornado can then form within this area of rotation.

Nat Webster and Ellen Bloodworth have led studies at Scan-Man to determine how the Searoc Beam can negative-

211

ly affect an active tornado. The easy answer they came up with is to heat the cold upper air to eliminate the contrast in the weather systems.

As their studies and experiments continued, they determined it is impractical, if not impossible to attack tornadoes one at a time. These rogue tornadoes are singular events that can occur anywhere in the U.S. Any one of these could be managed, given adequate forecasting. The Searoc beam could do its thing, as above, *before* the tornado has fully developed.

In the case of a band of tornadoes marching across a number of states, the Searoc Beam could broaden its effectiveness and either push the cold front north, or actually warm the entire cold front to render harmless the colliding of opposing fronts.

The team of Webster and Bloodworth did just that in the spring of 2012 when a band of potentially colliding fronts began to form over Texas. Forecasters sent warnings across the southern states all the way to the East Coast.

The Searoc Beam was mobilized. Scan-Man sent a notice to its subscribers to be aware that the Searoc Beam would be attempting to moderate the unstable atmosphere. Other Scan-Man satellites aided the evaluation of the atmosphere by barraging the Control Center with atmospheric temperatures at various altitudes and with readings that measured the differences in temperatures.

The Searoc Beam was initiated and broadened to cover the area of the initial front over Dallas/Fort Worth. The cold air above was warmed to nearly match the warm, moist air below. The beam then followed the front from west to east and thus negated the potential damage. Instead of tornado winds, the South experienced a healthy dose of rain.

The activity was a great success. The weather people this time understood Scan-Man' intentions and were able to modify their local forecasts accordingly. A collective sigh of relief across the South could be heard if you listened closely.

Once again the Scanner XII satellite proved its worth.

* * *

"Nat! Listen to this!" Ellen exclaimed when she rushed into their living quarters. "Maggie told me the most interesting news."

Webster became equally excited as he absorbed Ellen's story. "Let's call Odie."

Webster dialed Gallop's cell. As always, he was quick to answer.

"You are really onto something Nat," Gallop said. "If this is true, we have firmly connected Sasha and Harrington with the words 'Webster' and 'mouse.' Who is this Puff person?"

"She is Puff Chabus," Webster explained. "She lives in the Zenix Tower penthouse directly across the hall from Sasha."

"I'll call Ms. Chabus right away," Gallop said. "I want to meet her. Let me put you on hold while I call. I may need more info from you."

Two minutes later Gallop was back on the line. "Sorry folks. No answer. I left an urgent message with the Zenix operator. I'll get back to as soon as I can."

Webster and Ellen continued to speculate.

"I find it incredible that Puff Chabus in Boston would have such coincidental information," Ellen said. "This mystery is going very far afield."

"Probably not that far afield," Webster said. "It's less than twenty miles to Boston. Certainly its in easy commuting range."

"What are you saying, Nat? That this cat person could be living in Boston?"

"I don't know. If these words were next to the phone it could mean anything. The cat person could have even called that number and whoever was there would have written it down. In any case, it's somebody finding the words significant enough to write them down. I doubt if the cat person herself would have written them."

"Gosh I hate waiting. This is such important news," Ellen ruminated.

* * *

It was not a convenient time for Nat Webster to meet with the military. But, considering his attitude toward their interest in the Searoc Beam, there would never be a convenient time.

It was a large gathering at Scan-Man headquarters. Webster brought his board of directors, and General Armand Stringer brought his Joint Chiefs of each military branch and their respective top aides.

Webster immediately recognized he was outnumbered. But if this was going to be hand-to-hand combat, he had the advantage. The military was so loaded down with medals on their chests they wouldn't have a chance at rapid-movement conflict with the Scan-Man directors.

The meeting took place in the Control Room where the use of sophisticated graphic displays and software could be best presented.

"Welcome to Scan-Man," Webster began. "This is a first for our organization to have such a distinguished representation of the United States Armed Forces gathered here.

"General Stringer and I have been in correspondence regarding the Searoc Beam and its potential use in military activities on land and sea and in the air.

"You are all aware of the meteorological uses of the Searoc Beam. This has been a busy year during which we have successfully managed fires, floods, tornadoes and snowstorms. All this has been done with the single Searoc Beam that occupies the Scanner XII satellite. The success of the Searoc has encouraged us to broaden our Earth coverage by developing additional satellites that can carry and use the Searoc Beam. It will take a few years to design, build and implement these.

"The program today will consist of making use of the Searoc Beam and this you will be able to observe, in real time, on the screens in front of you.

"Following this, we will go out onto Peters Field where we will demonstrate the power of the Searoc Beam on an Army tank right before your eyes.

"General Stringer. Do you have anything to say at this point?"

"Thank you, Mr. Webster. I will restrain myself and save my talking until the end of your demonstration when I believe discussion will take place."

"Very good. Let's proceed," Webster said.

During the next hour the screens in the Control Room brightened and the Scan-Man crew put the Searoc Beam through various meteorological gymnastics that resulted in applause and gasps from those present.

The group then piled into buses and rode out onto Peters Field where the Army tank sat at the corner of a large area of concrete. It was a bright sunny day.

Webster spoke to the Control Center on his cell phone and told them to begin Demo 1 when ready.

"Demo 1 will use the Searoc Beam to penetrate the wall of this tank with a hole about one inch in diameter," Webster began on his megaphone.

"You will not see the beam in this bright light. At night it would appear as a laser beam. As we do this, any human in the path of the beam would be penetrated as well.

"The technicians in the Control Center have a full view of us and the tank. The first thing you will see is a circle of light on this side of the turret.

"There it is now!" The audience watched in wonder. It took three seconds to penetrate the two inches of armor. Paint around the hole was blistered and a small plume of smoke rose.

Someone said, "That was so fast, and it didn't make a sound!"

"You can walk over and examine the hole if you wish." Everyone wished.

General Stringer stood beside Webster. "I have never seen anything like this in all my years. So swift. So clean. So deadly."

"Now, if you will please back away," Webster warned, we will proceed with Demo 2. This will create a great deal of heat, so you must be well back."

Webster spoke to the control room again.

This time a bright light engulfed the entire tank. Before their very eyes the tank began to melt and smoke from the top down. Within fifty-five seconds, the tank was a molten red mass on the concrete, not much different from a small lava flow. It would take hours for the steel to cool.

The group was transfixed, including all of the directors, none of whom had ever seen this demonstration. Many a face had a gaping jaw at the results.

"This, ladies and gentlemen," Webster said, "is a glorification of the magnifying glass some of us played with as children. The principle is not that much different, just over a longer focal range with the very same energy source -- the sun."

Webster paused, allowing time for his audience to digest his words.

"Thank you for your attention. The busses are ready. Let's return to the Control Room for discussion."

* * *

Chief Wilson jumped to attention when his laptop tracker told him Harrington responded again.

He called Gallop.

"Harrington's new response to Sasha is, 'You've played enough. Do it!'"

"Here's what I want you to answer," Gallop said. "'It'll be world news in three days. Meow!'

"I don't know if we'll get a reply to this one, but call me if you do," he told the chief. "We are getting there."

* * *

"Thank you for getting back to me, Mrs. Chabus," Odie Gallop said. "I am a private detective who is working for Mr. Nat Webster. Mr. Webster is curious about your information that has filtered down by way of Maggie Billings, specifically about two words that you found on a telephone pad and read 'Webster' and 'mouse'.

"I also understand that you live on the top floor of the Zenix Tower directly across the hall from the person who was shot a few days ago. Is this true?"

"Yes."

"I would like to visit you and hear your story. What you have to say could be critical in saving a man's life. Would you be free this afternoon about two?"

There was a pause as Puff considered what was happening. "Yes, Mr. Gallop. I'll be here."

* * *

Gallop was doubly interested in the Zenix Tower. He was here a few nights earlier when he tracked Mildred/Sasha to the rear loading dock doors. It was here, also, that he talked with a friend who was the Tower manager and learned, among other things, that Mildred was called Sasha at the Tower. What he could not connect was the Tower Sasha with the Harrington Sasha. Mrs. Chabus' call promised to be of some significance regarding this.

Gallop stopped at the manager's office to see his friend, Darleen.

"Odie how nice." Darleen said. "Twice in three days. It's either feast or famine. Thanks for the drink the other night."

"A Puff Chabus lives in one of the penthouses," Gallop stated. "What can you tell me about her?"

"Her name says it," Darleen explained simply. "She's a little puffball who dances around waiting to be picked up by eligible males. She's the lonely widow."

"She was involved somehow with the residents in the condo across the hall?"

"Yes. She's a nosey one. It was Puff who called our security after Sasha was shot."

Gallop did a double take. "What? Sasha was shot?"

"The story is she was cleaning her gun and it accidentally went off." Darleen shuddered. "Took off the side of her face. Very ugly."

218

"Did she survive it?"

"I haven't kept up with it. She made a hell of a mess on her white carpet."

"Where is she now?"

"The last I knew she was at Mass General."

"Did she live with anybody?"

"Yes. She has a partner, Helena, who is a little short on brain power, but she is nice and very shy. They were good tenants."

"Is this Helena still occupying the condo?"

"Not at the moment. She's afraid to live alone. She's with her mother now, somewhere in the city."

"But they still own the condo."

"Yup. As long as the money keeps rolling in."

"I'd like to get a look at that condo, Darleen."

"I think I can help you. I have to check the smoke alarm batteries anyway."

"Good excuse."

* * *

They exited the elevator on the top floor.

"The only other condo is the door on the right. That belongs to Puff Chabus." Darleen explained, just before opening Sasha's door.

As she said this, Puff appeared at her door. Darleen introduced her to the detective.

Gallop said, "I'll be back in a while for our talk, Mrs. Chabus."

They turned and entered the other condo, shut the door, and left Puff behind.

"Unbelievable." Inside, Gallop remarked as he looked toward the window and its view, "It must be nice to have money. I haven't seen anything like this since I was in Vegas."

"Sasha was cleaning her gun right about here. The bullet hit her face and ended up in the ceiling right over there.

"I can just see where they repaired the hole," Gallop noted.

"And over here are photos of the girls."

Gallop turned. "Damn. This blows me away. Which one is which?"

"Sasha is the redhead. Helena has the long blonde hair."

"My God, they are beautiful!" Gallop gushed. "Just think of the depth of narcissism it takes to create a showcase like this -- displaying their sex life so overtly. It's amazing.

"I need a couple of pictures," Gallop said. "I think my iPhone can handle it emotionally."

"How are *you* handling it emotionally? Are these for your collection?" Darleen teased.

"I want their faces, Darleen. Only their faces. You wouldn't believe how drab this Sasha woman looks in the shipping department."

Gallop silently moved from room to room, occasionally giving his full attention to details that caught his eye. One of these was the telephone. Next to it was a pad of paper. No detective of any stature would ever bypass a pad next to a phone. He picked up the pad and held it to the light to look for impressions. He then found a lead pencil in the desk drawer and gently rubbed the graphite sideways across the pad. The indentations from the instrument that had written the last note were revealed. Two words. "Webster" and "mouse."

"Aha," Gallop said. "Here's the tie-in we need, that everyone has been talking about." He tore off the paper and put it in his pocket.

"Darleen, do you have any contact information on the police who were in on this?"

"Sure do. I have a name and a number."

Gallop made an impromptu reach for Darleen, put his arm around her, bent her backwards and kissed her on the cheek. "You are manna from heaven, Darleen."

They straightened up. Darleen looked overwhelmed. "Wow! What brought that on, Mr. Detective?"

"Your charm, beauty and information."

"Which one, specifically?" Darleen joked.

They looked at each other, aware that a new level in their relationship had transpired.

Gallop interrupted the spell. "Tell me, Darleen. Is Sasha's bike still stored under the stairs next to the loading dock?"

"Why? You want to steal that machine?"

"I'd like to. That is one cool bike."

"I guess it's still there. I haven't checked on it."

"Mind if I look at it?"

"I'll go with you."

"I tried to follow Sasha home the other night from her job. She took off like the cartoon roadrunner. She's a daredevil."

"I don't know her that well. I prefer handsome men."

Their next stop was the stairs next to the loading dock. Sasha's bike was still under the stairs. The light was poor, but Gallop used his tactile senses to admire the details of the machine.

"Whatever else this Sasha is," Gallop said, "her taste in two-wheel speed machines is exquisite."

The pair returned to the lobby.

"Well, I'm out of here, Darleen, darling. Thanks for the info."

"It's going to cost you another night out."

"Give me a few days, Sweetheart. Too many of those drinks affect my constitution."

"Oh, Odie darling. I don't want to upset any of your parts."

* * *

"Thank you for taking the time to see me Mrs. Chabus. You have a very nice place. Have you lived here long?"

"I came here soon after my husband died last December. So you're a detective? I've only known detectives through my reading. Frankly, I didn't know they came this handsome, if you know what I mean."

"Nor have I known widows who came as pretty as you, Mrs. Chabus."

"Oh, thank you. Can I get you a coffee or something else to drink?"

"No. Thank you." Gallop cleared his throat. "Has the condo across the hall had much activity lately?"

"Helena has been in and out. But she won't stay there."

"Helena?" Gallop was searching for Puff's insights.

"She lives with Sasha, but won't stay there alone."

"Is it also true that you spoke with one of residents of that condo and you have been inside that condo?"

"Helena. Yes."

"What I would like now is the full story of how you found this information and just what that information is."

"Well, my deceased husband," Puff began, "was a close friend of Nat's. They worked together at Scan-Man. You know what I mean? My husband was killed when the atrium at the hotel fell on him. He . . ."

"Is this related to your neighbor, Mrs. Chabus?"

"Not really. It's background information."

"Let's cut to the point, Mrs. Chabus, if you will, please."

222

"Well, the night of the shooting here at the Tower, I heard a loud noise and I looked out into the hall. I saw this woman with long blond hair running to the elevator. The door to her suite was left open. I only saw the back of the woman. She went right into the elevator.

"The door to her suite was open, you know? I was curious and went over to it and opened it further. There I saw this other woman on the floor bleeding like crazy, and her face was horribly damaged. In fact, one eyeball was hanging out of its socket.

"I saw that she was breathing. I ran back to my suite and called the hotel desk and reported someone had been shot.

"It was awful."

"What next?" Gallop urged.

"The Tower security came up and questioned me. Then the Boston police came up and questioned me. Then a bunch of other people came up and took the woman away, and some other people checked the place out and cleaned up the mess, you know what I mean?"

"Please Mrs. Chabus. What about the information you gave Maggie at the *Bulletin*?"

"That wasn't until the next day," Puff continued.

"The next day this woman with the long blond hair came back. I heard her get off the elevator so I looked out and saw her face for the first time. She was cute. Very pretty.

"I talked with her. Her name was Helena, she said. She also said she had no last name. Then it became strange. She said she was living with her momma, but she said she didn't know the address, only that she knew how to get there.

"She said that she lived in that suite and that her roommate's name was Sasha. She had no last name either, she said. But this Helena talked like a little girl, like she was mentally off balance. She asked me where Sasha was -- as if nothing had happened to her the day before. I just said I didn't know where she was. I think she was taken to Mass General."

"Mrs. Chabus? You do have the information I'm looking for, I presume?"

"Yes. Sorry. So this woman had a key and opened the door and peeked in. She didn't go in. But then she left. She left the door open and the key in the door!

"I am a curious person. I went in the room and the mess was all cleaned up. You should see the photos of these two women on the wall. They are all naked and in embarrassing poses. I was shocked. You know what I mean?

"I walked around the suite. It's a mirror image of mine. I went to the desk in the main room and that's where I found the note by the phone. It had two hand-written words on it -- 'Webster' and 'mouse'. I recognized 'Webster' of course and called Maggie to see if it meant anything. She didn't think so.

"There were a lot of unopened bills and stuff on the desk, but nothing with Sasha's or Helena's names on it. All the mail was addressed to a Mildred McCoy, which meant nothing to me. I forgot to mention this to Maggie. McCoy's address was a post office box, not the Tower.

"Then I just left the suite, locked it and took the key with me. I probably should have left the key in the room, but then somebody important might want to get in."

"Is that it, Mrs. Chabus?"

"I feel a little guilty. You know what I mean? I took the note by the phone as well as one of McCoy's pieces of mail."

"You took evidence?" Gallop asked.

"What? Do you think I should put it back?"

"It's too late. Will you mind showing it to me."

"Not at all. I want to get rid of it. It's right beside you on that table."

Gallop reached for the slips of paper. The two words were clearly written on it. "Is there any more you can tell me about the women next door?"

"After three months living here, the night of the accident was the first time I'd seen them. "Except for a little whooping and hollering now and then, they were very quiet."

"They threw parties?"

Puff looked puzzled. "Oh. You mean the occasional noise. No. They never had parties, but I guess they had wild arguments now and then, but it didn't last long."

"Well, thank you very much, Mrs. Chabus. This has been helpful."

"I like to help. And you. Please feel free to stop by when you're not tied up with business."

* * *

General Armand Stringer was uncharacteristically gleeful. He had found the needle in the haystack. He had discovered the ultimate weapon of the future. Visions of proverbial sugarplums danced in his head. His normally stern visage was, at least for the moment, broken in childish joy. He struggled to contain an enthusiasm he had not known since he was a cadet.

Webster recognized the General's excitement during the demonstrations. He watched now as Stringer forced himself to resume his accustomed demeanor.

"Nat," he said calmly. "Not a bad show. We might be able to find a use for this technology."

Webster was tempted to laugh in the General's face. But he could put on just as good an act.

"Well, there are a lot of imperfections and glitches we have yet to iron out. It could take years for this to be of any practical value."

The General looked surprised. "I don't mean to say that we're not interested. Certainly your demos have been very interesting."

Webster smiled. "We've had our technicians on this since day one, but their breakthrough estimates of completion are discouraging. You have to understand, Armand, what you have seen here is technology in the rough. We were fortunate to even have it operating today."

Webster watched the General's countenance fade. He almost felt sorry for the man.

"But how did you run these demos if the technology is so primitive, as you suggest?"

"Bandages and duct tape," Webster explained. "Anticipating your presence here today took a superhuman effort. I have to give great credit to our Searoc team for overcoming extraordinary odds to impress you. I'm sorry the results today didn't meet your expectations."

"Oh, but they did. I was very impressed."

"Well. I'm glad," Webster said. "As we progress in our development of this science, I'll keep you informed. In the years to come, I'm certain we will have a system that will better meet your 'expectations.'"

The General felt it was too late to express his initial excitement. He knew he had screwed up. A certain dignity had to be maintained if he was going to eventually negotiate to his advantage.

The buses carried the General and his retinue to their military transport. He and Webster shook hands and vowed to keep in touch.

It was Nat Webster's turn to be gleeful.

He was, at least until he saw Susan Morales speaking with the General. He made haste to see what was going on. He didn't trust that woman.

Webster interrupted their conversation with, "I see you have met one of our directors, General."

Both of them turned to Webster. "Ms. Morales was telling me information that was contrary to what you told me."

"And what did she tell you, General."

"She said that you were operational and that the technology could be available within months."

Webster looked sternly at her. "I'm certain Susan was trying to be upbeat after we heard your initial coolness to the project."

Webster now looked to the General with his back to Susan. "I ask that you ignore any information regarding this technology unless it comes directly from me. No one else is authorized to distribute confidential information."

"I thank you, Mr. Webster."

"I thank you, General Stringer. Susan will accompany you to your plane."

* * *

The right side of Sasha's face, including her eye, was covered with bandages.

"I can't look, Sasha," Helena sobbed. "I can't look at you."

They were at Mass General Hospital. Sasha had just been moved from Intensive Care to a semi-private room. Surgery on her face had been difficult with most of the cheekbone gone. Surgeons had taken skin from her thigh to temporarily cover the open area that was the cheek to help prevent infection. Without the bone support, the right side of her face was sunken. They managed to save the right eye but it was not in sync with the left. Doctors told her they had a lot more work ahead of them. Eventually, they might be able to graft a new cheekbone.

"Shut up, Helena. Just listen to me." Sasha's speech was slurred. Her jawbone had been knocked out of place and had been refitted.

"Yes, Sasha." Helena was crying.

"You owe me big-time, Helena. You did this to me and don't deny it. You owe me very big time."

"Yes, Sasha."

"I told them it was a friggin' accident. Do you hear me? I told them I was cleaning my gun and it went off. I didn't mention you."

"Yes, Sasha."

"That means you owe me big-time, you little idiot."

"Yes, Sasha."

"And stop saying that! You drive me crazy!"

"Yes ..."

"Now listen! I've got a job for you."

"Uh huh."

"Have you been back to the condo?"

Helena nodded.

"Listen! I've got a pistol hidden in my closet under the bottom shelf that holds my shoes. Lift the top of that shelf and inside is a gun, and it's loaded."

"I don't like guns, Sasha."

"You don't have to like guns to use guns."

"I'm afraid."

"You *can't* be afraid, you stupid little idiot! I've got a job for you. You have to do it for Sasha! You have no choice. You can use my bike."

Helena's face lit up. "I can?"

"Yes. Now, here's what I want you to do."

* * *

"Nat. This is Susan. Do you have a minute? I want to speak with you."

"Sure, Susan. Come on up."

Susan was not known for her appropriate dress choices. She was on the board of directors because of her brains, and not in small part because she was the token woman. Why she thought she looked good dressed as a sexy twenty-something baffled Webster. But the rest of the board apparently didn't object.

Today's outfit included skin-tight blue jeans, black high heels, and a tight tank top that outlined every feature of her breasts. Her hair was pulled tightly into a bouquet of wheat at the top of her head. Her perfume could easily have been applied more sparingly.

Webster often found her looks more amusing than anything else. He smiled when she pranced into his office, her heels click, click, clicking like a horse on cobblestone.

"I was embarrassed by what you said to both me and General Stringer at the demo the other day," she began. "You did everything you could to discourage the military from buying the Searoc."

"I did?" Webster said, playing innocent.

"Now don't try that with me," she said shaking a finger at him.

"Susan, knock it off," Webster said, becoming angry. "You know my philosophy. I am in no hurry to cater to the military and make weapons. I will put them off as long as I can. You were out of place by contradicting what I told him."

"I disagree. You screwed up by throwing away $5 billion in that Recovery Fund. Now you are throwing away billions more by turning away the military. What are we, some kind of non-profit?"

"That is your opinion, Susan," Webster said calmly.

"Well, I have my opinion and there are others on the board that think my way also."

"That may be, but I will be very sorry if you attempt to turn the board against me."

There was an uncomfortable pause. Susan moved around Webster's desk and sat on the corner of it facing him.

"Pardon me if I come on strong," she said sweetly, "but I work hard and I play hard." She leaned down toward him in his chair. "I can change my thinking if you'll just play house with me."

Webster stood abruptly, nearly toppling Susan. She caught her balance and stood.

"You can leave my office now," Webster said sternly. "You've said enough."

Susan slid off the desk, turned away and went to the door. She turned toward Webster. "You will regret this, you sonofabitch."

"I will take that as a threat, Ms. Morales."

She spun around and left the room, slamming the door.

I have to get rid of that woman, Webster thought.

* * *

The days passed by carefree for Robby and the McCulloughs. The school year was ending soon, and he looked forward to building a tree house with Grampy. They had already picked out two trees. This was going to be a big tree house. It would straddle two big elms not far from the house. Robby drew pictures in crayon of how it would look. He planned to invite his school friends over to enjoy it. It would have a fireman's pole. Grampy even suggested adding a zip line. He had a long cable in the barn that could be used.

Grammy began looking skeptical as the project grew on paper.

The school bus arrived. Robby plucked the mail from the mailbox. Old Rolf met him and licked his cheek. He spoke to Henrietta as he skipped down the drive and into the house.

The mail sat on the counter during chore time. Nothing much ever came in the mail. Finally, Mabel looked through it and noticed something that looked important. It was from the state. She opened and scanned through it. One line caught her attention. "You have been approved as foster parents for Robert Randolph."

Mabel couldn't contain herself. She ran out to the barn where Robby and Grampy were just finishing the milking.

"Hey, everybody! We have great news!"

Just the appearance of Mabel in the barn was enough for them to turn their heads. But to hear Mabel sound so excited really caught their attention. Even Henrietta, with a mouthful of hay, stopped chewing and turned her head in the stanchion for a look.

"Robby's been approved as our foster child!"

Frank nearly kicked over the milk bucket as he reached for Robby and hugged him. Then Mabel did the same to the two of them.

When they quieted down, Mabel told them they had a few papers to sign and then it would be official.

"We are going out for ice cream tonight," Frank announced. "This will be a big celebration."

* * *

"I'm here to see a woman by the name of Sasha. She has no last name," Gallop stated.

231

"Oh, yes," the gentleman at Information said. "You'll find her in room 614."

Sasha was asleep. The right side of her face and her jaw were heavily bandaged. Her nose and left profile were unmarked. Gallop took several photos of her face with his iPhone.

He went out to the nurses' station.

"I'd like some information on Sasha's condition," he said to a nurse, flashing his identification.

"You'll have to speak with Dr. Gandhi. He should be back from his rounds any time now. Oh, wait. Here he comes now."

"Sasha's right zygomatic bone is gone," Dr. Gandhi began. "Excuse me. Her right cheekbone is gone and part of her right eye support. We think we will be able to save the eye, but the cheekbone will have to be rebuilt over time.

"She is very lucky to be alive. The bullet entered at a sharp angle and glanced off. It did not touch the brain, the mandible or the ear."

"What's the recovery time?"

"I don't know that she'll ever be fully recovered. But she should be mobile in a few days if she is very careful. We're just trying to stabilize her now, and then we can begin to consider reconstruction."

"I need a photo of Sasha when she was first admitted," Gallop said. "You must have one."

Dr. Gandhi went to the nurse's station and asked for Sasha's file. "Yes. Here it is."

"If you would please hold the folder, Doctor, I'll get a photo of it." Gallop zeroed in and captured the gruesome image.

Gallop thanked him for his help.

* * *

Precinct 49 was chaotic as ever. Every time Gallop returned to his old workplace, he felt the satisfying relief of having escaped this turmoil.

"Hey, Gallop!" came a familiar voice behind him.

"Kelly, you old fart. How you doing?"

They exchanged pleasantries briefly and then Gallop asked for Captain O'Brien.

"Yeah. That's his office there."

"Thanks Kelly. Let's go out for a drink sometime."

"Yeah. Sounds good, Odie."

Gallop introduced himself to O'Brien.

"I'm checking out the situation that took place at the Zenix Tower a few days ago. A person named Sasha shot herself in the face cleaning her gun."

"I remember. That case is closed."

"I'd like to look at the report."

"Why not," O'Brien said resignedly. "Have a seat."

The captain shuffled through his file cabinet and came up with a file. "It was a pretty ugly scene."

Gallop studied the report. It was pretty bland. The janitor would have better information. "I see you were on the scene. The only evidence you took was the gun and an expended Remington 223 shell."

"Right. The victim was alone. It was the neighbor to reported the accident."

"How'd the neighbor get in?" Gallop asked.

"She said she had a key. They must have known each other. There was no evidence of foul play."

"On a more important matter," Gallop continued, "I need to see a judge about confiscating a laptop from an inmate out in Walpole. Can you set me up?"

"No problemo, Mr. Gallop. It sounds like a slam-dunk process to me. Hold on. I'll give Judge Clancy a call."

It took about ten minutes to find the judge, check his calendar and arrange to meet him.

"You are a one lucky guy, Gallop. He wants you to go over right now. Good luck to you."

"I thank you, O'Brien. I owe you one."

* * *

"Thank you for seeing me, Judge Clancy." Gallop began. "I have an investigation in which I'm gathering evidence for past murders and currently an attempted murder. The man I'm after is incarcerated in Walpole and has been using his laptop to arrange for a hired killing. I want to confiscate his laptop and search it for further evidence of offshore financial havens, names of hired assassins, and embezzlement of funds from Scan-Man where he was the former chairman. He is currently sentenced to ten years for attempting to scam the federal government of billions of dollars."

The judge looked through the computer printouts, asked a few questions and agreed the evidence warranted the removal of the laptop for retrieval of evidence.

The judge then called Walpole State Prison and ordered the immediate confiscation of Chandler Harrington's laptop to be held for pick up by Detective Odie Gallop.

"You can head out to Walpole immediately," the judge said. "They say they will have the laptop ready for you."

"I can't thank you enough," Gallop said.

* * *

'Things are looking good," Gallop began.

"Good?" Ellen asked.

234

"Better than good. It looks like you are out of danger for the time being."

'Time being?" Webster asked.

"Let's see if I can explain," Gallop began.

"Mildred McCoy is no longer at Scan-Man. She is also known as Sasha, the woman who shot and then beat up, Nat. Sasha accidentally shot herself a few days ago while cleaning her gun in her condo. She shot off the right side of her face, but she is still alive and is in Mass General. I have a picture of her face if you are interested.

"So, in brief, the person who has been threatening you is now out of commission for a long time. You will probably want to bring charges against her."

"Do you mean that we are finally free from this animal?"

"You're free until you press charges," Gallop said. "It will be a long time before Sasha/Mildred recovers, if ever."

"You've done a wonderful job, Odie," Webster said. "I'm very, very happy."

"We still have a long way to go," Gallop continued. "We are the only ones who know Sasha is guilty of attempted murder. And then we have to prove Harrington's involvement. I have just acquired Harrington's laptop. I expect to find a wealth of incriminating evidence on it.

"My mission today is simply to tell you that you are out of danger from Mildred/Sasha."

Gallop then went into details about Puff Chabus' involvement and Sasha's roommate, Helena.

* * *

"I think its time we called it quits, you know what I mean, Richard?"

"It's been a great ride, Puff," the Reverend said. "You've been very generous to me."

"You *do* spend a lot of time at your storefront. Do you consider it a success?"

"Most definitely. My regular flock is up to 50 of the faithful on weekends."

"I sure wish you had struck out for the big-time. I think you have it in you. A lot of churches are struggling. They need someone with the charisma you have to suck them in."

"I'd prefer to be *drawn* in, Puff. But, as we discussed many times, the white buildings with the white steeples and the white people are not what I'm after. To quote Emma Lazarus, 'Give me your tired, your poor, your huddled masses yearning to breathe free', et cetera."

"Our differences are too great, Richard. The one thing we do well together is hardly worth doing well together. There's a world out there waiting for me to explore. There are stores out there waiting for my credit card. There are parties to attend and friends to frolic with. I'm tired of living in this condo. The excitement I've had here recently is far too exciting, you know what I mean?"

"I know what you mean, Puff. I know what you mean."

"So where are you going to live?"

"There's an extra room in the back of the place where I can lay my tired bones. I have a hotplate and a student-size refrigerator. What more does a man of the cloth require? My needs are simple."

"Let's go to dinner tonight and celebrate the months we've had together," Puff said. "Then we can part gracefully."

* * *

Harrington was furious. He was distraught. He was helpless. The guards marched into his cell and grabbed his laptop despite his protests and requests for an explanation.

"We've got our orders, Pops," was all they said.

He now sat on the edge of his bunk with his head in his hands. Prison suddenly took on a new meaning. Life itself would take on new meaning when the contents of his laptop were examined. Everything about his personal and financial life was on that laptop.

"This is my death sentence," he mumbled to himself and he began to cry -- the first tears of any kind he had shed since he lost his parents.

Now be cursed himself. "I could have kept all the sensitive information on a memory stick that I could have kept hidden. But I didn't."

For the first time, he thought how his parents would now be disappointed in him. He knew better. He should have known. It is now too late.

"They will now have access to all my finances and also to Sasha's. They have my passwords. They will learn where my money came from. They will take everything I have. When I'm released, I will have no money. I will have nothing."

Each of his thoughts became progressively worse and he reviewed his losses.

He suddenly sat up straight, alert. "Jesus! They'll find all the correspondence with Sasha and with my Washington contact. I'll be re-tried. I'll be accused of murder. I'll be hanged. I'm a walking dead man!" He smeared tears when he wiped his face with the back of his hand.

"Shut up, Mr. big executive," came a voice from a nearby cell. "Cryin' ain't gonna help."

* * *

Helena was distraught after visiting Sasha in the hospital. They had been lovers, worshiping each other's bodies and souls. Sasha was dominant in their relationship.

Helena's mother had never told her, or anyone in the family, that she had dropped her daughter as a baby and her head had struck hard on the wood floor. As a result, the adult Helena retained a lot of her childishness and accepted the domination of Sasha.

Helena ran through the instructions Sasha had given her during their visit. She was eager to do whatever Sasha wanted, but now those instructions were tangled and confused. They were wrapped in the image of Sasha's distorted face.

She remembered Sasha said it was Helena's fault that Sasha looked like that. Helena did it. Helena did it. She heard it over and over. She didn't know how she did it.

All she recalled from that night of the big bang, was playing with Sasha's gun. Sasha said they were toys, Sasha's toys, and Helena could not play with them. She said they were guns, her guns, no one else's.

But Helena *did* play with the gun. She was playing with it when Sasha came home. Sasha saw her playing with the toy. When Sasha came in the door, she was angry and yelled at Helena. And then there was a big noise that scared her. It hurt her ears. She didn't know what made that big noise that frightened her.

Right after that Sasha lay down on the floor and went to sleep. But she had hurt herself. She looked awfully ugly. Helena thought she had better leave while Sasha slept. If she stayed, Sasha might hurt her for playing with toys she was told not to play with.

So she left and went home to Momma. Momma always made Helena feel better. It was always good to go home.

But she didn't dare tell momma what Sasha wanted her to do. She knew her momma would not like it. But Sasha was her friend and she wanted to do what Sasha said to do.

But now her momma just held her tight. Momma suspected something was bothering Helena, but then something was always bothering her. So Momma said everything was all right and told her not to worry.

Later, Helena went back to Sasha's condo, but Sasha wasn't there. She turned on the light. The room was empty and quiet and scary. She was afraid to go in alone.

Then this nice lady from across the hall talked to her. Sasha told Helena not to talk to other people. That's what she said. Do not talk to other people. So she walked away from this nice person and went back to Momma.

Some days passed and she heard Sasha was in the hospital. She took the bus across town and someone helped her find Sasha. Oh, Sasha looked terrible.

Sasha told Helena to do something. Sasha said she owed it to her because her broken face was Helena's fault. She said she had to do it. Sasha said there was a gun in the closet under her shoes. It was one of Sasha's toys. Now she said she could play with it. Now she said she could even use her bike! That made her very happy. Sasha wanted Helena to ride her bike like she did a few times before.

She tried to think of what Sasha wanted her to do with the gun. It was something about a man named Webster. Sasha wanted Helena to go to a place called Scan-Man and hurt Mr. Webster. Sasha said Helena owed Sasha big time. Helena had to do it. She had to find Scan-Man and hurt Mr. Webster with the gun, just like she did to Sasha. Helena had to do the big bang on Mr. Webster. Sasha gave her a folded piece of paper and said the information on the paper told how to get to this place.

Helena was so confused, so mixed up with bangs and ugly faces and hurts and had-tos and don't-dos and toys and noise and smelly hospitals, and sick Sashas.

She didn't know what to do.

* * *

Puff Chabus hadn't been to Hollandson since the snowstorm. It was here, on that memorable Christmas Eve at the hotel, that she met and made friends with Rev. Richard Masters.

But Rev. Dick, as his flock called him, was now part of her past. She was after something new. She drove by the Hollandson Motor Hotel and saw that it was being reconstructed. Everything in town was so strange to her. She had only seen parts of it, and that was under a deep snow.

She thought she might stop by the *Bulletin* office. Maybe her old lover from her college days, Phil Billings, might be around and they could chat a bit. Hopefully Maggie would be out on assignment.

She swung her sporty red BMW through town. The top was down. She wore a big hat that was battened down with a red ribbon chinstrap. She was very pretty in her colorful spring dress, all fancied up with buttons and bows.

It was just about noon and a diner was in sight. She decided on a little lunch. She had had only black coffee for breakfast to keep her figure as glorious as it had always been.

Luckily there was a slot right in front. She pulled into it and stepped out of the car. As soon as she entered the diner, all eyes turned in her direction. She answered with a big smile and went to the only booth available -- in the far corner -- and sat facing the length of the room.

Jack Thompson beat his two waitresses to the booth and greeted the lady. "Mornin' Miss. I'm Jack, the proprietor of this fine establishment. Can I get you a coffee to start?"

"You may, Jack. Make it black, if you know what I mean. My name is Puff."

Jack was back in moment. "Here ya go, Puff. Careful. It's hot. You know what you want? The menu's right there."

"Jack, you can make me an iceberg lettuce sandwich, on wheat bread untoasted, with mayonnaise. Please cut it in quarters. And, if you have a cucumber, you can put a slice on each of the quarters."

Jack thought for a minute. "Puff. I don't think anyone has *ever* ordered such a creation here. But since this is a fine establishment, I will create it for you -- if I remember how." Jack laughed.

Puff looked around, searching every face for one she might know. She sat low in the booth and had trouble seeing over people's heads. She looked out the window at the cars and walkers passing by.

One person grabbed her attention. It was a soldier in uniform. He was standing over her car looking at it. He walked from side to side and stuck his head in by the steering wheel -- probably looking at the mileage, she thought. Then he stood up straight and looked in her direction. God, he was handsome. He had a mustache, was cleanly shaven and had a rakish look to him. For the heck of it, she wiggled her fingers at him. He winked.

He came in and walked directly to Puff's table. He gave a mock bow and took off his cap. "My name's Redford. Captain Redford. You can call me whatever you want, young lady. Er, is this seat taken? If not, may I?"

"You may have that seat, Captain. It's my pleasure, if you know what I mean."

Redford slid into the opposite seat. "Are you from around here?"

"Yes and no. I was here in December in the snow, and I'm just passing through today."

"Should I be afraid of your husband?"

Puff giggled. "No husband, Captain. I'm as free as can be."

"I'm glad to hear that. I'm as free as the Army lets me be, which isn't much. I'm stationed at Peters Field. I was here through the snowstorm."

"It is nice to have so much in common," Puff laughed.

"That little red car out there wouldn't happen to be yours, would it?"

"It is mine. My dream machine."

Jack returned with a disappointed look drooping his face. "Here's my creation, Puff. I hope you like it.

"And Captain Redford," Jack said. "Would you like a lettuce sandwich with cucumber slices on it?"

"Jack. Give me the regular. A Corona Light and a liverwurst piled high on white with horseradish and mustard."

"How do you want it cut?"

"What do mean?"

"The sandwich. See Puff's? It's cut in quarters."

"Oh. Don't bother cutting mine. I have a big mouth."

The three laughed.

"Comin' up."

"So, tell me, Puff. What brought you out to Hollandson on this beautiful spring day?"

"I needed the ride. Boston was getting stale."

"So you're from Boston."

"Off and on. I went to college in Boston and I have friends there, but I don't call it home. My husband and I were from the Midwest -- St. Louis to be precise."

"I thought you said you weren't married."

242

"I'm not. He was killed in the collapse of the hotel atrium last December. He was the president of the NSA."

"NSA?"

"The National Scientific Association."

"Oh. That's out of my class. Was he a professor type?"

"He was. We talked different languages and pretty much went our own ways. His interest in science bored me. And he wasn't interested in shopping, going to plays, and driving fast cars."

"I think you and I have a lot in common, Puff. You gonna take me for a ride in your buggy?"

"If you don't smell of liverwurst."

Redford laughed out loud. "Puff. You kill me. I like you."

"How about *your* wife?"

"Good try. No. I've never been married. I move around too much. I'm here. I'm there. I fly helicopters. Oh, that reminds me. You were here in December. Do you know a couple girls who live here in town? One is Maggie and the other is Ellen, I think. Oh yeah. I think Maggie has a newspaper here."

"Yes. I do know them."

"Well, last December they needed a ride into Boston in the middle of that storm. I flew them in my chopper and they jumped out over Boston Harbor! Can you believe it? They were some dames. Er, you don't skydive do you?"

Puff laughed. "That's the very last thing I'd do."

"I'm with you. The last thing a pilot wants to do is jump out of his aircraft."

Puff had finished her sandwich by the time Redford's was delivered.

"I don't need this liverwurst," Redford said. "Let's get out of here. The food's my treat."

"Thank you, Captain."

Puff handed Redford the keys. "You drive, Captain."

"Why thank you, young lady."

* * *

Odie Gallop became more exuberant the deeper he dug into Harrington's computer files. Everything was here to convict both him and Sasha of several murders. Here were all his passwords to the offshore and local bank accounts, the total of which was several million dollars. Information was here on how and when he embezzled money from Scan-Man to finance his and Sasha's high living styles and future security.

Gallop learned that Mildred McCoy was initially hired to work as a full-time employee in shipping at Scan-Man. It was here she met Harrington who convinced her to work for him and enjoy a high living style and other benefits. She then switched to part-time work that became a front for her and a means for Harrington to keep track of her.

* * *

"I want a baby or two," Maggie said one evening to Phil. "We've talked about it a lot but we've never put our minds to it -- so to speak."

"Oh, good!" Phil said. "I've been looking forward to a few months of continuous sex."

"I'm ready for children now. I don't want to become too old to play with them. I also think it will liven up our marriage."

"I'm for livening up my sex life if that's what it takes. I'm putting in my bid right now for a boy."

"Hey, Wait a minute! I want a little girl I can dress up in pretty clothes."

244

"No, no. Let's order a boy so I can play baseball and basketball with him."

"Let's compromise. Let's do twins -- one boy, one girl. That would be ideal."

"Oh, oh. Beware. What if we had triplets?"

"We've looked at our family histories. There are no twins and certainly no triplets."

"What if you need fertilization drugs?"

"Let's not talk about that. Think positive."

"Who? Me?"

"Let's be serious," Maggie said. "This will be a big responsibility. Are you ready to get up in the middle of the night to cuddle a screaming, hungry baby?"

"But wait! You're going to breast feed aren't you? That means *you* get up."

"Not necessarily. I might pump milk."

"What? And take the joy away from the baby nursing on your lovely breasts?"

"I'm ready to be a mother. I'll be thirty-three when she's born. That means I'll be fifty-three when she's in college. I could be a grandmother at sixty-three or even earlier."

"We're well established in a business of our own," Phil continued. "We have twenty years to save for college; thirty years to save for retirement. In forty years we'll have kids old enough so we can move in with them."

"Be quiet. Our parents may be thinking of moving in with us."

"Not with a screaming baby or two."

"Sure they will. Grandparents can hardly wait to take care of their grandchildren."

"So, future mother, where do we stand?"

"Once we get going, there's no turning around."

"I'm ready."

"Me too. Lets go out and celebrate."

"Don't we have to do this at home, upstairs?"

"Plenty of time for that later."

"You are a tease, future mother."

* * *

"Nat. Have you ever heard of 'Sky and Sea Industries'?"

"Yes. They are a recent start-up hoping to capitalize on a share of our business."

"Aren't you worried about them taking business away from us?"

"Not yet. But they have some good people working for them."

"I read that they envision a variation of our Searoc Beam that they would be eager to sell to the military."

"It took us twenty years to get where we are. It'll probably take them close to that to catch up."

"But they are building on what already exists," Ellen rationalized. "It took you years to build something that works."

"You could very well be right. It does bother me that someone is willing to create another killing machine. But there's not much I can do about it."

"You seem so blazé, Nat. Don't you care?"

"Of course I care, but what do you expect me to do, picket their building?"

"We could start up a PR program against another killing machine," Ellen pursued. "I'll bet there are dozens of groups around the world who would support such it. We can graphically demonstrate just how a new killing machine could start another arms race. We don't have to take this lying down. We can fight it."

"We could also stir up hornet's nest that could back-fire."

"It could, I suppose. But it's you, Nat, who has a strong belief of what is good and what is bad. If you support the good, shouldn't you attempt to overcome the evil? A killing machine is evil."

"OK, OK," Webster gave in. "You are probably right. Why don't you put something together? Get a group in the Brain Trust together and see what ideas are sparked. I'll support it."

"I think I will. It will get me out of my rut."

* * *

Puff, with Captain Redford at the wheel, followed Rte. 117 west. Redford loved the way the little sports car managed the corners and then accelerated on the straightaways. They were a happy looking pair on a joy ride with no real destination in mind. Redford was in his glory. He had never driven a BMW. It sure beat his clunker.

They stopped at a dairy bar in Stow and each had a small dish of ice cream. They were silent as they ate. Each looked at the other, smiled and looked down again.

Redford broke the silence. "I really like you, Puff. You're fun, good-looking, dress pretty and you have a nice car. Where do we go from here?"

"Are you talking about the drive or our relationship?"

"You hot ticket. What I want to know is, do you want to come back to my BOQ?"

"Your BBQ?" Puff laughed.

Redford answered with a laugh. "I'll be straight with you, Puff. I really want to know you better. How about coming back to my pad with me?"

Puff said nothing. She studied him.

"Why not? I like you -- you hot ticket," she finally said.

Another roar out of Redford. "Sweetheart, you and I are going to get along just great. Let's go home."

Redford drove a little faster on the return route on the two-lane winding road. Puff didn't complain. She liked going fast. She was confident in Redford's driving. He had to be a good driver. He drove helicopters.

She thought of what Redford would be like in bed. Would he be slow and gentle like the Reverend? Would be inept like her poor dead husband? Would he be slam, bang thank-you ma'am? Or maybe there would be surprises. Surely this Army guy had been around. He probably had a girl in every port or, in his case, every miserable backwash town that the Army polluted.

She squirmed in her seat and looked at the captain. What if he had AIDS or some other ugly disease? That's not the surprise she wanted. He must be my age so why hasn't he been married? Does he just pick up his bedmates along with their diseases here and there? No wonder he likes me. He probably thinks I'm a virgin because I was married to an inept scientist -- an older man.

Look at him, she thought. He is as handsome as they come. He could pass for Clark Gable in a dark bar. There has to be something wrong with him. He's too good to be true. Do I want to take a chance on a one-night stand with a possibly diseased guy?

"Let's stop by the diner and you can pick up your car," she said.

"Nah," he said. "I can pick it up later."

"Please. I'd really like to do that. I can follow you to your BBQ."

"Sweetheart. There's plenty of time to switch cars. We're on a mission and I hate to interrupt it."

248

Puff was now frightened. "Captain!" she was angry. "I do not want to go to your BOQ. I want you to stop at the diner."

"What are you talking about, Puff? Ten minutes ago you said you really liked me. What's wrong?"

"I can't go through with it. I'm frightened."

Redford slowed the car and looked at her. "What's wrong? I'm a fun, easy-going guy. I never hurt a flea."

"I'm sure you are, but I can't do it."

Now Redford was angry. "You are a goddamned tease. You got me excited for nothing. You're a bitch!"

He jerked the steering wheel sharply left and right, making the tires squeal. He accelerated again and drove even faster. He rapidly came up behind a car and passed it on a curve.

Puff screamed. "Stop it. You're going to kill us!"

"Good," the captain snarled. "I hope I do!"

Puff screamed again. "Slow down, you idiot!"

They came up fast behind another car and turned into the other lane to pass. The cars were side-by-side when a car facing them suddenly appeared. The captain floored the accelerator and squeezed right, between the two cars, forcing both to turn into their respective ditches.

Puff continued to scream. She was shaking in fear.

He slowed now, and they were soon at the diner. He recklessly swung into a parking spot. Puff was crying.

"OK, bitch. I've had my fun," he said getting out of the car and slamming the door. "Some guys would have killed you for playing your teasing game. Oh, God I hate your kind. That's what I get for picking up a sweet little thing. Give me a goddamned tramp any day!"

He left. Puff was still shaking. She didn't move until he had driven away. She didn't know if she could drive all the way back to Boston.

It was early evening. If the hotel had been open, she would have gone to stay there for the night.

She thought of Maggie and Phil. Maybe she could stay with them. She called.

Phil answered. "Well, I don't know. I'll have to ask Maggie."

"I don't think I can drive back to Boston. I've just had a terrible experience."

"Let me ask Maggie. I only hesitate because of our past relationship."

A minute passed. Maggie came on the phone. "Of course you can spend the night here."

Maggie gave directions.

"Thank you very much, Maggie. It's been a rough day, if you know what I mean."

"You can tell us when you get here."

* * *

No one had ever treated Puff as badly as Redford had. It was very frightening. Her relationship with men had always been cordial. Flirting with men was what she did. She admitted she was a flirt. She loved to tease men and she had always gotten away with it. She enjoyed playing the cute and loveable girl. To that end she dressed in little-girl clothes with puffy sleeves, flared hems and low necklines.

Her late husband, Freddie, didn't mind. He knew he possessed her and she liked being possessed. Freddie was her financial security and his revered position as president of the NSA insured her safe flirtation. He was happy in his own world of science and she was content in her world of parties and up-scale shopping.

Her first love in college was Phil Billings. But she eventually rejected him because he showed no promise as a hunter and gatherer in her social aspirations.

But then Phil had rejected her when Puff wanted a one-night-stand during the December NSA convention. He had walked away from her when she had earnestly wanted him. This really baffled her, because when they were in college, she had him totally under her spell.

Captain Redford was the first man with whom she experienced violence. Redford apparently wanted Puff for one purpose only. When his true nature came out, it frightened her -- she had never before been frightened by a man. Her men had always been gentlemen at the very least. Her little-girl act had failed with Redford. She had almost been killed in his anger. She shuddered at what might have happened in his BOQ. She had learned a harsh lesson.

Now, as she anticipated visiting the Billings, she wondered if this was the right thing to do. She certainly didn't want to upset Maggie who had always been cordial to her. Phil, respectful of Maggie's feelings, had let her make the visit decision. That was nice. Phil had always been a nice guy. Back in college though, nice guys, in her opinion, didn't often make it in an aggressive world.

Maggie appeared to be the aggressor in her relationship with Phil. Phil needed leadership. In college she led Phil around like an Arab with a camel. Phil was obedient and she got her way at a price she was willing to pay in bed now and then. She wondered if she could ever get Phil interested in her again, for a one-night stand, or something.

She wondered about the Billings' sex life. They had no children. Who knows? Maybe Maggie couldn't have children. She never seemed very sexy. Certainly she never dressed that way. But that, of course, was no indication of her sexual activity.

Look at herself. She never had children either. Actually, she never wanted children. She couldn't imagine herself as a parent. Both she and Freddie were far too busy for children they had told themselves.

But that was then. This was now. Would she ever want to get married again? What kind of man would she want to marry? A Freddie? No. A Reverend? No. Certainly not a helicopter pilot! A Phil? Maybe -- if they still made Phils these days. At her age now, she had a different outlook on a Phil-type, but that could be because she was already secure financially.

* * *

Nat Webster is a happy man. He is happy with his job. He is happy with Ellen. He is happy with their small group of friends. And, most of all, he is happy that the Sasha creature has been found and is out of commission.

He has to make a decision about Ellen. He loves her. He loves everything about her. Smart and beautiful are the obvious. Intelligent and creative? She has it. The spark of fun? You bet. Loving and giving? It couldn't be better. Stable and grounded? She's a rock. Trustworthy, loyal, helpful, friendly, courteous, kind, obedient, cheerful, thrifty, brave, clean and quite possibly reverent. She'd make a great Scout.

It is time I asked her to marry me.

Susan Morales is a major problem. I should have fired her after our last meeting. Her attempts to date me are out of place and crude. Thus far she has been very helpful on the board, a good idea person and she's my token woman. Firing an elected board member is a tedious and politically ugly experience, and she knows that. At the moment I'd rather think about other things.

And then there is Lois. What a cute, smart little person. I can't wait to see her paper. She has to be at least eighteen. What a mix of emotions she exhibits. She has an apparent immaturity in love, and a developing maturity in technical innovation. She couldn't have thought up that Searoc alternative during our brief visit. She must have been at it for some time. She is worth cultivating.

And now there's Sky & Sea Industries. I knew it was coming. I met its president at the last NSA meeting. He told me his plans. Competition, I keep telling myself, is good. Most established businesses hate competition because it forces us to rise from our nests of laziness and improve our own products and marketing.

So with S&S on the prowl, I'm looking for innovations here, such as the one Lois just happened to mention. I've learned that outside thinking by problem solvers is most effective when working at the margins of their fields. As a result, I have my Brain Trust that is made up of a spectrum professional engineers and scientists. They are charged with looking at technical problems with the aim of finding solutions.

I'm not afraid of competition. I thrive on competition. It's my driving force. I'm attempting to instill that in all my employees.

* * *

"Captain O'Brien. This is Odie Gallop."

"Hey, Odie. What's up?"

"Need a couple officers and an arrest warrant for Mildred McCoy, alias Sasha. The charge is murder, attempted murder and other things. She is currently at Mass General. We will also need a 24-hour guard outside her door until she is released from the hospital."

"She was the victim, Odie."

"I have the evidence to substantiate everything, Captain."

"Your word's as good as gold, Odie."

"Can I meet you at the Mass General front door in a couple hours? I'll explain everything later."

"We'll be there."

"I appreciate it. Thanks, O'Brien."

Odie notified Mass General security that an arrest was going to take place and they arranged to meet each other.

* * *

Marsha Randolph bought a cute little Shih Tzu. She had been walking aimlessly in the mall when puppies playing in the pet shop window caught her eye. She paused for a moment and watched them tumble and roll and summersault. Their activity made Marsha smile -- her first smile in months.

Her pause lengthened into a linger. The linger extended into minutes. She was captivated. She envied their carefree activity. Her mind wandered back to her childhood when she had asked her parents for a puppy. They had said no, they take too much care. She watched with envy as her friends walked their pets, played and talked to them.

And now, as she walked the streets of Naples, she became more aware of the many adults who led their pets on leashes. Some carried them in mini-strollers. They dressed them, painted their toenails and tied ribbons in their fur. The pets were part of their families. She even heard of one that sat with them at the dinner table.

Marsha awakened to the realization that a dog might make a wonderful companion for her. It would be a special friend that never complained, talked back, or placed undue demands on her. It would be something she could love and cuddle and, yes, even play with.

As she watched, one of the puppies waddled over to the window and looked at Marsha. She brought her finger to the window and met its nose. The puppy rose on its hind legs and pawed at the window. Its soft, brown eyes met Marsha's. He wants me, Marsha thought.

She made a decision. She had to have him. She entered the store. A hit tune from the Sixties came into her head and she hummed it. "How much is that doggie in the window?"

A young girl approached her. "Can I help you?"

"I'm interested in the white puppy in the front window."

"Let me get it for you."

A moment later Marsha was holding the squirming puppy awkwardly. She had never held a puppy. It was lively. It stood up in her arms and licked her face. "Oh, my. It's so active."

"Have you ever had a puppy?" the girl asked.

"No. Never." Marsha was losing control of this wriggling creature that was climbing up to her shoulder.

"I don't want to talk you out of this, but puppies require a lot of attention and care," the girl explained.

"Here," Marsha said. "He's too much."

The girl returned the dog to the front window. She returned and studied Marsha. "We do have some more mature dogs that are housebroken. Would you like to see them?"

They went to the back of the store and through a door. Marsha recoiled at the barking and yapping when the animals saw them. The girl noticed Marsha's reaction.

"Over here we have cute little fella," the girl said. He's a Shih Tzu, and he's housebroken. He rarely barks. His disposition is also quiet. Do you have any children?"

Marsha hesitated. "No."

"He'd make a nice companion for you."

Marsha reached down and patted the dog's head. He was little bigger than the puppy she had just held. The dog licked her hand.

The girl took the dog out of the cage and handed it to Marsha. It nestled quietly in her arms and looked up into her eyes. Marsha imagined it saying, "Take me, please."

"Let me get a leash. You can take him for a trial walk."

Moments later Marsha was led through the mall. She watched the hurried little steps of the short legs. She came to a bench. She stopped, sat and lifted the dog into her arms. It gently lifted its head and licked her face, then settled down quietly into her lap. "You are for me," she said to the dog. At these words, the animal looked up at her. From that point on, Marsha swore that Winky winked at her.

* * *

"I'm so sorry, Maggie," Puff apologized. "I forgot all about it being dinnertime, you know? I can come back later."

"Don't be silly. You come right in. We have plenty of food." Maggie paused. "Phil, Puff's here."

Phil appeared. "Hi, Puff." There were no hugs or handshakes.

"Come on in and have a seat," Maggie offered. "We want to hear what happened. Dinner won't be ready for a while yet."

They went into the den and sat down. Maggie and Phil faced Puff and waited for her to begin.

"It was so stupid of me. I asked for it. And it could have been so much worse." Puff was downcast. "It was Captain Redford."

"Oh, no," Maggie said.

Puff looked up. "He said he knew you and Ellen. He said he flew you into town and you two jumped out of his helicopter."

"That's the story. He's a rake, a womanizer."

"That's what I found out the hard way," Puff said.

"OK. But go on with your story."

"I drove out from Boston. It was a nice day and I thought I'd drive through Hollandson to see what the town was like without snow. By chance, I stopped at the diner. Jack was very kind and waited on me himself, you know?"

"That's old Jack -- looking after the pretty women."

"I sat at the end booth so I could get a view of everything. What I saw was this handsome soldier get out of his car. He looked in my direction and stupidly I waved to him. He gave me that smile, if you know what I mean, came into the diner and came right over to my booth and sat down."

"I'm not surprised. He's a lady-killer," Maggie said.

"Well anyway, one thing led to another, and we got along pretty good. He asked if that was my Beemer. He suggested I take him for a ride in it. I figured why not?

"Then came my biggest mistake. I handed him my keys. Everything was fine at first. We drove out to Stow and stopped for an ice cream.

"At some point during our conversation he suggested we go back to his living quarters at Peters Field. Again, I stupidly said, 'Why not?' On the drive back I began to get cold feet. I didn't think I was that dumb. I didn't want sex with this guy. I imagined the diseases he might have and all kinds of other stuff. I said no. I asked him to stop at the diner and we'd go our own ways.

"Well, let me tell you, this was not what he wanted to hear. He drove my car like a drunkard. He swerved and speeded and passed cars on curves and scared me to death. He swore at me and called me names but he did get out at the diner and slammed the door.

"I was shaking like a leaf, you know what I mean? I didn't think I could drive all the way back to Boston. That's when I called you."

"Oh, Puff. That's terrible," Maggie consoled.

Phil looked at Maggie. "And you rode with this guy in a helicopter?"

"I was so stupid, stupid, stupid!" Puff beat herself up. "I had never done anything like that in my life." She paused. "Well maybe once or twice. But none of them were like this guy, you know?"

"Wow. Excuse me," Maggie said. "I have to check the dinner."

Puff and Phil looked at each other.

"Do you think I'm a bitch?" Puff asked.

"You are our guest tonight, Puff. I don't want to spoil a nice evening by getting into that. Let's just say we've had our differences."

"Touché, Phil."

"Where are you living in town?"

"I'm at the Zenix Towers on Summer Street."

"Gosh that name sounds familiar," Phil said. "It's been in the papers lately. There was a shooting there."

"Oh, God. I don't want to get into that now, you know. It happened across the hall from me."

"Did you see anything?"

"I saw everything, Phil. It was terrible, you know."

"How do you get into these things, Puff?"

"Well at least this time it wasn't my fault. I just heard a shot and I investigated."

"What did you see?"

258

Puff was excited to see that she had Phil on the edge of his chair. "One woman had shot off half of another woman's face."

"And you saw that?" Phil said with a gasp.

Puff raised her hand to stop the questions. "Wait till Maggie has a chance to hear it."

"Jesus, Puff. You *are* a tease."

She glared at him.

"You've *always* been a tease," he continued.

Puff got up and went into the kitchen. "If you'll excuse me, I think I'll go home now. I think it's best for all of us. I don't even have a change of clothes with me."

"Did Phil say something?"

"I think it's best for me to leave. I just hope I haven't put you out."

"No. You haven't put me out and I want you to stay."

"Thank you. But Phil and I can't be in the same room together."

"It's that bad, huh?"

"I'm afraid so, Maggie. I don't want to ruin your evening too."

"That's too bad. Wait a minute. I'll give you something to take home."

"Thank you, but I'm on my way."

Maggie ushered Puff out the front door. Phil had disappeared from the room.

"Goodbye, Maggie. I hope you and I can have a heart-to-heart sometime."

"We'll see. We'll see."

Maggie watched as Puff started up the Beemer with a roar and then crawled out the drive. It was just getting dark.

Phil returned and followed Maggie into the kitchen. He watched her remove one place setting from the table and waited for her to say something.

259

"Aren't you going to say something, Maggie?"

"No. What can I say?"

"OK. OK. It doesn't matter. She's gone."

"Will you please pour us some milk?" Maggie asked.

"Yes, dear," Phil smirked.

* * *

The gaggle of uniformed men assembled outside Sasha's closed door. The door opened and a nurse scampered out, nodding that the patient was present.

In they went. Officer O'Brien made the official announcement that Sasha was under arrest for murder, attempted murder and other crimes. She was also told that an armed guard would be placed outside her door, and would continue to be present until she was released from the hospital, at which time she would be taken to prison to await trial. They shackled her to the bed.

Mildred/Sasha would have screamed at the group and unleashed a volley of curses but for her fragile facial condition. Instead, she uttered expletives through her teeth and then sank back onto her bed in resignation.

Gallop's duties fulfilled, he shook hands with Captain O'Brien and left.

* * *

"I'm surprised you're delivering the paper so quickly," Webster said, glancing through its dozen or more pages.

"One always finds time to do the things one wants to do, to paraphrase someone's saying, Mr. Webster."

"Sage advice, Lois. Please give me a few minutes to browse through this."

Lois was anxious again. She noted that she was sitting in the same chair beside his desk that she sat in the day she was so nervous and made such a fool of herself. As she sat, she watched this man's handsome face and its muscles move in their unique ways as he read. His eyebrows went up and down. He blinked. He smiled. He nodded. His lips moved. His cheeks moved. His was a face in constant motion she decided. But then again, maybe she had never noticed anyone else's face as closely as Mr. Webster's.

He put her paper down on the desk and turned to her. He had a smile. A smile is good. What was he going to say?

"Frankly, I'm amazed at the maturity of your paper. It is well beyond what I expected of an undergraduate intern. When did you first begin thinking of this?"

She twisted in her chair. "It has to be a year ago. Interning at Scan-Man has been my first goal since I began my technology studies at school. I'll be a senior this fall. I used the Internet a lot and scoured it for anything related to the Searoc Beam."

Webster chuckled. "I was unaware this information was so easily available."

It was Lois' turn to chuckle, but hers was not as effective as his -- in her mind. "With web sites like WikiLeaks, you know, there's plenty of information around -- especially with the ultra-high interest there is in your weather modification."

"Lois. You are not the girl who came into my office a week ago. You show such maturity now, whereas on the first visit you came across, at least initially, as a lot younger person -- maybe even childish, if you'll excuse the comparison."

"I can't answer that, Mr. Webster. If I can also be frank, you recall I was fixated on human love and the emotion of love. Human love is totally unrelated to my love of technology and science. Yes. I admit I was childish, or at least immature. But that was then. This is now."

"I think you have the foundation of a workable concept. I` think a portable Searoc may be something that is worth pursuing."

"I'm flattered. Thank you."

"I'm not trying to flatter you, Lois. I'm giving you credit for what you have accomplished in this paper."

"Thank you again."

"What I'd like to do is consult on this with some of my people. There may be an opportunity for you to work with one or more of them, not only on this project, but also to be introduced to other projects we have in the works. Frankly, Lois, I think you have an innovative mind. We can always use innovative minds here."

"I'm thrilled. Does this mean I won't be delivering packages to you any more?"

"Yes. The packages I want from you are ideas and they rarely come in boxes through the shipping department."

Webster stood. Lois stood.

"May I have another one of your hugs, Mr. Webster?"

Webster put out his arms and took Lois in. She put her head against his chest and felt the beat of his heart. He then released her.

"Thank you. I needed that."

Webster smiled at her. "I'm glad, but please don't expect this to continue. Remember. This is a business environment and you and I are part of that. Nothing more."

"Of course. I understand."

* * *

Ellen had not thought much about her all-woman assent on Mount Everest that was fast approaching -- less than a year away now, next May. A reminder arrived in an e-mail from the team leader. They were scheduled to leave for a training climb on Mount McKinley on July 16 -- less than a month away.

Where has time gone? she thought. She smiled. All the adventures at home had distracted her.

"I'm not going to leave you while these threat notes continue," she told Webster.

"Ellen. There is nothing you can do about the threats by staying here," Webster reasoned. "Odie is hard at work. I want you to go. You've been planning this for, what? Three years?"

"Yes. It's my life dream. I feel prepared but I need the McKinley experience. But you're my dream also, Nat. I don't want to come home to find it exploded."

"That's very nice of you, my sweet, but it's not necessary. I want you to go."

Throughout Ellen's ten years of serious hiking, friends and acquaintances have asked her why she climbed mountains.

"It's far more than 'because it's there.' It's a challenge I need," was her answer. "I think we all need challenges to keep us mentally fit. Challenges, of course, have a broad range depending on the individual.

"Life itself is nothing but challenges. Simply getting out of bed in the morning for a person crippled with arthritis can be a challenge. Getting good grades in school is always a challenge. Think about it," she explains to the inquirer.

"My life on a mountainside, whether it be Mount Chocorua in New Hampshire, or a summit in the Himalayas, is a thrill. For me, the mountain air clears the brain, exercises the lungs, strengthens the legs, and gives a sense of accomplishment like no other. To do this with a few like-minded hikers increases the enjoyment."

"You don't have to convince me," Webster said. "I understand passion. I have my own, of course. But you'll never catch me on a mountain."

"Opposites certainly attract," Ellen said. "Maybe that's why I find you so interesting."

"Only 'interesting'?" Webster asked.

"Oh, stop teasing. You know what I mean."

* * *

The McCullough household was packed with kids and their parents. Robby had invited twelve of his best friends at school to his tenth birthday party. There was plenty of room. Most activities were outdoors. Robby had his new tree house to show off. Henrietta made herself available for milking lessons. And the hens went into overtime to provide enough eggs so everyone was able to collect some.

Then there was Mabel's cake, the centerpiece for the celebration. The cake was four tiers high and all the boys' and girls' first names were inscribed around the tiers.

The weather could not have been better. The children and their parents began arriving at eleven. Frank was in charge of the outdoor activities. He directed everyone to the tree house. There, he gave each of the parents duties in supervision, specifically, each had to be responsible for their own children.

Everyone gathered round the tree house.

"I want to say somethin'," Frank said, holding his arms up. "This here tree house project took a lot of good people to put it together. All of you men here put in a lot of hours to make this dream of Robby's to come true. I am truly grateful. This is the biggest and the bestest tree house in the state, I'm sure.

"Everybody chip in and keep an eye on all the kids. Safety first. We sure don't want nobody hurt."

The tree house required very close attention. In fact, some parents wouldn't let their kids climb the ladder at first, until they saw others do it. One girl was stuck on the fireman's pole. She wouldn't go down and she wouldn't go up. She just hung on and screamed. They had to get a ladder to help her.

The tree house was unusually large. It was constructed between two huge elms. An eight-by-eight beam ran between the trees and provided the main support.

"With the help of some of the men here," Frank explained to one mother, "we raised that beam so that one end lay on a crossbeam fifteen feet up the tree. The other end was set at an angle on the other tree. I then hooked up my Chevy to a strong rope and pulled the trees apart enough so the beam dropped down to the level on the other crossbeam. And, Lordy me! We had our foundation. It was just regular construction after that."

To access the tree house, there was an aluminum ladder that led up and into a fenced-in deck. The only 'house' part of the structure was a small enclosure in one corner that could hold two or three children, sitting.

But, in addition to the tree house itself were the fireman's pole and the zip line. With the parents stationed at critical points in these activities, there was a constant motion of kids going up the ladder and then down the pole or along the zip line.

The latter traveled along a cable from the tree house for about a hundred feet to another elm. The child sat in a suspended swing seat, pushed off the deck, and then zipped along until near the end of the short ride to where the pulley was gently braked with a spring. The child then slid off the swing seat and dropped a foot or fell into the arms of an anxious, waiting parent. The swing seat was then pulled with a long rope back to the tree house where someone grabbed it for the next rider.

The day was like no other for both the parents and children. At first, there had been a great deal of trepidation, of course, for these young parents. But Frank and Mabel anticipated this and prepared accordingly. There were no accidents.

Most of the children, not to mention their parents, had never retrieved eggs from beneath a sitting hen. Children were escorted into the henhouse two at a time and, amid giggles and shyness, they filled their little baskets. Yes, a few eggs were dropped and broken, followed by a few tears, but generally this event went well.

Milking Henrietta was far more difficult for the kids than Frank had anticipated. Robby gave a demonstration, and even squirted the cat. But the unpracticed ten-year-old hands just couldn't manage. Some of the parents tried milking with mixed, but happy, success.

The finale was the birthday party itself. Two of the men carried the cake out to the picnic table that was spread with a red-checkered tablecloth.

There were ten candles in a circle on the top tier.

"Hey look, everybody!" Robby said gleefully. "All your names are on the cake!"

The kids gathered around excitedly and studied the display until they found their names.

Grampy Frank lit the ten candles. There was a little breeze blowing. A candle here and there would go out and then he'd relight it. The kids watched, fascinated.

"OK, Robby," Frank said. "Do you think you can blow these candles out before the wind does it? Make a wish first."

Robby climbed onto a chair to get him at the right height and Frank put his hands on Robby's waist to keep him from falling into the cake. Robby then blew hard and out they went. Cheers followed.

Mabel had the cake knife in her hand. "How many of you want cake and ice cream?"

The kids danced around and cheered.

"How many of you *don't* want cake and ice cream?" she teased.

Robby raised his hand and cheered.

Mabel looked at him.

"Just kidding Grammy," Robby said and laughed.

They sat in folding chairs or on the ground. It didn't matter. They were all happy. This was perfect celebration for Robby who had found family and friends here in Hollandson.

There was only one disappointment for Mabel. She expressed it to Frank later. "We didn't get a birthday card or a present from Robby's mom. Don't you think that's strange? Robby never mentioned it. And I'm certainly not going to say anything. What a shame."

* * *

It was Ellen who found the new death threat note. It was addressed to her, Ellen Bloodworth, and was amongst the morning mail at their home address.

"Oh my God!" she said as she unfolded and read the typewritten note.

She called Webster. "It's terrible. It's disgusting. I can't read it to you. I've never seen such racial hate," she said with a sigh.

"I'll call Odie. We'll both come over to the house." Webster said. "In the meantime, don't do any more touching of the letter or the envelope. Leave it where it now lies. I'm sure Odie will want to have it checked for fingerprints."

* * *

"You're right," Gallop said. "Such profanity and racial epithets are very rare these days. The envelope has a Portsmouth, New Hampshire postal cancellation. We may be moving our investigation out of state now.

"Nat. I'd like you to call personnel and have them give you a list of all employees with New Hampshire home addresses. Of course, any Massachusetts resident could have mailed this letter in Portsmouth. And, I don't know what makes me think this is an employee. But, that'll be a start."

"This may be a stupid question, Odie," Webster said, But, should we be nervous?"

"All I can honestly say, Nat, is all threats should be taken seriously."

"Do you have any thoughts on why *I* received this note?" Ellen asked.

"Sure I do," Gallop said. "One, it could simply be from someone who hates Blacks. Two, it is more likely another method of attacking Nat. To attack the person he loves is the ultimate attack on Nat."

"You're right, Odie," Webster said. "I feel this in the gut, far more than I felt the other attacks. And then add the racial slurs to it and it gets me all riled up. It's all I can do to keep myself from putting my fist through this wall."

"Don't punch the walls," Gallop warned. "That would be just what they want. They want you to get angry and violent and become someone other than your true self. Don't give in to it. In the end it will do you more harm than them."

"Sage advice, Odie," Ellen said. "Thank you."

"I'll get to work on this."

* * *

"I need a beer or two tonight," Webster said, as they sat at a table in a dark corner of the elegant Blue Moon restaurant in Hollandson.

"What a refreshing change from Jack's diner," Ellen said. "It's so good to see linen tablecloths and napkins. Are you sure we can afford this?"

"How are you coping, Sweetheart?" Webster asked.

Ellen reached across the table and clasped his hands. "Oh, Nat. When is this ever going to end?"

"How long's it been since the last one?"

"A week? Ten days? A month? I don't know. It was just before we called in Odie, anyway," Ellen said.

Webster poured his Guinness into a glass. Ellen raised her glass of Chablis. They clinked. "I don't find much to cheer about. This could be either an inside or an outside job. I may be naive, but I just can't believe anyone at Scan-Man is villainous enough to pull a stunt like this. It has to be someone from the outside."

"If that's the case," Ellen reasoned, "all these new camera installations will help at work. Maybe we ought to have cameras set up at both our houses. Where do you stop on this? And we don't know anything. And we don't know if Odie is making any progress."

"That's a good excuse to change the subject," Webster said. "Do you know what you're going to order?"

"Yup. I'm going for the Seafood Salad."

"Again? You have that every time."

"When I find something good I stick with it."

"Boring," Webster groaned. "Cripes, this is a long menu."

"I know. I know. You like a menu with ten items on it."

"Not tonight. I want something different."

"Hey. You're closing your eyes and pointing?" Ellen asked.

"Why not? Let's see what happens."

Ellen watched him to make sure he didn't peek.

Webster's finger found the menu. He opened his eyes and burst out laughing. "You know what I hit? Seafood Salad."

"You going to order that?"

"And copy you? No way. I think I'll do the Blue Crab. I feel like fighting with my meal."

"You did fight with it the last time, if I remember. They had overdone it and the legs didn't snap, they just bent."

"I remember. I'll remind them this time."

The waiter arrived and Ellen ordered her Seafood Salad.

"And I'll have the Blue Crab. But, I want the legs to snap open."

"I'll tell the chef, Mr. Webster. He'll make 'em just like you want."

"Thank you. Oh. I'll have another Guinness."

"And you Miss Ellen?"

"No. I'm all set. Thanks."

"OK. Where were we?"

"You were telling me how much you loved me."

Webster laughed. "I thought I was crabbing about you."

"Ha. Ha."

* * *

"I can't help it Sasha. I can't remember."

"You are the stupidest person I've ever known. Look what you did to me. Look at me, you idiot! I've only got half a face and one good eye. *You* did this to me!"

270

Helena cowered in her chair at the side of the bed. A nurse appeared. "*Please* be quiet! You're disturbing the other patients."

"Oh, screw you," Sasha mumbled under her breath. The nurse turned quickly and left. Helena remained hunched in her chair, crying quietly.

"Helena! Sit up and listen. You hear me! Sit up and look at me. Stop the goddamn crying."

Helena slowly straightened up, her face blotchy and wet with tears.

"Now look at me. Look me in the eye. Stare at me, hard!"

Helena grimaced as she looked.

"It looks great, doesn't it? How would *you* like to look like this?" Sasha laughed -- an ugly laugh through her contorted jaw. "Now you listen, Helena. Listen very carefully. I'm going to tell you once again what I want you to do. What you *must* do."

Sasha slowly and patiently told Helena the plan. Helena strained to listen. It was difficult. Her attention span was brief. Sasha's voice came and went. She'd hear what Sasha was saying, and then she studied Sasha's face. Sasha's voice returned, but then disappeared when the flowers on the table distracted her. Then Sasha's arm moved and Helena was again distracted.

"It's very simple, Helena. It's something even a dimwit like you can understand.

"Now repeat it back to me so I know you have it."

Helena haltingly repeated what she remembered.

"Oh, Jesus," Sasha groaned. "Why do I try? You've got most of it. You've got enough if it. Let's try it once more. Now listen, Helena."

This time Sasha abbreviated her instructions. Helena nodded.

"And you still have my note?"

Helena nodded again.

"One more thing," Sasha said. "Don't say anything to Momma about this. This is a secret between you and me. Do you understand? Don't tell *anyone* about the wonderful thing you are doing for Sasha. Sasha is so proud of you, Helena.

"OK. Now get the hell out of here and do what Sasha told you. You're a good girl Helena. I like you a lot even though you're stupid."

Helena left. She was happy Sasha still liked her. She couldn't help it if she couldn't remember things. She tried very hard to remember. All her life she had tried to remember. But Sasha liked her and that was most important. She would try real hard to do what Sasha wanted.

Her face finally brightened when she thought of the motorcycle. She thought how lucky she was that Sasha was letting her use her bike. That would be fun.

Helena went home. She was staying with Momma until Sasha got out of the hospital. She didn't want to stay at the Zenix alone. It was too spooky. She had bad memories of Sasha's condo -- memories that came and went -- like flashes. She would go there later to pick up the gun and the motorcycle and get out fast before the memories caught up with her.

She was happy. She was going to make Sasha happy.

* * *

It was another lovely day in Naples, Florida. Marsha Randolph was out early with Winky, briskly walking Fifth Avenue South with other early risers and their pets.

Pets were the attraction. They were the catalyst of conversations. A dog walker never passed another without a stop and a greeting. And, with heads down, the owners watched their pets mill around each other and do what dogs do instinctively.

Marsha easily picked up the rhythm of Southwest Florida's most prestigious avenue, crediting Winky with helping her make friends and giving her the incentive for welcoming each new day.

In particular, she had met a man. He was quite a bit older than Marsha, but he was a gentleman and Winky liked his dachshund. After a few meetings, the man asked if she'd join him for coffee at one of the many outdoor cafes along the avenue.

They enjoyed each other's company. His name was Clarence Lynch. He was widower, a retired book publisher, and an active art collector. He was a major donor to the annual Naples National Art Festival, ranked as one of the top ten fine art festivals in the United States.

But more importantly to Marsha, he was the open door to Naples society, an introduction to a group she desperately missed since the series of disasters in Hollandson. Their coffees were frequently interrupted by Clarence's friends and acquaintances, each of whom he formally introduced to Marsha.

Marsha provided Clarence with an edited version of her background. She said she was a widow, which might be interpreted as such with Ed's sad condition. She said she was childless, which might also be interpreted as such because of the responsibility of Robert being taken from her.

It appeared that Marsha's negative personality had disappeared along with her responsibilities. Her sweetness and intense interest in Clarence's every word helped develop their relationship.

Clarence lived well. Following their third coffee date, he invited her, as a new resident, to tour the Naples area with him in his Rolls Royce. Marsha likened the ride to what she imagined it would be like to float through the air on a cloud. They drove through neighborhoods lined with the addresses of Hollywood stars. They viewed Royal Harbor's waterfront homes on the Gulf of Mexico and other streets with homes on deep-water canals. They swung through Port Royal, one of the most prestigious and exclusive communities in the country.

They stopped at The Port Royal, a private club, for lunch. Again, Clarence's presence caused other guests to greet him and meet his companion. Clarence, it appeared, was smitten by the lovely, newly arrived widow.

When, in the middle of the afternoon, Marsha returned to her condo and Winky, she was all aglow. She picked up her pet and danced around the room.

"And I have you to thank for all of this, Winky dear."

She picked up her calendar. Clarence had suggested they go away for a few days. Scanning the month she saw a reminder a week earlier for Robert's tenth birthday.

"Oh, my," she said. She had forgotten Robert's birthday. "Well, Winky. There's nothing we can do about that now."

* * *

"What happened between you and Puff the other night?"

"I thought you'd never ask," Phil said. "She was being her same old nasty self."

"Oh?"

"After you went into the kitchen, she asked me if I thought she was a 'bitch.' She was referring to her unfortunate day with the captain. I told her I had no comment on the 'bitch' term. I said I wanted a pleasant evening."

"In essence, then," Maggie said, "you agreed she was a bitch."

"I guess."

"And that after you said you wanted a pleasant evening." Maggie paused. "Anything else?"

"I told her she was a tease."

"Were you saying she was teasing Redford?"

"She could have interpreted it as that, but it really was about another story she was telling about her encounter with the shooter in the Zenix Towers we've been reading about."

"Yes?"

"She began to tell me about the encounter and went into some gory detail. Then she stopped and didn't want to tell me any more until she could tell us both at the same time."

"What's wrong with that?"

"Just the way she said it. All the time I'd known her she'd get me hooked on a story and then stop. So I told her she'd always been a tease."

"I'd say you were the impolite host," Maggie suggested, calmly. "You only had to put up with her for a few hours -- actually a few *minutes* while I was in the kitchen."

"OK. OK. You win," Phil apologized. "Puff and I can't be in the same room together."

"That's what she said."

"She's gone. Let's forget it."

Silence.

"You said she had an encounter with the shooter in the Zenix Tower?"

"Aha! So *you're* interested!"

"A bit."

"There's not much more because I was left in suspense. Puff said she saw the shooter leave the condo across the hall from where she lives. Puff looked into the room and saw another woman who had half her face shot off.

"That's all she told me," Phil concluded.

"So now we'll never hear the end of her story. Good going, Phil."

"It was in the papers."

"Her story wasn't."

"I'm not going to win this one," Phil said in surrender.

Silence.

"Phil," Maggie sighed. "Our marriage is not a win-lose. It's win-win. I just feel sorry for Puff. She has been at loose ends since her husband died in the atrium collapse. I was just trying to be a friend to her. We might try to get together sometime for coffee or a drink."

"That sounds good. Please don't invite me."

"I think that is a given."

Silence.

"Let's go to a movie tonight," Maggie suggested. "We haven't seen 'The King's Speech' yet. All our friends have been talking about it and, as usual, we're the last to see the most popular shows."

"That's because we're discriminating," Phil commented.

"Yeah. Right. It's because we're so cheap we wait till the box office prices go down, or it appears on television and we have to watch hours of commercials. Change your shirt. We're going out. The dishes can wait. It's playing at the downtown cinema."

* * *

"So, when do you expect your version of the Searoc Beam to be up and running?" General Stringer asked his host at Sky & Sea Industries.

"Sir, we can be up and running in five or six years."

"Well, that's a disappointment. As you know, Scan-Man's Searoc is up and running as we speak. I have seen it operate. It is exactly what we need."

"I've heard that Scan-Man is reluctant to sell its technology for military purposes."

"That's why I am here," the General said. "Competition is good. I applaud you for your offer to award a contract to the military. But, five to six years is an eternity. It's longer than World War II!"

"We understand that, Sir. But you have to consider that our version will be more advanced than Scan-Man's."

"I expect Scan-Man's version will be more advanced in five to six years," the General added. "Have you considered increasing your staff to speed up development?"

"We don't have the funds to do that."

"What have you done to raise additional funds?"

"Oh, we have people out there looking for financial sources."

"Young man," Stringer said disparagingly. "I applaud your entrepreneurial spirit. It takes guts to compete with a fully developed enterprise when you only have a shoestring to work with."

"Have you, General, considered influencing the military to invest funds in this enterprise you are so interested in? I would guess that with the right investment we could produce a competing product -- let's say in one or two years."

"I can't see us getting into speculation," Stringer said. "We have been burned any number of times investing in promises that never materialize.

"It just occurred to me," Stringer continued, "the former chairman at Scan-Man is now doing time for trying to get government money to fund R&D for the Searoc Beam technology that already existed. I don't think anyone will fund your technology when it already exists at Scan-Man."

"Thank you for your honesty, General. Sky & Sea will continue along its present course. It will be interesting to re-evaluate the situation when our technology comes to maturity."

"That it will. Good luck."

* * *

"What the hell do you want?" It was Puff calling Phil on his cell phone.

"Well that wasn't a very nice greeting."

"It wasn't intended to be."

"I'm sorry." There was a pause. "Phil I *must* see you."

"Why *must* you see me?"

"I have to talk to you."

"About what?"

"Oh, Phil," she was crying. "I want to talk about us."

"About us?" Phil was incredulous.

"Don't you feel anything for me any more?"

"Puff. I'm a married man."

"You didn't answer my question."

"Yes. I feel something for you. But I feel more for my wife."

"Phil. I'm *begging* you. Please see me."

"This is ridiculous, Puff."

"Phil. I'm begging you on hands and knees. I have never done that before for anyone. Please, Phil."

"Wow. This must be important."

"It is."

"Where do you want to meet?"

"Find an excuse and come into town. I want to tell you more about confronting this killer."

"Is that why you want to see me?"

"No. It's more than that. I can't tell you over the phone."

"Are you in trouble?"

"You might say that."

"What's that mean?"

"It means I have to speak with you -- soon!"

"Are you teasing me again?"

"I am not teasing you. I am begging you."

"I may regret this, Puff. But I'll take a chance."

"Oh, Phil. You are the best, you know what I mean?"

"*I don't* know if I know what you mean. But I'll give you a call when I'm ready."

Phil hung up.

I am weak, Phil thought, replacing his cell phone in his belt holder. I am very weak. I can't help myself. I know exactly what that sexy little thing wants. The temptation is too much. I'll hate myself for this. Just thinking about this makes me a wife cheater. That little woman has done things to me that Maggie never heard of. I hate myself. I hate myself for even thinking of this.

* * *

Odie Gallop was on the trail again. Scan-Man records indicated only one employee lived in Portsmouth, N.H. It was Susan Morales. He had her address. It was a single-family, located well out of town in the suburbs.

Gallop was determined to take a chance and try to enter the house without breaking in. Maybe a door or a cellar window was left unlocked. It was worth a check. Susan, he knew, was at work.

It was trash day in the suburbs of Portsmouth. Susan had her trash barrel and recycling at the end of her driveway. It was then a thought hit him.

He stopped his car, got out and opened the top of the barrel. It contained several white plastic trash bags. This was a long-shot. The top one was obviously kitchen garbage. He lifted another. It was very lightweight. He ripped it open. It was office trash -- papers and notes. There were some crumpled sheets of paper. He unfolded a couple. Unfinished typewritten letters. He didn't have time to search the bag now. He put it in his car. He lifted another bag. It too was light. Without even opening it he put that in his car. The same with a fourth bag.

He put the first bag back into the barrel, secured the cover and left. No one saw him, or at least *he* saw no one. There was a difference. Some people look out their windows at the slightest noise. They have good reason, many times, to be suspicious. Odie, he thought, was a perfect example.

* * *

"How the hell did you pull that off?"

"What did you do to him?"

"What do *you* know about Searoc Beams?"

"It's not fair."

"Do you think we could do that?"

Lois' friends misunderstood. They totally misjudged Lois. They just didn't get it.

"We're not going to see you any more," one girl said. "You'll be stuck in a lab somewhere."

"I made a fool out of myself the other day when I delivered Mr. Webster's package," Lois said. "We girls made such a big deal of him, I was paralyzed when I went to his office. I even cried! I felt like a little kid.

"You guys had fooled me into thinking I could put the make on Mr. Webster. I believed you. I felt like a child in his presence. Put the make on him? Are you kidding me?

"He was the one who comforted me and put me at ease. He still represents the man of my dreams, but I totally respect him for not taking advantage of me. I was very vulnerable. He could have done anything with me. But he didn't. He made me feel like a woman, not a girl. He gave me respect. He discovered my brain, not my panties.

"Let me put it this way," Lois said. "I delivered a package to Mr. Webster. He opened the box and took out a book titled 'Thermodynamics', a book that he wrote. I told him the subject must be related to the Searoc. He was surprised I knew that.

"We got into a conversation and it came out that I had a new idea for the Searoc Beam. My idea was to make it portable, not something that you could carry, but something you could mount on a truck -- like they do with television, beaming signals by way of satellites. This is something I was working on at college. I based my research on Scan-Man and what they were doing with weather modification.

"He said the idea sounded interesting and he asked me to write a paper on it, which I did. I gave him the paper and he liked it. He said he was going to assign me to a bunch of idea people who I will work with for the rest of this internship. What happens after that depends, I suppose, on how I fit in with this group."

"Wow," was the collective response.

"Mr. Webster is really a wonderful man," Lois continued. He's very thoughtful and kind and willing to help people who have good ideas.

"In my own case, I had done some research for one of my classes in school. I chose the Scan-Man's Searoc Beam just by chance. At the time I had never dreamed of interning here. While doing this research it hit me that a portable, Earth-based beam might be possible. So I focused on how this might work. There are an awful lot of technical details to overcome yet, but with a bit of luck we may have something here.

"How about you guys," Lois asked. "You're all going into your senior year. What research papers have you worked on?"

This began a flurry of discussion. Each of them had indeed done research on something relating to space science. After all, it was that interest that steered them in the direction of Scan-Man. Their time in the shipping department was actually minimal. Most of their time was within other departments with other specialties.

"Have you ever mentioned your research papers to anyone here?" Lois asked.

"No."

"Why not?"

"No one asked."

"Have you seen anything happening here that might relate to what you've studied?"

"Some things are a little related."

"How serious are you guys about working in this technology? If I were you," Lois said, "I'd try to relate it. Take the initiative. Show your best side. How else are you ever going to impress anyone? You got me going. Get yourselves going."

* * *

Sasha had sunk into a deep depression. She avoided looking at herself whenever she used the bathroom. She didn't need anyone to tell her she was the ugliest woman in the world. The doctors told her they planned more surgery to build up new cheek and upper jawbones. There would then be plastic surgery to cover over these new bones to fill out her face. This would take months and perhaps years to accomplish. Meanwhile, she would have to wear the bandages.

In addition, they told her they could not promise a return to her original beauty. But, they said, new techniques were being invented every day and wonders were known to happen.

She was still a young woman, Sasha thought, not yet thirty. Except for her face, her body was still lithe and muscular. She had lived to move fast, to race her bike, to have the wind blow in her face. She yearned to be attractive to other women.

They told her she could go to the hospital gym. They said she was mobile and could go whenever she wanted. Sure, sure, Sasha thought. The true reason for the bandages was to protect other patients from being exposed to the nightmare she had become. She visualized herself playing the male lead role in 'Phantom of the Opera', but someone removed her bandages. The audience was aghast, panicked and ran from the theater. She was left on stage alone with her ugliness.

Her face hurt most of the time. Her jaw was very painful. She could not chew. As a result the foods she ate were mashed, pulverized, pureed and probably stepped on as well -- at least they tasted that way.

The doctors said her face was very fragile, like a fine wine glass. Be careful moving the jaw. Don't sleep on your right side. The structure is very sensitive as new tissue grows.

She hated hospitals, but she really had no choice. The doctors wanted her to stay for the next few weeks. Infection was the real danger now. They wanted her around so they could work on her face whenever it was convenient.

She could walk the halls. She went to the gym and lifted weights and rode the stationary bike. This brought life back into her limbs. She felt better, but then she always had to return to the hospital room.

She thought of Chandler Harrington in the pen. Until her accident she had always kept in touch with him. She had known him by way of her Scan-Man job in the shipping department. Something, she didn't remember what, brought this unlikely pair together. Maybe it was a package she delivered to his office. She may have told him her love of guns. Whatever it was, they got into a long conversation and the next thing she knew she was working for him on freelance jobs outside Scan-Man. She was his hired gun. He paid her well, $50,000 per job plus expenses, deposited directly into a blind checking account he had set up for her offshore.

She never knew the people she shot or why Harrington wanted them hit. It was none of her business. It was a kick. The best job she ever had. It turned her on. Nat Webster was the only hit she had actually met. She had nothing against Webster. It was just that she hated men -- especially powerful men -- men who controlled women. Harrington was the exception. There was something about him she liked. He wasn't married. Most of the men with power, that she was aware of, were physically soft -- pathetic worms -- incapable of physical combat. Webster was soft. She took him down easily. She could have taken him blindfolded and with one hand behind her back.

Webster was the first assignment with which she played cat and mouse. The game added spice to the regular aim, shoot, kill and run. She loved it. And the fun included knowing it was pure hell for Webster. The night she caught him in the parking lot -- that was a thrill. It was a disappointment that Webster never hit her. She would have preferred some resistance. What kind of a man just stands there and looks stupid? But she sure smashed the daylights out of him. What a turn-on. God, he was soft. Obviously he'd never spent a day in the gym. So easy. A few smacks in the face, a knee to the groin, and an uppercut to the chin. It felt good, but it was pathetic. She liked a good fight. Webster had no fight.

It was Helena who had fight. She and Helena had combat once a week and they tore into each other. Then they made love and wound up their activity with a few martinis. The good life.

But now that was over. A lot was over for Sasha. Things would never be the same. They would never put Humpty Dumpty together again, she thought. Her love life was over. Helena was horrified when she saw Sasha. That was proof of love lost. Hell. She couldn't force Helena to make love to her.

What does life really offer me now? she thought. Nothing, was the conclusion. She should kill herself. Too bad Helena was such a poor shot. I should have been killed. Maybe I should have given her training. She really thought it was a big bang toy. What an idiot she was. Brainless, but a good lover.

How can a person kill herself in a hospital? Put a sign on your chest that says, "Do not resuscitate!" and then take a handful of pills? In the early morning, when the nurses are half asleep, I could grab the keys from one of them, get into the medicine closet and take a mouthful of oxycodone.

But, she didn't want to do that until Helena carried out her final plan.

Phil had never lost his attraction to Puff. He had always been attracted to women that oozed sex appeal. He admitted it was his weakness, but it had never been at the expense of his marriage. He had always been faithful to Maggie. He had rarely wanted to cheat on her. Now, after a decade of marriage, their sex life was, at best, ho hum. The thrill was gone.

Maggie and Phil had recently decided it was time to have babies while they were still in their early thirties. Maggie went off the pill and their lovemaking, or baby making if you will, increased substantially. But that did not mean it was more exciting or thrilling. It simply meant more frequency. In fact, the increased frequency over the weeks became more of a chore to both of them. The goal was not the enjoyment of the process. It was the need, the pressure, and the mutual desire to simply get pregnant.

Phil perhaps felt the duty and the boredom of the ritual more than Maggie. Phil had to use his imagination to achieve the critical stage of his duties. Maggie had little passion and imagination when it came to sex. The tried and proven missionary position suited her just fine. When Phil suggested alternative positions, his wife was just not interested.

Phil, on the other hand, had sexual experiences throughout college. His long-time partner was Puff. She was quite the opposite of Maggie in this respect. Her imagination and passion knew no bounds. Anything that produced the desired effect was fine with her. Phil had been her eager student. As he remembered it, Puff was exciting, fun, passionate, gentle and was an expert at teasing a man into a frenzy.

Such experiences were not easy for Phil to forget or even suppress. Images of those experiences lingered in the intervening years. During his otherwise happy marriage, those images took on a very practical value. They helped him enjoy his sex life with Maggie.

Phil was now entering the Zenix Tower in Boston. Visions of sugar plums danced in his head. The security desk was expecting him. He took the elevator to the top floor. It opened into a hallway. There were two doors he was considering when Puff popped out of one of them.

She ran to him and, to his surprise, she leaped and wrapped her legs around his waist and her arms around his neck. Phil wrapped his arms around her and nearly lost his balance. Fortunately she was only half his weight and the momentum of the contact was minimal. She kissed him on the cheek, the neck and the tip of his nose. Her perfume reminded Phil of a similar scent from their college years.

She unwrapped, stood back, and displayed her standard little-girl outfit. But the neck was cut low showing much of her big-girl attributes. In fact, as Phil looked at her, she was dressed as she was in the old days.

They went into her suite and Puff gave a tour. The huge main room furnishings, the decor, the views were well beyond what Phil had ever imagined. Maggie's and his home in Hollandson was strictly suburban ordinary.

"I decorated it myself," Puff explained.

The kitchen was behind a long bar, or counter, at the end of the main room. A 180-degree view of Boston and the harbor spread over two adjacent wall windows. Smaller rooms were at the far end. One was an office. Another was a guest room. There were utility rooms. And then there was the "mistress" bedroom, as she called it. It was straight out of a Las Vegas nightmare, filled with lacy pillows, stuffed animals, thick carpet, fluffy curtains, and a dressing table with lights and make-up bottles. The bed was king-size and much higher than usual and, in Phil's opinion, decorated with a lot of soft, fuzzy, stuffed things. Everything was ultra feminine -- strictly Puff, as Phil would say.

"Well," Puff said. "What do you think?"

Phil looked around. "I think your husband left you very well off. This place is extraordinary."

Puff was a little nervous. "Let me fix us some drinks. I have everything. What do you prefer these days?"

"Do you have any beer?"

"I do. Do you still drink Bud Light?"

"That's fine."

"Have a seat while I get it."

Phil chose a chair that took in the entire view. He was near the window, a twenty-three-story drop before the view swept toward the ocean. A schooner was crossing the horizon, heeling in the breeze.

Puff returned. "Oh, let's sit on the couch, Phil. It's much more comfortable."

Actually, Phil thought, he was already very comfortable. But he moved anyway. She sat after he was seated. She kicked off her heels and swung her legs up and across his lap.

Phil was surprised, but he shouldn't have been. He knew Puff was after something -- most likely him.

'Take off your shoes too, so we can sit like we used to."

Phil was obedient again. He lifted her legs and swung his up to either side of Puff. They were now facing each other, leaning back into the pillows, her legs crossing his. They sipped on their drinks, wordlessly at first.

Her legs were short, so her feet were in his lap. Every little while she'd wriggle them. Each time she did, Puff could feel him respond increasingly. At the same time she allowed her knees to separate just a bit, allowing more and more to be exposed.

Phil noticed this, but let it all happen. It was one of her many teasing games that she played with him years ago. More sips, more wriggling, more exposure.

"You begged me to come here," Phil finally said. "You wanted to tell me something."

She smiled. "Haven't I expressed myself enough all ready, if you know what I mean?" she said nodding at her feet.

"Is that all you have to say?"

"Do I have to say anything?"

"It would be nice."

There was a pause as both thought.

"Are you happy with Maggie?"

"I am. In fact, we are working toward having children."

"That's an awkward way to put it."

"You know what I mean."

"Do you think you could ever be happy with me, Phil?"

"Is this what you wanted to say to me?"

She looked at him and smiled. "What I begged you for was for us to re-live old times. I'm so frustrated. It is possible that we've both had terrible sex lives since we stopped seeing each other. Do you remember how wonderful that was?"

"It's foremost in my memory sometimes," Phil smiled.

"What is it that makes you happy with Maggie?"

"The simple answer is, everything you don't have."

"Phil. I'm going to beg again. I want to re-live the way it used to be with us just one more time."

"Then what?"

"We can decide that later."

"In other words, you want to lure me into your nest and wrap me in a cocoon of your charms."

"Don't say that." Puff whined. "You make me sound like the spider and the fly."

289

"Puff. Be realistic. You want to spend the night with me in the hope that your charms will be enough for me to leave Maggie. You want me in your ivory tower."

"Phil. Listen. I have lots of money. You wouldn't have to work. We can travel the world without any worries. We can do anything we want together."

"How about children?"

Puff glared at him. "You know my answer to that."

"What would we talk about? Do you read anything? Are you up on world affairs? Do you watch the evening news? Do you have any girlfriends to do things with? How about friends? Do you have *any* friends?"

Puff was crying.

"I remember when you chummed around with a gaggle of girls. But I also remember how you treated them. You told me you scanned the N.Y. Times *Book Review,* then led your friends to believe you actually read the book itself. You *bragged* about that, hoping they'd think you were some kind of intellectual."

Through her tears Puff said, "Couldn't I just be your mistress. I'd be here whenever you wanted me. You don't even have to love me. You'd still have your freedom. You can..."

"I'll ignore that."

By now they both had their feet on the floor and sat at opposite ends of the couch.

"I'm sorry Puff. I don't want to be mean to you. But I want you to understand there is a lot more to life than sex. There's no question I'd like to take you to bed, but I won't. It's because I love someone else very much. Sure I have a tough time resisting temptation, but so far I've succeeded. And I feel very good about that. I thought I'd hate myself when I came here and gave in to your charms. But I don't and I didn't.

"I seem to remember we had a conversation something like this not too long ago, Puff, and I haven't forgotten it."

They were both quiet for a moment.

"You are right, Phil. You are absolutely right. Do you think I can change the way I am? Do you think I can change from what I have always been to someone new? Is that possible, Phil?"

"I can't answer that, Puff. It's up to you.

"Well. I'm on my way. I'm going home to my wife with a clear conscience. I'm going to tell her where I've been and what happened between us. I expect she'll understand."

* * *

Maggie swung the Bronco into the Hollandson Motor Hotel parking lot.

"Will you look at that, Phil? I can't believe they put the new atrium up so fast. It is gorgeous."

As they walked toward the entrance a man met them.

"Hello. Maggie?"

"Mr. Crumm, I presume."

"You've got it. I'm the new manager."

"This is my husband, Phil."

"Nice to meet you, Mr. Crumm."

"Please. Call me Henry. Thank you for coming. You're the very first visitors to view the completed work. As you know, we're having an open house gala next weekend. It's my hope that you can give us a spread in the *Bulletin*."

"We can't believe you completed it in such a short time," Phil said.

"Our goal was to finish it in time for the National Scientific Association Summer Conference. They committed to holding their July conference here if we could meet a June

15 completion deadline. So we tripled the workers we usually hire on a hotel construction and, as you can see, we're home free."

"The atrium is spectacular," Maggie said. "You don't know this, Mr. Crumm, but I was on the 5th floor with a balcony into the atrium the night it collapsed."

"Oh, my. That must have been frightening."

"It was far more frightening for those *in* the atrium," Maggie said. "There were a dozen deaths."

"I'd prefer to concentrate on what has happened since that terribly night, Maggie. We have increased the structural integrity of the atrium. Let's go inside."

As they toured the atrium, the lobby, the Cloven Hoof Tavern, the conference and dining rooms, Maggie was again amazed at the beauty. Her most recent memories were from that week in December when the place was filled with refugees from the pileups on Rte. 128 when the first inches of several feet of snow began the highway slowdowns. It took only a single car to skid sideways on an off-ramp to block all the following cars. It was just a chain reaction, she remembered.

But now, the place was as clean and spacious as any big city hotel. There was not a hint of the past.

The tour was over. Phil had taken his photos and Maggie her notes.

"We are impressed, Mr. Crumm," Maggie said. "It looks like you'll get the center spread this Thursday, in time for the open house. Do you have any descriptive material I can take?"

"You've got it," Crumm said, handing her a fistful of paper. "Thank you for coming. I look forward to seeing the spread."

* * *

"I went into town yesterday to have a talk with Puff."

"Oh? I thought you two couldn't stand being in the same room together."

"That's mostly true. She begged me to meet with her. We met at her roof-top condo."

"She begged you?"

"She did. She was embarrassed about the night she was here, as was I."

"As was I also," said Maggie.

"You know that she has always acted and dressed like a sexy little thing. And I will admit that I can be attracted to sexy little things."

"Do I want to hear this when we are struggling to create babies?"

"I just want to get this off my chest."

"Go on, I guess."

"As it turned out, Puff was trying to lure me into her nest for a one-night stand."

"Surprise, surprise. Yes?"

"Let me quickly say that she failed. Instead I gave her a lecture on why she can't find a decent man. I advised her to wear a mature woman's clothes and stop trying to lure men by acting sexy."

"What a hero you are! God's gift to stray women! How many women have been on your lecture tour?"

"Maggie! Come on! I'm trying to be honest and up front with you."

"Is this reasonable? Can anyone really be changed?"

"I gave up smoking for you."

"You did. Congratulations," Maggie said. "So now you are in her condo and she does something to draw you into bed with her."

"She was frank. She came right out and said she was frustrated with her lack of a sex life and she wanted to do a one night stand with me."

"Interesting. So you said, 'Not me, Baby. Sexy as you are, you'll never get me into your bed. I have full control of my sexual urges.'"

"Please, Maggie. I did turn her down. I told her my one love was you and that we are trying to start a family."

"Am I supposed to congratulate you for your sexual restraint?"

"Do what you want? Here I am, guilt free and more in love with you than ever."

Maggie was in thought. Phil looked at her anxiously. Maggie looked up and searched Phil's face. She wondered if he had visited Puff previously without her knowledge. He was such a jerk sometimes. Was she being suckered by this 'sexy little thing?' Did Phil *really* have control over his sexual urges? She was well aware of how he often wanted to do these strange things with her that she was not comfortable with. Where did he learn about those things? How much is Puff able to manipulate him? Is Puff a threat to their marriage? Maybe we shouldn't have children. Maybe I should kick Phil out and let him play with his sex image for the rest of his life.

"Sometimes I think you are quite naive, Phil. I believe your story. I am sorry that you met with her at all, given what little I know of her, and of your former relationship. I think it is naive of you to believe you can change someone like Puff. How she acts must be so ingrained in her. Do you think you could change me into something different?"

"The difference between you and her is significant," Phil said. "She has no man, no friends, no family, no love. She's looking for love in all the wrong places, to paraphrase the song. You have all those things. I don't know if she can change. It all depends on how badly she wants to."

294

Maggie searched Phil's face again. "I trust you, Phil. I love you. Let's leave Puff out of our lives. I'm serious, Phil. I don't want you to see her again."

"As Mr. Crumm at the hotel said, 'You've got it.'"

* * *

Back at his apartment, Gallop methodically went through the trash bags he had collected from Susan's house. One by one, he un-balled and smoothed out typewritten correspondence and hand-written notes. As he neared the bottom of the bag he saw Webster's name. He smoothed the paper some more and read it.

It was a love letter, dated two months earlier. Susan had composed it, in her handwriting, to Nat Webster. It was two pages long and described in detail her passion for him. She said she knew the risk she was taking by writing him and prayed that he could see how wonderful his life would be with a white woman.

She went on to say that she would do anything for his love, including arranging for the disappearance of that black girl. She was the only impediment Susan saw in their relationship, and the memory of Ellen would soon fade once he experienced white-girl love in her arms.

Greatly encouraged, Gallop went through the rest of the papers. These included drafts of the love letter that experimented with various high-emotion words as well as drafts of the racial death threats.

On reading all of the drafts, one stood out particularly. It said she would even kill Ellen in order to get Webster's love.

Individually, these writings were incriminating. Grouped together, they told the story of a lonely woman obsessed with matching up with the one man she wanted to possess.

"Once in a great while," Gallop said to himself, "a detective's luck unearths a trove of invaluable evidence."

* * *

Marsha received the call in the middle of the afternoon.

"Mrs. Randolph," the voice said. "This is Barbara MacAdoo from the rest home. We have some very good news for you."

Oh, good, Marsha thought. Ed's finally died. She sat up attentively.

"Yes?"

"Your husband has made a remarkable recovery. He's not one hundred percent yet, but his doctors say he no longer needs nursing home care. He can now come home with you."

That was all Marsha heard. She fainted and dropped the phone. When she recovered, the phone was beeping. The memory of the call returned.

"Impossible," she said to herself. "I won't hear of it! This is some kind of practical joke. I *do not* want to hear it. It didn't happen."

Thoughts raced through her mind. This is total destruction of the beautiful life I have found down here. Total, absolute destruction! What am I supposed to do now?

She thought of changing her address, not to leave Naples, but just to find somewhere they couldn't find her. The thought of leaving Clarence was unbearable. The life he had built for her was a life she had always dreamed of. She didn't want Ed back. She didn't want the responsibility. She didn't want things the way they used to be.

296

The phone rang again. She considered not answering it. She thought of ripping it out of the wall. She finally answered.

"Mrs. Randolph?"

"Yes."

"Somehow we got cut off."

"Yes."

"As I was saying, your husband has pretty much recovered. He is ready to go home. He is able to feed and cloth himself, manage his bodily functions and all the other essentials. He appears to have full recollection of his life with you and your son, Robert, and he is anxious to see you. He's so sweet. He's a real loving man. He won't be able to drive for a while, but with a little of your attention everything will be fine."

"Yes."

"I understand you now live in Florida. When will you be able to come for him?"

"Yes."

"Mrs. Randolph?"

"Yes?"

"Are you all right?"

A long pause.

"Please call me tomorrow. I have to take all this in."

"Mrs. Randolph?"

"Yes."

"Do you *want* your husband home?"

Another long pause. Marsha wanted to say no. She desperately wanted to say no. What would happen if she did say no?

"I won't be able to care for him."

"I beg your pardon?"

"I don't think I am capable of taking care of my husband."

297

"That would be a problem, Mrs. Randolph. This is something we need to discuss. What is the earliest you can visit us here?"

"I don't know. I just can't cope with this."

"Mrs. Randolph? Please give us a call tomorrow when you are feeling better. I realize you need time to think. OK?"

"OK. Goodbye."

Marsha was in a daze of depression. She lay on the couch immobile. Winky jumped up onto her chest, startling her, and reflexively she knocked the dog to the floor. She didn't care. Her life was over.

The phone rang again. Let it ring, she thought. But it couldn't be the nursing home all ready.

"Hello?"

"Marsha. Hello, my darling."

"Oh, Clarence." She sat up again. "Thank you for calling."

"If you're free I'd like to take you out to dinner."

Marsha was cheered. "For you, Sweetheart, I'm always free."

"Oh, good. Why don't I pick you up in an hour? I have a special treat for you."

"I just love treats, Clarence. I'll be ready with bells on."

"Love and kisses."

"To you too."

She hung up. In less than a minute, she made up her mind. "I am not going to visit that nursing home," she vowed out loud. "I am not going to live the rest of my life with Ed. They can come and take me away, but I will *not* go willingly!"

Marsha called the phone company. "I want to change my phone number. I've had too many harassing calls."

She made a note to tell Clarence her new number.

She picked up Winky and held him close. "I'm sorry Winky. Mommy feels much better now."

* * *

Robby knew something was wrong when Old Rolf didn't greet him when he jumped off the bus. Grampy McCullough met him without his usual smile.

"Where's Old Rolf, Grampy?"

"Bad news, Robby," Grampy said slowly. "Old Rolf went to doggy heaven this mornin'."

"Oh, no. I loved Old Rolf. He was always with me."

"He was always with me too, Robby. He was an old friend. But Rolf was old, lame and tired, Robby. He was nearly twice your age, and in doggie years he was almost one hundred years old."

"That's old. What are we going to do?"

"I think we're goin' to go get his cousin."

"His cousin?"

"Old Rolf was a Golden Retriever. His cousin is also a Golden. Maybe we'll go downtown to the pet shop to see if we can find his cousin."

"How old is his cousin?"

"Oh. He's just a puppy. But I think he might know us when we find him."

"Really?"

"Yup. That's the way things are. They have a way of knowin' you when you find them. You just wait. I'm guessin' that you'd like a lively little puppy."

"Oh, yes. But I'm still going to miss Old Rolf."

"I hope you'll miss him. I know he'd like that."

Robby began to skip along the drive again.

Into the house they went. Grammy was at the kitchen counter.

299

"I know what you're making, Grammy. Chocolate chip cookies."

"What a smart boy you are. You want one or two."

"Two, please."

"Careful. They just came out of the oven."

"Grammy?"

"What, Chocolate Face."

"Do you want to help us find Old Rolf's cousin? He's a puppy."

Mabel was puzzled for a moment. Then a smile came over her face. "Of course. I'll be glad to help."

* * *

"Hello Maggie? This is Puff."

Maggie couldn't believe it. How did she dare call after what Phil had told her?

"Yes, Puff," she returned coldly.

"When I was at your house a week ago we talked about getting together for coffee sometime."

"I recall it was your suggestion for a 'heart to heart.' I don't remember agreeing to it."

"Oh, you know what I mean. Just a woman to woman talk about things, Maggie."

"Like what, my husband?" Maggie jabbed.

Silence on the other end.

"Phil told me about his visit to your lovely condo," Maggie continued.

"Oh. That was nothing. Nothing happened."

"Nothing except your attempt to seduce my husband."

"That's all over with, you know? I need to talk about woman things."

"I don't think I'm your woman, Puff. You've gone too far with this. You're not part of my marriage or my life. We don't care to see you any more."

Maggie heard her softly crying. "Puff," Maggie interrupted. "You are an expert at pulling heartstrings. You are a manipulator. But it's not going to work with me. I'd advise seeing a psychologist."

"But you're a psychologist of sorts, Maggie. I admire you and everything you do. You're down to earth, practical. I am going to try to be like you. Phil told me I had to change if I wanted to find a man and be happy. I need your advice."

"Sorry, Puff. I can't help you. Please do not bother either of us again. Goodbye." Maggie hung up.

Hopefully, Maggie thought, they wouldn't hear from Puff again. On the other hand, it wouldn't really surprise her if she did reappear.

* * *

Frank McCullough was caretaker at the landfill fifteen hours a week, year round. The job was boring on weekdays. He loved Saturdays because that was when the children came with their parents and he handed out candy. He loved their giggling, their shyness, and their joy of living. The landfill was like a town meeting on Saturdays. Even the politicians came here to look for votes. Frank kept the place tidy. He picked up papers that were blowing around. That job was easier on Saturdays because Frank showed the children how to make a game of it.

Now that he was living with the McCulloughs, Robby joined Frank for the four hours on Saturdays. Here he met his school friends and introduced them to his Grampy. Old Rolf had always accompanied Frank, but that was to be no more, and Robby noticed the void.

301

"Can we bring Old Rolf's cousin when we find him, Grampy?"

"Of course. I think your friends will enjoy the new one too. That puppy will have a lot of energy. You'll have a hard time keeping up with him."

When the weather was decent, Frank occupied his free time sitting outside the little shed on an overturned plastic can. That was where he did his whittling. Last year he created a six-foot chain, hand hewn from the slim trunk of a young oak. He rarely had time to work at it on Saturdays. It was too busy. But that was the day when he displayed his work of art.

Last Christmas the house was full of people including two boys. Frank had separated the chain into two lengths. He gave them to Francisco and Robby. They had seen Frank working on them day after day. The boys were thrilled.

* * *

"Phil!" Maggie called urgently from the bathroom. "Phil! Come here! Quick!"

Phil ran down the stairs and dashed through the hallway skidding on the waxed floor and bouncing off the hall wall. "What's the matter Maggie?"

"I'm pregnant!"

"What?"

"Yes! I'm pregnant!" Her eyes were sparkling. Her face was radiant."

"How do you know?"

"These little testing things. See the color on the paper? That color means I'm pregnant."

"That was awfully fast."

"How long do you think it takes to get pregnant?"

"Gee. I don't know. Does this mean our sex life is over?"

"It means we have to wait another few weeks to be really certain."

"But, I mean, we're through tumbling in the sheets?"

"No. But it'll be a few weeks before we know for certain. It *is* early. And I don't know how accurate these things really are."

"Oh, good," Phil smiled. "I was worried."

Maggie looked at Phil. "Aren't you happy we're going to be parents?"

"Of course I am." He put his arms around her. "I was just kidding about the sex thing."

"Sure you were," Maggie smiled.

* * *

"Damn it all!" Webster tore the note from his office door without reading it. "I'm getting very tired of all these hollow threats," Webster grumbled.

Ellen patted the pouch at her waist, assuring herself their protection was still with her.

"What makes you think they're hollow threats, Nat? You didn't even read it."

Webster opened the crumpled note and read:

The time has come for me to wipe your
nigger girlfriend off the map.
Then you will be next.

"I think you had better read it, Ellen." He handed it to her.

"This sounds very serious, Nat. We're now into racial slurs."

"I'm calling Odie again," Nat said. "He's going to get very tired of hearing from us."

They went into the office. "Hey! Wait!" Ellen dashed out of the office and looked up at the ceiling. "Nat! The video camera is there. Let's check it out. This may be it."

Nat made the call. "Augustine. Check the video outside my office. Someone was at my door last night."

"Will do, Boss."

* * *

"I looked at the tape, Boss. It was a woman. She's sticking something to you door."

An electric current ran through Webster's spine. "Who is she, Augustine?"

"I don't know her."

The cat! Webster thought. She's reappeared.

"Where are you, Augustine? I want to see that video."

"Sure thing, Boss. I'm in B342."

"I'll be right down." He turned to Ellen. "Let's go. This should be very interesting."

* * *

Robby was talk, talk, talk during breakfast. Today was Saturday. This was the day they were going to the mall to find Old Rolf's cousin.

"How big will he be, Grampy?"

"Well, I don't know. Probably little."

"Can we keep him in the house, Grammy? He's probably too small to stay in the barn with Henrietta."

304

"Sure, he can stay here," Grammy said. "We'll put a bed right beside the couch."

"What color with he be?"

"He's a Golden Retriever. He'll be yellowish without the gray hairs that Old Rolf had on his face."

"Finish your breakfast, Robby," Grammy said. "You're going to need a lot of energy to play with this little guy."

"When do we go?"

"Right after the landfill."

"Oh." Robby was disappointed.

They arrived at the mall just after lunch. Robby led the way. He remembered exactly where the pet shop was. He had looked at the puppies every time he had gone to the mall but never thought of getting one.

There were dozens of dogs, from puppies to full-size orphans. Robby was the center of the dogs' attention also. Robby knew what a Golden looked like, but he didn't see one.

"They don't have a Golden here," Robby said sadly.

"Let's ask the girl."

"Yes," she said. "We have one right here. Remember. They're puppies. They don't look like the grown up Goldens."

"There he is, Grammy and Grampy," Robby shouted out, jumping up and down. "Look, he knows me. You can tell he's Old Rolf's cousin." Robby put his nose to the glass. The puppy did the same with his tail wagging like a flag in a high wind. "Can we get him?"

Grammy said, "Let's ask the girl if you can hold him."

"Sure you can," she said, and went behind the cages and brought him out on a leash.

The girl held him first and let Robby pet him. They were nose to wet nose. She passed the puppy to Robby, who knew exactly how to hold him. He giggled, the dog wiggled, and the their bond was sealed.

Robby set the puppy on the floor and followed it around the room. They picked out another collar and a leash and were soon on their way home with the puppy in a little cardboard house.

"Remember, Robby," Grampy warned. "He's not house-trained yet, so we have to be careful."

"Can we name him Rolf? I think Old Rolf would like that."

"I'd like that too, Robby," Grampy said. "Rolf it is."

* * *

Augustine turned on the video. Webster didn't believe his eyes at first. He rubbed them and looked again.

"Good God!" he said. "That's Susan Morales!"

"She's one of your directors, isn't she?" Ellen asked.

"She is. I just can't believe this."

Webster watched the video again. It clearly showed her entering the scene with a sheet of paper in her hand, going up to the door and attaching it with tape.

He fell back in his chair. "I have to call Odie right away."

He used Augustine's phone.

"Odie? Nat. I have news for you. I'm looking at the video surveillance and we've found the person who's been posting the threat notes."

"You know who it is?"

"I do."

"That is great news," Gallop said. "And that piece of information pretty much wraps up my investigation. When can I come by?"

"The sooner the better, Odie. I want to get this damned mess out of the way."

* * *

After he learned that Susan Morales was in her office, Webster announced an urgent meeting of all board members who were present. They assembled in the small conference room. Susan Morales was among them.

"What's this all about? What could be so urgent?" Peter Posednik asked no one in particular.

Head shaking and shoulder shrugging. Everyone was in the dark.

Then Webster, Gallop and Ellen walked into the room. Gallop and Ellen took two seats in the front row.

"Ladies and gentlemen," Webster began. "I want to introduce Detective Odie Gallop. He is a private investigator. As you all know, I have been the subject of death threats for several months. We now have learned who is responsible for this vile activity."

Webster paused and looked around the room. Susan looked very uncomfortable and was squirming in her chair.

"That person is Mildred McCoy, also known as Sasha. She worked in our shipping department. She has now been arrested and will be charged with several heinous crimes.

"Personally, I feel much better having found this person thanks to Mr. Gallop.

"But there is another reason I have called you all together. The death threats have continued after Ms. McCoy was taken out of circulation. It appears someone else in this company has continued to post death threats.

"I have something to show you all."

The video began. It clearly showed Susan approaching Webster's office door and then Susan's face as she turned and left.

Susan rose silently from her chair and headed for the door.

Odie Gallop left his chair and intercepted Susan at the door. "You are under arrest, Ms. Morales, for threatening the life of Nat Webster."

Gasps and mumbles of surprise rose from the directors as Gallop placed handcuffs on her.

"I was only leaving a regular memo on Nat's door," Susan complained.

"Please sit down, Ms. Morales," Gallop said. He led her to a front row seat.

Gallop reached for several sheets of paper on a nearby table.

"I have here some threats notes. Some are handwritten in Ms. Morales' handwriting."

Susan interrupted. "Where did you get those?"

Gallop turned to Susan. "You should be more careful how you dispose of sensitive materials, Ms. Morales."

He continued. "The writing compares favorable with handwritten memos Ms. Morales has given to Mr. Webster over the months. The others are computer typed."

"It was meant to be a joke," Susan said, breaking down into sobs. "I didn't mean to scare anyone."

* * *

Mabel McCullough heard the soft knock and went to the door. It was a man who looked a little familiar. He was carrying a suitcase.

"Mrs. McCullough. Don't you remember me? I'm Ed Randolph."

308

"Oh, my gosh. You come on in, Mr. Randolph. It's good to see you."

"Is Robert here?"

"He's at school but I expect him home pretty soon. What brings you here Mr. Randolph?"

"Well. I've just been released from the nursing home. They told me I should come here, where Robert is."

"Where are you gonna stay now that you're out?"

"I don't have a place to stay. I was hoping I could stay here for a while."

"Have you called your wife, Marsha?"

"The home called her but it seems that she moved and doesn't want to see me."

"Well, that's a fit, ain't it?" Mabel said. "Do you have any funds for travel or livin'?"

"They gave me money from the last payment Marsha made to the place, but they said that was all there was and Marsha wasn't going to be sending any more money."

"Oh, my. Well why don't you make yourself at home here and we'll see what we're gonna do when Robby and Frank get here."

"Thank you very much. I appreciate your hospitality."

"Have you had anythin' to eat?"

"That apple pie smells real good."

Mabel gave Randolph a slice. It was still warm.

"Want a piece of cheese with it?"

"That sounds good too. Thank you."

Mabel returned to the work area behind the counter. She didn't know what to think about Mr. Randolph. Did he think he could stay here forever? Did he think Robby would welcome him? Did he think he and Robby could go off and live together somewhere? Why didn't Marsha want him? He sure looks a lot better now than when he was here during the snow storm. Frank will be home in another hour. Then Frank and Mr. Randolph can greet Robby when he gets off the bus.

* * *

Puff had enough of sitting around in her empty condo. She had to mix with people. Her first thought was the hotel lobby. Just by sitting there she had the comfort of people coming and going. They had plenty of magazines she could browse. She might even meet someone.

She spruced up and took the plunge. She sat at one end of a couch, a move some might interpret as inviting, rather than sitting in the middle.

The lobby was busy with salesmen and executives, bankers and well-dressed women -- all in a rush. She was a bit jealous. She had nothing to rush to. But maybe they were envious of her as well. She skimmed some magazines, looking up now and then.

From where she sat, she could see into the lounge. It had a happy throng, probably winding down after work. But it was packed -- too sardiney for her liking. Too noisy as well.

A young man, probably in his mid-twenties, dressed casually, but clean and neatly pressed, approached her and politely asked if he could join her. He had short reddish hair in the current fashion of having it brushed upward in the middle. He had a pleasant smile and a tenor voice.

"Why certainly. Be my guest."

He carried a book under his arm.

"Are you traveling?" he asked.

"She turned to him and said, "No. I live here in Boston."

"So do I," he said. "I'm down on the waterfront near the aquarium."

"Are you a student?" she asked.

310

"Oh, no. I'm an author. I write for a living."

"Is that your book?" she asked.

"It's not only mine, but I wrote it."

Puff looked puzzled.

"That was a play on words. Yes. I wrote it."

"May I see it?"

He handed the book to her. It was titled "Death on the 12:05."

"And you're Michael Rock?"

"I am. And what's your name?"

"Puff Chabus." She flipped through the pages. "What brings you to the Zenix Towers, Mr. Rock?"

"I have a book signing here at four."

"Oh. That's nice. Is this your first book?"

"No. I've written several."

"I presume this is a mystery or a thriller?"

"It is -- it's very frightening," he said with a mysterious voice that made them both laugh.

"Do you read much?" Rock asked.

Instinctively she searched her mind for some of the reviews she had recently read. "I'm a John Grisham fan."

"You're not alone."

She looked puzzled again.

He answered with, "He sells an enviable number of books."

"I know what you mean."

"Tell me. If you're free, would you like to come to my book talk and signing? I'm always afraid no one will show up. I have to be there in a few minutes."

"I'd like that. I've never been to book talk."

Mr. Rock's presentation went very well. He had the audience in awe as he read several suspenseful selections from his new book. About ninety people attended and gave him a fine reception. The bookstore sold to more than half of those present, including Puff. Rock was elated at the success of the event.

"Congratulations," Puff said at the end. "I really enjoyed that."

"Will you join me for a celebration drink?" he asked.

"I will. I've always wanted to talk with an author."

The young man was very pleasant and excited about his life and work. Puff learned he was not only single but wasn't dating anyone. He said he spent too much of his time writing. He obviously enjoyed her company. She loved to hear him talk about writing and the interesting people he knew.

The evening passed by quickly as did several drinks.

Mr. Rock looked at his watch. "Oh, my gosh. It's getting late. I should let you go."

"No need for you to run," Puff said. "Come on up to my place. I'm here on the top floor."

"You are? That's cool. I'd like to see it."

As they walked to the elevators, Puff took his hand.

* * *

Odie Gallop stopped the next day to see Webster. He was smiling.

"I believe you'll find Ms. Morales' letter of resignation in your correspondence," Gallop said. "Will you press charges? This is a very serious offense."

"Yes, I will," Webster said. "A threat is one thing which under some circumstances can be excused, but when it is combines with racism of the most vulgar kind, it is unforgiveable."

"Very good.

"One other thing," Gallop continued. "Regarding Mildred/Sasha, she has been arrested and a guard has been placed outside her hospital room door. When she is released from the MGH, she will be jailed until trial. She has been charged with murder and attempted murder. Currently, she is a very sick puppy with half her face gone. It is unlikely she will ever get well."

"That is the best news I've heard in months, Odie. I owe this all to you. I guess that ties everything up," Webster said.

"It appears that way, but you never know," Gallop said with a glimmer in his eyes. "You just never know."

The men shook hands and embraced.

* * *

"Nat," Ellen said with a big smile. "We're finally free! I'm free to go on the Mount McKinley expedition. We're scheduled to leave at the end of this month."

"That's good news, Baby. I was afraid you'd opt to sit around here with me gathering excess fatty tissue." Webster smiled. "Then you'd look funny in your jumpsuit. So, this still leaves us a couple weeks to celebrate our new-found freedom together."

"The on-again off-again fears I've had over the months is draining right out of me, Nat. I can feel it. I'm a new person. We're a new couple."

"Where's your gun?"

"Oh. That! I put it away. But, someday I might want to go shooting rats at the dump."

"Did Annie Oakley ever shoot rats?"

"I don't know. Why don't you Google it sometime."

"No. I'd prefer to Google you." Webster grabbed her around the waist and pulled her to him."

"If this is Googling, I like it."

* * *

Helena anxiously returned to the Zenix Tower condo following Sasha's instructions. But the door was locked and she couldn't find her key. It was not in her purse. Sasha told her she had to get into the suite. She kept trying the door handle but it wouldn't open. She looked in her purse again.

Puff heard the elevator and gently eased her door open. It was the girl with the long hair! "Helena!" she said, "What's the matter?" The girl was crying.

Helena looked up, startled, but then recognized Puff as someone who had been nice to her and even knew her name. Still crying, she said, "I can't get in. I lost my key. Sasha says I have to get it."

"Wait, Helena. I think I have the key in here." Puff retrieved it from the table by her door and handed it to Helena. "You left it in the lock the last time you were here."

"Oh, thank you." Helena was now all smiles.

"What do you have to get?" Puff asked.

"Sasha told me I had to get her toy from the closet." All business now, Helena entered the room.

Nosey person that she was, Puff followed Helena. "What toy is that, Helena?"

Helena turned to Puff, "The big bang toy."

Puff was startled now. Was Helena talking about a gun? Was there still a gun in the room?

"Do you mean a gun?"

Helena looked at Puff. "Yes. Sasha's gun. Sasha told me to get it."

Oh, God! What should I do? I shouldn't have given her the key, Puff thought.

Helena turned suddenly to Puff. "You go! You can't come in here with me. This is Sasha's room. Sasha said I couldn't see anybody. You get out," she demanded, pointing to the door.

Puff was again startled at the change in Helena. She was a very angry person.

"Get out!" she demanded loudly.

Puff ran for the door, suddenly shaking in fear. She took one last look behind her. Helena had turned and was on the other side of the room. Puff ran across the hall to her open door.

"Oh, what have I done?" she cried to herself. "I have to call the cops. Something bad is going to happen."

* * *

Frank McCullough returned from the Landfill. He greeted Ed Randolph cordially and Mabel related what Ed had told her. Then it was time to meet Robby. The two of them walked to the end of the drive.

"We call him Robby and he calls us Grampy and Grammy."

"That's nice," Randolph said.

"Robby has legally become our foster child, Mr. Randolph."

"Oh. I see."

The bus arrived and Robby jumped off. He looked at the man, puzzled. "Father?"

"Yes, Robert. They let me out. I'm all better."

Robby walked slowly over to his father and put his arms around him. His father held Robby to him. It was not exactly a warm greeting.

"It's been a while, Robert. You've grown a lot. You're a handsome boy."

"Yes, Father. I really like it here on the farm. I can show you around when I do my chores. And I have a tree house with a zip line and a fireman's pole."

"I want to see that."

"Grampy and our friends built it together."

"You must have a lot of friends."

"How long are you going to stay, Father?"

"I don't know. It's up to these people, I guess," he said gesturing to Frank.

"You're not going to see Mother?"

"Your mother doesn't want me."

Frank interrupted. "Well. Let's get back to the house. It's time for a little pie and ice cream. Right, Robby?"

A long discussion took place over the food. All four contributed. A lot of issues were covered.

"This all boils down to one thing, Mr. Randolph," Frank said. "Can we all get along as a family?"

Frank paused and studied Randolph. He seemed like a pleasant, agreeable man.

"If you are handy at all, Mr. Randolph, there are a lot of things to be fixed up on this property, a lot of wood to be cut, a garden to tend, a lot of snow to be shoveled. I can't do as much as I used to.

"Mabel and I agree you can stay on with us if you can do your share of the work. Robby has been a wonderful worker. He takes care of the animals and milks the cow. He's polite and always eager to help. As I said, he is our foster child.

"Does all this make sense to you, Mr. Randolph?"

"I have a lot to learn, but I will try."

"What do you think, Robby?" Mabel asked.

"It's not like it used to be, Father. We don't have Turk and Francisco. There will be a lot of work and we can do it together."

"If you are happy about you father staying with us, Robby, we are happy," Mabel concluded.

"I'm happy, Grammy."

* * *

Helena forgot the Puff incident as her brief attention span returned to her mission. She was happy, but still anxious. She never liked being in this room alone. It was spooky. Everything looked the same, but without Sasha, it was scary.

She went to Sasha's desk and found the photo in the bottom drawer. He was a nice looking man. She didn't know why Sasha wanted to big bang this nice man.

She then went to the closet and carefully raised the bottom shelf that held the shoes. There was Sasha's toy. It was a lot smaller than the toy she used with Sasha. She hesitated. She didn't want to touch it. It was scary. She dropped the shelf and put her hands over her ears as she remembered the noise the toy made. Recovering, she very slowly picked it up being careful not to let it make a big noise. Just holding the gun instantly brought back the image of Sasha's mangled face. She gingerly placed the gun in her small backpack.

Helena looked in her pocket and found the piece of paper that told her how to find the man in the picture. When she found him, she had to take the gun out of the backpack and point it at the man in the picture just like she did with Sasha.

Helena cried again. She didn't want to do this. But she knew she must because Sasha told her Helena owed her big-time.

* * *

Puff's hands were shaking just like they did when Captain Redford yelled at her. It took her three tries to hit the correct 911 numbers.

"This is Puff Chabus in the Zenix Towers on Summer Street."

"Is that Summer Street, Boston?"

"Yes. Of course."

"What number?"

"I don't know what number. It's a huge tower on the waterfront, for God sake."

"OK ma'am. Please be calm. What is the problem?"

"There's a woman across the hall from me who is looking for a gun. I think she's going to hurt somebody. Please send the cops fast. We are on the top floor."

As Puff said this she heard the door across the hall slam closed.

"Oh," she continued. "It's probably too late. I heard her leave."

"Please describe this woman"

"Well, she is tall and has long blond hair down her back..."

Puff heard the elevator click.

"Oh, forget it. She's gone now." Puff hung up.

* * *

Helena was in high spirits as she sped Sasha's bike across the city. It wasn't often she had this thrill. Sasha mostly kept it to herself. She loved this bike. It was quiet and fast and exciting. It must have cost a lot of money. She had always wished she could have one just like this. But Sasha had the money. Helena didn't have any money -- only what Sasha gave her.

It was early afternoon when she arrived at Scan-Man. She had been so consumed with the pleasure of riding she flew past the Hollandson exit and had to backtrack. She had almost forgotten what Sasha had told her to do. But as that thought returned, she became very nervous again. She didn't want to do this. But Sasha would hurt her if she didn't.

She hesitatingly asked the woman at the desk for Mr. Webster.

"Who will I say is asking?"

Sasha didn't tell her this question would be asked, but she knew the answer: "My name is Helena."

The security woman looked curiously at Helena and recognized her nervousness. She called. Webster answered. "There's a lady here who would like to see you. She says her name is Helena." Then in a whisper, she said, "She seems strange -- awfully nervous."

It was like a hammer had hit him in the chest. Helena! It can't be *the* Helena, he thought.

"Does she have a last name?"

The woman asked, "What's your last name?"

"I don't have a last name."

"No last name, Mr. Webster."

This will be interesting, Webster thought. He turned to Ellen and whispered, "Helena's here. She wants to see me."

"Whoah!" was Ellen surprised reaction. "What the dickens is she doing here?"

"I guess we're going to find out." Webster returned to the operator. "I'll be right down."

Ellen had stopped wearing her sidearm after Susan Morales had been fired and the threats seemed distant. She thought of retrieving the weapon now, but then brushed off the idea of danger.

"This is ridiculous. It can't be."

"I'm going with you," Ellen said determinedly.

As they exited the elevator into the lobby, the woman at the desk pointed to Helena.

The girl with the blond hair was sitting. When she recognized Webster, she slipped one hand into the backpack that lay across her lap. He looked like a kind man, but Sasha had told her to hurt him. She must hurt him.

319

She was shaking. She remained seated. She was ready. Her hand was sweating. Webster and a woman with him were standing still just looking at her.

"Helena," Webster said. He smiled and put his hand out to her.

Helena automatically smiled at Webster's pleasant face, then looked down and began to sob.

Then, without any warning, she jumped up from her chair and ran for the door, her backpack in hand. Astonished, Webster and Ellen watched her run through the doors.

They looked at each other and then ran after her, calling her name. When they saw her again she was mounting her motorcycle, and then, gone.

Webster sighed. "What do you make of all that, Ellen?"

"I'm wondering why she wanted to see us," Ellen replied. "Did she want to tell us something she thought we should know? How did she find out about us? Why should she care about people she has never met?"

* * *

"Hold it right there, ma'am. What do you want?"

Helena was startled. "What?"

"If you are a visitor, I have to have the nurse check you before you go in."

"I want to see my friend," Helena said.

"You can," the officer said. "Just leave your bag out here with me."

A nurse came over to Helena. "I'm going to have to check you for security reasons, ma'am. Please raise your arms."

The nurse checked her clothing. "That's all there is. Thank you."

"Now ma'am. Please leave you backpack out here with me."

Helena looked frightened. The gun was still in it.

"It's OK. I'm not going to eat it. It's just that you can't take it into the room."

Helena hesitated again and then decided it would be OK to leave it.

"You can go in now, ma'am. Please leave the door open."

* * *

"Did you do it?" Sasha asked.

Helena simply hung her head.

"I should have known you couldn't do a simple job," Sasha said through her teeth. "You're a simpleton who can't do crap. You are an idiot."

Helena was crying. Through her tears she tried to explain. "When I saw Mr. Webster, I just couldn't do it. I know he's a nice man. I didn't want to hurt him with your toy."

Helena paused. "Why do you have a policeman out there?"

"It's none of your business. It's a waste of time for me to tell you anything. You really piss me off."

"I'm sorry, Sasha."

"That's enough. Shut up and listen."

"Yes, Sasha."

"Here's what I want you to do. I'm giving you one last chance."

* * *

A bike and two riders arrive at the Scan-Man loading dock doors. It is late afternoon. One rider enters the shipping

321

room and passes through quickly amid the bustle of end-of-day activity.

No one questions the person, who appears to know exactly where to go. This person leaves the shipping area, enters the main hallway, and presses the elevator button for the fourth floor. A minute later the rider steps out and heads for Nat Webster's office.

Without knocking, this person walks right in and comes to an abrupt stop. Webster is not at his desk. A look around reveals a steaming cup of coffee on his desk. The rider takes a seat next to the desk, back to the door.

Webster's door opens again and Ellen enters. She is startled when she sees someone seated next to Nat's desk.

"May I help you?" Ellen asks.

The person sitting gets up, turns, and faces Ellen. Ellen is shocked when she sees the face. She knows at once who it is.

"You are Sasha!" she gasps.

At that moment, Webster appears in the doorway, walks in and sees the two women.

"What the hell is going on?" Then, "You are Sasha!" Webster exclaims.

Without a word of warning Sasha bypasses Ellen and springs toward Webster.

The movement is so fast Webster has no time to think. This ugly creature is nearly upon him. With a violent reflexive swing of his arm to protect himself, Webster's fist hits hard at the left side of Sasha's jaw. As it hits, the lower jaw and Sasha's right bandaged cheek collapses and is ripped from her face.

Sasha lets out a ghastly scream. Half her face swings wildly free, dangling by a patch of skin.

Without hesitation, Ellen springs and tackles Sasha from the rear, sending her crashing to the floor where she hits face first.

Webster is stupefied. He doesn't know what happened. What he sees on the floor is nothing but horror. Ellen stands. Sasha is motionless. For the first time they both see the horrifying result of Webster's hit.

Ellen puts her arm around Webster's waist. Both are shaking.

* * *

"We caught Helena in the loading dock area waiting for Sasha," Odie said. "She was keeping watch on Sasha's magnificent Ducati.

"Nat, I apologize for Sasha escaping from the hospital. The two of them overpowered the hospital room guard. Helena piloted Sasha out here on that machine. Helena had a revolver in her backpack that the guard was holding for her. Apparently he never checked its contents.

"Sasha will have to have her face taped together again. It was pretty mangled when they scraped it up off your floor.

"She's been sent to Boston City Hospital this time, and will be kept in leg shackles. It is difficult to feel sorry for this monster. She just may never survive her self-created ordeal."

* * *

"This has been one hell of an exciting week," Webster sighed as he raised his glass of wine to Ellen's. "Odie was right when he said, 'You just never know.'"

"I'm curious," Ellen said. "I thought you said you would never hit a woman."

Webster smiled. "It's true. Let me tell you something. That was no woman. That was a monster -- a cunning killer."

"I agree. It's OK to hit a cunning killer."

"Truthfully, Baby, that hit was not intentional."

"What?"

"It was *reactional*, if I may coin an descriptive word. When I jerked my fist up, it was simply to protect myself. It was quite by accident that I hit her. Sasha's face was surprisingly fragile."

"My superhero," Ellen swooned. "You won't take credit for saving the life of your helpless girlfriend."

"*You* were the one who felled her. Don't ruin my pacifist reputation."

"Yes, my sweet, exciting it was. Hopefully we'll never see a repeat."

"I just realized, you didn't have your gun with you. What would Annie Oakley say?"

"That's another thing my daddy taught me. Use a weapon only as a last resort." Ellen smiled.

"Sasha wasn't a last resort?"

"I suppose she could have been."

"Yet you saved my life, you know," Webster said.

"Only by tackling her. You are a life worth saving. You were the one who put her out of commission."

"I propose we do something about this mutual feeling of love and respect while we're both still alive," Webster said.

"And what is that, my darling?"

"I propose we get married as soon as possible, Baby, before you take off for Mount McKinley."

A big smile crossed Ellen's face. "I'll say cheers to that."

They clasped their hands across the table. "You may have to wait a while for the ring."

"Why?"

"I haven't bought it."

"Is that because your proposal is a surprise to you?"

"Do you think I'd admit that? Actually, I haven't had time to go shopping."

"You're forgiven, but you realize you've broken all the rules of making a proposal."

"I did?"

"You're a goof. I'll take you shopping tomorrow. Then you can make a proper proposal. I want to see you on your knees with a diamond in your hand."

"Oh, the demands you put on me."

Ellen gave Webster a long look. "I'm having second thoughts about going on the McKinley and Nepal expeditions."

"What? Why? You've been looking forward to that for years."

"They're too dangerous."

Webster laughed. "And what was today?"

"That danger doesn't count. If we're going to get married, I have to think more about my safety. I want to save myself for you."

"I won't hear of it, Baby. I want you to go. Having you participate in these events is exciting to me also. I can't believe you're weaseling out of a little mountain exercise." Webster smiled.

"You are a tease, Massa. I'm just trying to be sensible."

"How boring. You let *me* be the sensible one. We can't both be sensible. Opposites attract. If you become sensible, we'll both be boring. Go do your thing."

"Then you don't mind if I raise a little hell with the girls?"

"Of course not. I encourage you to be yourself. That's why I am marrying you -- because you are you."

END OF BOOK TWO

The warmth and bright daffodils of late spring have brought new life to Hollandson. Reconstruction is fully underway. It has been a long winter.

Odie Gallop's investigations for Nat Webster reached a satisfactory conclusion. But Odie may soon be recalled to help Nat. This time the scope is international as terrorists take an interest in Scan-Man technology.

Nat Webster is preparing for a congressional hearing on the safety of weather modification. He is not entirely certain San-Man will be allowed to continue its experiments in the United States. If Congress does indeed issue a ban, it will probably mean the Searoc Beam has little use -- except, of course, if the military has an interest in it. The issue is certain to stir international debate, and maybe something violent.

Chandler Harrington is certain to spend most of his life in prison for numerous crimes including embezzlement and abetting murder. Embezzled Scan-Man funds discovered so far total $10 million.

A court case is pending for Mildred McCoy, alias Sasha, for several murders outside of Hollandson. Her face is healing but no reconstruction is planned. It appears she will live with her ugliness forever.

Helena has been turned over to her mother for care, funds for which will be provided from a portion of Sasha's bank account. Her mother has been told she must not allow her daughter to visit Sasha in prison or elsewhere under any circumstances.

Susan Morales is facing several serious charges, including the threatening a person's life. The vengeance of her written attacks, along with her racial epithets, are compounding her legal problems.

Ellen has finally joined a group of like-minded women and is spending three weeks on Mount McKinley in Alaska rehearsing for a later attack on Mount Everest.

Maggie and Phil continue to publish the Hollandson *Bulletin*. They are eagerly preparing for their first child. For Phil, fatherhood has not become all that he had imagined.

Puff Chabus made a brief try at becoming more conservative in her life style, but, in the end, she felt it did not fit her personality. Her current thinking is to attend the July NSA meeting and circulate among the intellectuals she had met through her husband when she was happily married to Dr. Chabus.

Marsha Randolph remains in Naples, Florida. The Nursing Home is no longer seeking her because her husband left on his own accord. She is fully involved with Clarence and Naples Society. The Naples *Press* has gradually become interested in Marsha's relationship with Clarence and has begun gentle questioning of her past.

The McCullough family, that now includes Robby and Ed Randolph, is doing well. Doctors say Ed's mental condition shows signs of full recovery. As the mists covering his past evaporate, Ed is asking more often about Marsha. He is also wondering what has happened to his finances. He is a willing learner on farm matters and McCullough's customers enjoy talking with him. He and Robby grow closer by the day.

Acknowledgements

Several people have contributed to the creation of *Cunning Killer*. In addition to my wife, Carol Seaman, who put up with my long hours and fluctuating temperament during the creation of this work, I gratefully thank: My long-time friend and fellow writer, Roger Hale, who did the editing of the initial draft. Fellow traveler and publisher, Clif Gaskill, who read the second and third drafts and offered invaluable advice on the characters and the pace of the novel. And my final reader and copyeditor, Barbara Peterson, who massaged the text to bring the book to this author's satisfaction. Any typos or errors found in the present text are solely the responsibility of the author who did the final reading and editing.